MIRRORS

SONYA DEULINA WILLIAMS

chandra

ISBN: 9781949964134
Published by Chandra Press LLC
www.chandrapress.com
www.facebook.com/officialchandrapress

TABLE OF CONTENTS

FOREWORD

"All men dream, but not equally. Those who dream by night in the dusty recesses of their minds, wake in the day to find that it was vanity: but the dreamers of the day are dangerous men, for they may act on their dreams with open eyes, to make them possible."

T.E. Lawrence

ACKNOWLEDGEMENTS

Writing this book has sent me on a journey that I would have never expected, the process to publication was equally mind-bending. I could not have succeeded in this endeavor without the love, support, insight, and inspiration from my friends and family. You know who you are. You all have been the bread, water, air, and peace of mind, that has helped me push past numerous barriers and produce something that I am truly proud of. I love you all. I also want to say a special thank you to my publisher Erik, who has put countless hours of his time, energy, and money on the line to make this happen. Thank you for believing in my story and for believing in me. We did it!

1. Waking Life: The Usual Grind

The alarm blared its clamorous 6:35 a.m. in neon-blue. Sarah's shift started in less than thirty minutes. She pushed the snooze button for the fourth time. There was something strenuous beyond belief about opening her eyes and climbing out of bed, no matter how many hours of sleep she got the night before. It didn't help that her shift at NC Roasters Coffee Shop started at 7:00 a.m. Sarah pushed the covers aside, shoving her insistent terrier, Drano, onto the floor. He looked up at her questioningly, having no awareness of the irritation he was inducing.

"Why bother with this alarm clock when I have you?" Sarah shook the clock threateningly at the unaffected canine. "Okay. Okay... let's go!" Sarah rolled over the side of the bed and opened the sliding glass door to the back yard. She rubbed the sleep from her eyes, as Drano bounded out, sniffed the grass, and then raised a curious ear at a rustling in the leaves.

Sarah remembered the day she got Drano. He was barely bigger than the palm of her hand and filled with inexhaustible amounts of energy. Six years later, he was still, equally neurotic.

"Come on, go already." Sarah looked at her phone impatiently. She was going to be late again. Drano looked over at her and stuck his tongue out tauntingly, displaying his innocent canine grin. Sarah smiled back in a way that let Drano know that he would be meeting his maker if he didn't move along. Drano then, by pure coincidence, found a choice spot to do his business and trotted back into the apartment. Sarah walked to her chaise lounge and began pulling on her uniform, which lay in a crinkled pile.

~~~

She pushed open the glass door of the coffee shop, smudging the clean glass, brushing the sweaty strands of hair from her forehead with her other hand. She was drenched from the overly brisk walk she had not planned on taking that morning. She checked her phone again. "Shit, I'm really late." With swiftly moving fingers, she clocked in and began the morning brews. *Only three more hours till my break with Bri.*

It was safe to say that Sarah didn't like her job. Plus, she hated coffee so the free brew was not an added incentive to her like it was for the perpetually hungover college students she worked with. Unfortunately, her journalism career with local paper, *Resonance Weekly,* wasn't paying the bills.

The coffee shop had a fifties diner vibe. Each table displayed a yellow and red carnation. The floors had a red and white checkerboard pattern and the register was old-fashioned and popped open with a loud ring. There were various pastries and fresh baked pies in the glass case near the front counter. The walls were covered in re-purposed sculptures, made by a local artist, consisting of old tin plates, forks, spoons and knives. They were shaped into portraits of old movie stars. There was even one formed around a working clock, which resembled Elvis Presley. An old jukebox sat near the front door that had been broken for years. According to the manager, it was there for decoration.

"Hi Rollo," Sarah said to the middle-aged man fiddling with three bags of colorful balloons in the front booth.

"Hiya, Sarah! How are you this morning? Would you like a balloon?"

"Sure!"

Rollo grinned and reached into one of the opened bags.

"What color would you like?"

"I'll take a green one today."

"Okay, here you go! You enjoy that Sarah," Rollo said enthusiastically as he fished out the balloon.

Rollo was a simply-dressed, middle-aged white man, with curly gray hair and a mustache. He came in when the coffee shop opened every morning with his balloons, greeting and striking up conversations with every customer who would walk in. He would offer up his balloons and derive great pleasure when they were accepted and blown up in front of him. He especially loved kids, as they were the most genuinely thrilled to receive one.

Sarah wasn't exactly sure if he had a special quirk or if there was something wrong with him. All she knew was that he was kind to everyone he met, and he loved people. Sarah never refused him. Her house had amassed quite a number of balloons over the years, and on Rollo's birthday, the staff would blow them up and put them around the restaurant for him, which made him so excited, you would think he just won a Ferrari.

The hours went by quickly. Sarah remained largely behind the counter making coffee and handing out pastries, wiping down the counter and brewing more coffee. She liked this part of the morning, it was busy, and she didn't notice the time passing. After a while, the parade of customers stopped, and Sarah went to the back to restock and then zipped back to the front of the restaurant to wipe down the tables.

Sarah heard the bell ring as Brianne (Bri) confidently walked in, her four-inch heels clacking on the linoleum.

"Anne, I'm going to take my break now," Sarah yelled back into the kitchen to her manager.

"Okay, but did you wipe down the counters?" came the muffled reply, subdued by the clanging of dishes.

"Yes ma'am!" she yelled back, rolling her eyes.

Bri was always the punctual sister, never feeling the need to rush around to get places, because she was simply always ahead of schedule. The two were pretty close and Bri would come to visit Sarah at work at least once a month, just to chat with her. Bri smiled and smoothed back her sleek, platinum blonde hair behind her diamond studded ears. Although Sarah and her sister looked somewhat alike, no one would take them for siblings. Brianne was tall and confident, always dressed in designer labels. Today it was a sleek, mid-length red dress, with a plunging neckline that revealed a flashy, gold Chanel necklace. She was not plump, but had a full, curvaceous figure, unlike Sarah, who was thin and petite.

Her sister's hair was always perfectly straightened or curled, and her makeup flawlessly and expertly refined. Sarah, on the other hand, would wear the same ripped jeans four days in a row. They were usually accompanied by some arbitrary graphic-T she'd owned since middle school. Needless to say, she did not buy herself clothes often. Her nails were short and uneven, because she bit them, out of nervous habit or boredom, and makeup was definitely not on the daily agenda.

Bri always donned a bronze, summer tan, mostly from her weekly trips to the tanning bed and her monthly rendezvous to exotic beaches, accompanied by equally exotic and affluent lovers. She would have torrid and short-lived affairs with them, and then move on to the next eligible bachelor. Sarah was pale, from spending too much time reading in her basement.

"Hey Bri! Just wait just one second. I just need to finish wiping down the tables." Sarah leaned over the white table, scrubbing the crumbs off the surface in circular motions with her rag.

"Okay, sounds good." Bri sat down at one of the window booths, carefully crossing her legs and gold strappy wedge heals under the table. She clacked her cherry red nails down on the table a few times, impatiently, then picked them up, inspecting them for stickiness.

"So how was that wine and painting class last week?" Sarah asked sitting down, slinging the rag over her shoulder.

"Great, actually. My painting was pretty terrible, though. I think I might have done more *wine* than painting." Bri laughed and threw her arms up in the air. "Oh, and I wanted to show you something." She rummaged through her large Coach purse for a few seconds. "So... I was going through the attic trying to find the old family photo albums and I came across this." Bri pulled out a golden pocket watch and dangled it in front of Sarah, flashing her a childish grin.

"Oh, wow. Dad's old pocket watch," Sarah said in surprise. A trace of pain passed across her face.

"Yeah, and I wanted to give it to you. Here, look at the picture inside." Bri popped open the watch.

"Dad and I on a fishing trip," Sarah replied in a monotone voice.

She remembered that trip so clearly. It was one of the few they had taken together. She could see it now: her father scribbling in his notebook and neglecting his fishing rod, her seven-year-old self, yelling out as the bob started going under; her father throwing his notebook down in a frazzled heap; watching him reel that fish in with so much finesse; screeching in delight as the fish squirmed in her hands.

"Yeah, I know how you always loved those trips. I thought you should have it."

Bri was a city girl, and the rugged outdoors had no appeal for her. Her finely manicured hands would scarcely touch a dirty dish, let alone a slimy river trout.

"Thanks."

The image of the caught fish dangling from the line was gone and replacing it was the splayed bloody carcass on a wooden table, Dad removing the guts using a pocketknife and his bare hands.

"Hey, I thought you'd be happy," said Bri in confusion, when she noticed Sarah's crestfallen face.

"I am, it's just, I don't know, seeing him— hurts. You know that's why I keep his stuff at your house."

"Sarah, it's been four years, I just thought..." Bri stammered and dropped her hands down on the table in exasperation.

"You just thought— I would have gotten over it by now. He's only been gone for four years Bri. Four years is not that long in the grand scheme of things."

"No, I just thought—"

"No, I get it. Thanks. Really, thanks." Sarah grabbed the watch and got up quickly, turning her back to Bri and squeezing her eyes shut. She remembered her father, sitting in the living room, popping open the golden pocket watch and exclaiming, "It's half past noon, let's have some tea, Sarah!" That pocket watch was given to him by his father and he carried it wherever he went. Sometimes he would rub his thumb over it while he worked or was lost in thought. Bri should have remembered how much this watch meant. *God, how could Bri be so nonchalant about all this*?!

"Sarah I'm sorry... I know it still hurts, but I just thought you might want to have this..."

Sarah turned around slowly, steadying her shaking voice. "Bri, Dad is not just a memory. He's still out there somewhere. I know it."

"Sarah, you're not still looking, are you?"

"Well, can you blame me? He's our father and I don't understand how you and Mom just forgot about him, when there's no evidence he's dead."

"Sarah," Bri looked at Sarah blankly before continuing. "We've been over this. We've done all we can and it's time to move on now. I'm really concerned that you're stuck on this again. Have you been seeing your therapist?"

Sarah's mouth moved inaudibly for a moment, before she finally spoke. "Look Bri, I have to get back to work. I'll see you later."

There were no words left in her to continue the conversation. This wound was as raw as it had always been. The day her father disappeared, or rather the day she had last seen him, was etched into her mind with cinematographic precision, even though she had not suspected anything was wrong then. She remembered her pain and confusion when she realized weeks later, that he was truly missing. The pain that followed had torn her heart and very existence asunder, as did the weeks that dragged on and nothing turned up, as did every time something or someone reminded her of that time. To deal with this life bending pain, she had developed a skill of repressing those emotions, and had honed it to a point of near mastery. She still had to live her life, after all.

~~~

With the idea of a nice visit with her sister shattered, the rest of the afternoon crept by slowly. Still, she did not have time to mope. Sarah left the shop that afternoon feeling despondent and queasy from the conversation that morning and from her stomach growling. She had almost forgotten to text her mom to check on Drano, almost. It was one of her longer days and she had no time to stop by her house in the interim. She had forgotten her lunch that day and frankly had forgotten to eat altogether. She checked her reflection in the huge, reflective glass sides of a financial investments building in downtown Raleigh, for visible signs of distress, and after straightening out her skirt and tucking her hair behind her ears neatly, she picked up her pace.

The walk to her second job was short; she didn't even need a bike. The temperature outside that afternoon was rising quickly, and Sarah wrapped her jacket around her waist. She didn't drive much, only when she went out on assignments, which was usually a couple of times a week.

The sidewalk was narrow where she walked and to either side grew petite magnolia trees and beds of fuchsia, purple and yellow pansies, and geraniums. Downtown Raleigh was beautiful; the perfect combination of industrial and natural. The air was crisp and clean.

Forrester Care Psychiatric Hospital was just a block away from *Resonance Weekly*. It towered above her, large and gray, nestled in the middle of downtown, with a good-sized enclosed green space around it. It was a modern building and reminded her more of some corporate high rise than a psychiatric hospital. The rectangular building was six stories of reflective glass windows and steel frame. The entrance had an elaborate glass canopy that gave it an artistic touch. The gardens around the building were also at a sharp contrast to the sleek industrial design of the building. Rows of multicolored blooms lined the walkway and entrance to the building.

The construction crew was back again. Two men standing near the entrance, wearing yellow hard hats, wiped the sweat off their faces and took large gulps of blue Gatorade. One of them, a short, bald man in his mid-twenties, began to speak. Sarah slowed her pace. As a journalist and a naturally curious person, she was prone to eavesdropping.

"Mike, there's nothing wrong with your back, that thing was just really heavy. You're in your early forties, come on man..."

"Yeah, I don't know why they need all that damn heavy equipment. What the hell are they building in there anyway?"

"I don't know, but that last machine we installed was weird. Have you ever seen anything like it?"

"No way, and I've worked inside a lot of hospitals. And what about all those glass rooms we built last month?"

The two men turned to look in Sarah's direction. She looked straight ahead and increased her pace. *What in the world are they building in there, some kind of research lab?*

Sarah hated that building. It was where they held her father all those years. For such a large building, you would think the hospital would be out in the country somewhere with some real acreage around it. Last time her father was in there, he stayed for three months. They called it a psychotic break. Sarah knew he was sick, but it wasn't so cut and dried. He did his best work when he had his so-called psychotic breaks. In fact, he kept busy even while in the hospital, gumming his medication when he could, to remain clear-minded. Sarah remembered her father complaining about the hospital. It was hard to take him seriously during one of his episodes, but he was emphatic that the doctors prescribed medication despite repeated patient complaints and said his pleas to the psychiatrist to switch medications due to "brain fog" went unanswered. Her father also talked about hushed conversations between staff, and the strange looks they exchanged when the director of the hospital left the room. He swore that there was something amiss about that place. Sarah wondered if her father might have been on to something. Maybe there was a way to find out.

~~~

Sarah continued at a brisk pace to the front doors of the eleven story, black steel and glass downtown high-rise, where *Resonance Weekly* was housed. She rehearsed her pitch silently as she made her way up the elevator to the fifth floor. The elevator opened and she walked slowly across the black linoleum hallway past the bathrooms and breakroom where he could smell hot coffee brewing. *Resonance Weekly* was a modern office with bright slate gray walls adorned with large abstract paintings and contrasting black floors. There were always fresh cut flowers stationed around the elevators, usually white lilies, tulips or orchids, that one of the interns would set up. She could hear the murmur of voices down the hall. Teams of writers and editors were busy pitching stories, writing, and discussing new ideas. She heard Jerry, one of the senior staff writers, erupt in laughter.

Sarah paused for a minute to inhale deeply before walking up to her boss' desk. Mr. Chesterfield was a well-intentioned man, but meticulous to a fault. She thought he had a case of Obsessive-Compulsive Disorder, as nothing was ever out of place on his desk, ever. And if you moved anything, he would become very disturbed and come after you like one of those Roomba vacuum robots, cleaning up after your every step. He was also very finicky about deadlines, understandably so, being the Editor-in-Chief. The newspaper business had to be run like a tight ship. He also had a weakness for controversial stories, and Sarah hoped her pitch would work on him.

"Good morning, Mr. Chesterfield, how was your weekend?"

"Good, good..." Mr. Chesterfield took a gulp of coffee from his mug and carefully smoothed his thick walrus-like mustache neatly into place with a napkin. "Veronica and I caught the game last night at Mitch's. How about you?"

"Oh, you know, not too much going on... but I think I may have come across an interesting story." Sarah squeezed her hands together nervously, then rubbed the sweat off on the sides of her pants.

"Really? Well, let's hear it then."

She paused for a moment and stared at him, getting focused, the way she always did before an important moment.

Chesterfield raised his eyebrows at her to say, "Well get on with it, then."

"Okay. Well, I was on the way in, actually, when I walked by the construction site at Forrester Care Psychiatric Hospital and overheard the strangest conversation," Sarah paused for a moment, thinking of the angle she wanted to take.

Mr. Chesterfield rested his chin on his hand, like the pensive Rodin statue. "Mhmm... well, go on."

"We still don't know what exactly they're adding onto the building. It's been under wraps for months... it's so secretive, even they don't know what they're building. I know we didn't get much information from our last reporter. I think we can go deeper."

"That's been going on for months now, Sarah. We've already had a reporter down there."

"I know, but I overheard two construction workers talking about the glass rooms and some large piece of hospital equipment they were installing. They had no idea what it was, even though they had apparently done these kinds of jobs before. I'm telling you, boss, something doesn't add up." Sarah continued, praying this would clinch it. "No one's talking about it or paying any attention to it anymore. The residents don't know what's going on, the workers don't know, and more importantly the public doesn't know. It seems like there could be a story under there somewhere. There could be a classified research project, like testing a new therapy or medication or maybe there's going to be some big reveal coming and I could get ahead of it.

"Okay. But 'could be' is not good enough for this business... if you can find a story there, I'll give you a chance. I'll give you one week to scope it out. Gather as much information as you can and present it to me on Monday with an original angle. If there's a good story there, then I'll pay you to write it."

"Deal!" Sarah turned and walked out of the office, feeling giddy. This was exactly the type of story that got her blood pumping, a mystery. Investigative journalism was her favorite style of writing and what she pictured herself doing on a full-time basis. In that moment, she felt just like Nellie Bly, her idol. She would get to do some real detective work.

2. Dream Life: Side Effects

S amantha, who always went by Sam, reached her hand over to push the snooze button, knocking the bottle of pills to the floor. "Ughh," she groaned. She hated getting up in the mornings; the sleeping pills made her drowsy, but nothing else seemed to do the trick.

Sam moaned and rolled over to look at the clock. Realizing how late it was, she sprang out of bed as if released from a tightly bound coil. She ran to the closet and pulled on her white, button-down blouse, tucking her shirt clumsily into her wool pencil skirt as she stepped into her black satin heels. She quickly combed her shoulder-length brown hair, still straightened from the day before, into a sleek ponytail. She ran into the bathroom and glanced into the mirror over the sink. *I can do this, I know I can do this... but I have to look the part,* Sam thought.

Quickly, she brushed her teeth, washed her face and applied a thin layer of coral lipstick to her thin lips. "The proposal, where did I put the proposal?!" She riffled through her cabinet, finding her blue folder labeled *Balixa: A New Day Every Day.*

It was Sam's third year at the pharmaceutical firm, and she had moved up to a lead position in the marketing department: Product Marketing Manager. She was now in charge of presenting the next generation of sleeping medication to the FDA and the meeting was starting in thirty minutes. It was one of those meetings that carried a tremendous amount of weight. This drug being approved would mean a multi-billion-dollar deal for her firm.

She was using the drug herself, the samples that is, and honestly nothing had worked better for her insomnia, and with fewer side effects. She had been using this medication for about a month now, but the dreams she was having were strange and vivid. So much so, that she had been keeping a dream journal to record them. It was her psychologist's idea.

Her therapist was one of those free-spirited, Woodstock-generation types. To Sam, it made sense why Dr. Shandi was drawn to the profession. She seemed she revel in the insights gained from subconscious exploration in therapy, as much as Sam imagined she would revel in the insights from her glory days at Ayahuasca healing retreats in Brazil. She was unconventional and quite intelligent, but had a sort of blistering, in your face way about her. But she was good, and definitely worth the one-hundred-fifty dollars a week.

~~~

Later that day, Sam met her husband Elijah for dinner. The air conditioning unit was blasting on that unusually hot September evening as Sam's yellow cab pulled up to Le Gordon, the city's upscale French bistro. It was their usual Friday night spot. Sam liked to think that she was a fairly grounded person. She grew up in a middle-class family and was happy. Elijah, on the other hand, grew up insanely wealthy and the lifestyle he introduced her to certainly had its appeal. Tonight's dinner would likely be another fantastic example.

Sam was adopted at birth and was told that her birth mother was too sick to take care of her and her father was not willing to shoulder the burden at the time. Her adoptive parents never really told her much about them; why her mother was sick and why her father did not want her. But Sam never really cared to find out why. Her entire life, she knew and accepted her family as her one and only.

Sam's adoptive parents were middle-of-the-road, upper middle class, suburban dwellers. Her father believed in the American Dream, making your own fortune, with no safety nets. So, as soon as Sam turned eighteen, she was cast out of the nest. She paid for college on her own, took out student loans, graduated top of her class, and found a dingy apartment in the center of the city. It was not ideal, and it took about three years of working one menial job after another before she landed in the pharmaceutical firm.

Her careers, in chronological order, were: assistant bookkeeper, pet store sales associate, waitress (a total bust), and then when her luck began to change: receptionist, marketing assistant, and then finally, product marketing manager of the biggest drug to hit the market in years. She had finally found her niche.

Her older adopted brother Michael, on the other hand, was more of a ragamuffin, bumming his way around the country, going from job to job, just to make enough money to eat. Sam believed he left the nest too early, but her parents said that he would have had the same destiny regardless of how long they would have let him live at home. He was currently salmon fishing somewhere off the coast of Alaska.

"We'll start with a bottle of your house Cab," Elijah said smiling at the waiter, who had promptly returned to the table upon seeing Sam arrive.

"No, make it the champagne," Sam chimed in.

"So, the meeting went well then?"

Elijah took an oversized bite of his heavily buttered roll.

"Yes, very well. I mean, the FDA seemed convinced. Of course, they still need to review all the paperwork, which will take months, but I did my job, and they were definitely pleased. The studies spoke for themselves, and like I said, if vivid dreams are the biggest side effect, these things will be on shelves this year."

"I'm so proud of you!" Elijah leaned in across the table and clasped Sam's hands in his. "So, what's in this thing for you?" Elijah winked at her.

"They haven't really told me yet, but I'm pretty sure I will be getting a massive bonus, at least, and more big projects."

"Okay, so you know what this means? We need to celebrate this weekend! It's a good time for you to take a break, right?"

Elijah was intelligent, in a sly fox kind of way. He had a cool demeanor and was always thoughtful. Sam was instantly drawn to him when they met. They had the type of relationship Sam had always envisioned for herself. Sure, he was different then the guys she was used to dating, more refined because of his upbringing, which intimidated her initially. She had been at Blakeley Pharmaceuticals for about two months when they met.

She remembered running out on her thirty-minute lunch break as a receptionist and bumping into Elijah on her way back to the building, tuna fish sandwich in one hand and coffee in the other. She spilled hot coffee all over his shirt and dropped tuna salad on his shoe and he was the one who bought her lunch afterwards. She remembered reaching down to pick up the cup and sandwich and then meeting him there on the sidewalk at eye level, his ice-blue eyes rendering her speechless. He was strikingly handsome with an impeccably crisp, dark gray suit, thick brown hair smoothed back, a hint of five o'clock shadow, and of course his pale, piercing blue eyes, a clarity she had never seen before. She could only stammer out an awkward apology. Elijah was unfazed. Sam wondered if he was used to women swooning and turning into blubbering idiots around him. She was wary that he might be a womanizer from the start, but, fortunately, that perception quickly changed when she got to know him.

She remembered her beach wedding on Long Island; the white curtains on the wedding arch billowing in the breeze, passing looks of love to each other through squinting eyes in the setting sun. It was the perfect day, a dropped tray of champagne glasses and the last-minute DJ cancellation non-withstanding. The usual wedding disasters that sometimes occur did not faze them one bit.

"Sam?"

"Oh sorry."

Sam was prone to daydreaming, or as her family often put it, going on autopilot. She had been doing it since she was a little girl; it was where she did her best thinking.

"I mean, I doubt I'll get any projects for the next week or so. Where do you want to go?"

"It's a surprise. You're going to love it."

"Oh, wow, but how did you know that the deal would—"

"Like you implied, it was a no-brainer."

Sam smiled and shook her head slightly. Elijah had all the faith in the world in her. Sometimes his assumptions and planning were bordering on obnoxious, but she figured there were worse qualities a husband could have. The rest of the night flew by the way nights do when a person is truly in the moment.

Sam and Elijah left the restaurant and stayed up late that night packing for the next morning. Elijah suggested she pack sports clothes and hiking shoes.

~ ~ ~

They left after 11am that morning, because Sam overslept. It was her body's attempt to recover the lost hours of sleep from pulling late-nighters earlier that week. She was grateful Elijah let her sleep in, knowing that he was silently stewing with impatience about the hours of precious vacation time lost. The trip took a total of six and a half hours, including two bathroom stops and a thirty-minute traffic jam.

The sky was beginning to burst open in tangerine orange at the horizon, when Sam and Elijah pulled up to the dock.

"Okay, you can open your eyes now."

"Oh my god! Are we at...? Bear Creek? Wow, I haven't been here since..."

"Since you were a kid, right?"

"Yeah, last time I went camping with my parents was when I was... twelve, I think. How did you know that I still liked camping?"

"I didn't. But I know we never do this kind of thing and you said you used to love it..."

"I did, I mean, I do. This is great! Thank you." She reached over and kissed Elijah. "Wait, I didn't see you pack a tent?"

Elijah laughed. "I actually got us a cabin."

"Oh, well that's perfect, too!"

"I know you said you used to go tent camping, but I figured you'd prefer the comfort of this, after the week you had, and it's kind of cold."

Sam knew that Elijah would hate tent camping: the mosquito attacks, sleeping on a pad, the trek to the bathrooms in the dark. She loved it though. Her father would take her and Michael as kids and she learned to love all the little things about it: gathering wood and building up the fire, being the first one to assemble her tent.

"And tomorrow I'm taking you to the waterfalls."

"Silver Falls hot spring?"

"Exactly. Sliding off waterfalls is precisely the therapy we need. Plus, you'll sleep like a baby. I promise."

"I don't think I'll have any trouble falling asleep after the week I've had. Elijah... this isn't going to be one of those vacations where you drag me out of bed before sunrise is it?"

A hint of dread came through in her voice. Elijah was an adventure vacationer. He looked at every vacation as an opportunity to cram as much activity as possible in as little time as possible, no matter where he went.

Not this time, Sam thought. This was her vacation, and this was the perfect time to relax and just lay around, without the constant sound of traffic outside her window.

"Well actually...I was thinking we could get up at dawn to get a head start on all the fun," Elijah replied menacingly.

"Elijah!"

He laughed, cracking one of his huge, devious smiles.

"I'm sleeping in till noon."

3. Waking Life: Stuck in the Attic

It's not that she wanted to intentionally lie to her sister. She, in fact, wasn't looking for her father at the moment. She had tried therapy to process her grief and move on, but it was too hard. As her therapist had put it during their last session, she did not want to move on. It was easier for her to hold on to the hope that her father was still out there, than consider any of the alternatives. So, repression it was. It's what she had been doing on and off, for years, but now all those memories came flooding back.

Sarah went down to her basement and sat down on a stool in front of a bulletin board pinned to the wall and covered in a dusty white sheet. She sighed as she unpinned the sheet to reveal a collage of overlapping pictures of her father, Hurston Davis. In addition, there were newspaper cutouts, patents, research articles, and even awards and certificates he had received for his work in Neurobiology. It was a hodgepodge of everything she could get her hands on that might give her some clue as to where he might have gone.

Now that she had the pocket watch, the anguish she now felt was as much of a motivator as it was a painful reminder of his disappearance. Sarah leaned on the table beside the bulletin board and tried to catch her breath. It had been four years since she had seen her father.

The last time she saw him, he was sitting in this very spot, muttering to himself. He was working in Texas at the time on some classified research and was back in Raleigh, staying with Sarah for a stint of four days. She was twenty-four at the time, exactly four years ago. He did his work in the evenings, so as not to take away from the time they had together. She remembered checking on him at 11:00 p.m. He had his composition notebooks opened up before him and was writing with a fervor. She could not break him from his spell. He refused all food that evening, considering it a distraction. When she came to check on him early that morning, he was gone. He had left a note written in hurried handwriting that he had a major breakthrough in his research and had to go. This type of behavior was not necessarily surprising to Sarah, but when his messages became shorter and less frequent, she knew something was wrong. After a couple weeks, he stopped responding all together and his phone went straight to voicemail. From then on, it was radio silence.

Sarah was a daddy's girl, while Bri was closer to their mother. Everyone said Sarah was just like her father and had inherited some of his less-desirable traits, like her propensity to be late, talk to herself, and obsess over things she had no control over. Her sister was worried about her more than anyone else and looked out for her over the years, making sure she wasn't spending all her time sucked into the vacuum of the basement, glued to a project, and making sure she got her "essential" monthly manicure. Sarah knew that Bri was trying to keep her feeling positive, and she really did love and appreciate her for her efforts.

The private investigator Sarah had hired had given up hope long before she was no longer able pay him. She took the pocket watch out of her jacket and rubbed her thumb over the embossed train on the front. It took her back twenty-two years.

She was six, staring out of the train window as the trees flew past her at rocket speed. It was her family's first move to a real house. Before that, it was apartment living and frequent moves to avoid increasing rent in the city.

North Carolina was different, more greenery, more peace. She remembered eleven-year-old Bri holding her hand as they stepped off the Amtrak. Their first real house was something Sarah would always remember: an old, blue, two-story home, nestled on one and a half acres, with a porch swing in the backyard and weeping willows in the front. There were pencil marks on the kitchen door frame leading into the living room, tracking Sarah and Bri's growth over the years. The 1940's home was small and required too much work, according to her parents, which is why the family moved three years later, when Sarah's mother found a higher paying job in the city.

~~~

The bedroom clock read quarter till three in the morning, and Sarah was lying wide awake staring at the ceiling, her thumb fixedly rubbing the embossed train of the pocket watch.

The phone rang.

"Hello?"

"Hey baby, you're still awake?" Her boyfriend Joey was calling late again.

"Yeah, I can't sleep."

"Are you still upset with Bri? Have you talked to her since she gave you the pocket watch?"

"No."

"You want me to come over?"

"Joey, it's three in the morning."

Three months ago, Joey began working second shift at a highway truck stop restaurant as a line cook.

"It's okay, I want to come over. It's been three days."

"I know. I just really need to get some sleep."

"Okay... you've been really distant lately."

"Look Joey, I'll call you tomorrow after work, okay?"

"Okay... goodnight. I love you."

"Goodnight." Sarah hung up and threw her phone down on her bed. She didn't want to be mean. Joey meant well and was just concerned about her. In fact, she usually saw him at least once a day, so three days apart was actually a fairly long stretch for their relationship. When she met him, he was living with, and taking care of, his aging grandmother who refused to go into assisted living. He moved in with her since the rest of the family refused to shoulder the burden.

She was instantly attracted to him in that profound carnal way when they bumped into each other at the local taco stand outside her apartment complex. He was tall and slim, with wavy, medium-length, brown hair and chestnut brown eyes. He had a bronze complexion and reminded her of someone who would be surfing or lounging on the beach, just laid back. He was also clumsy and ended up wearing his taco when they met. Sarah just happened to be at the right place, at the right time with those napkins on that fateful day. When she learned his story, she felt like she could relate.

Joey had a profound dedication to and respect for his elders. Sarah was close to her grandfather growing up and would sit on the porch listening to his stories for hours, while everyone else went about their business, brushing him off with a polite smile or nod, then scattering. The story repeated with her father; only Sarah had stayed to listen. Her family would never admit to how they acted, but Sarah knew deep in their hearts they were well aware. Her father was almost like an elderly man himself, even though he was middle-aged. Sarah listened when no one else would listen and paid attention when her father could not be bothered with the functions of basic living when he got absorbed in his work.

Joey knew how Sarah got from time to time and wanted to make sure she didn't go off the deep end. They had known each other for four years, and at this point in their relationship, Joey knew it all: her searches, her history with her father, and her propensity to become hyper-focused. Her journalism job provided her with a convenient cover whenever she did go into one of her search modes. When her family wondered why she had no time to see them, she would use work as an excuse. The truth was that she had the time, but when the obsessive tendencies took over, she developed tunnel vision and she was becoming more deeply committed to finding her father by the minute. *This time, it will be different.*

~~~

It had been a week since she had spoken with her sister.

"Oh crap!" Sarah scrambled out of bed and immediately fell to the floor, Drano yelped in pain and wiggled out from under her legs. "Drano, not today!" She was going to be late for work again. Every day this week she had been sleeping through the alarm clock and waking up at least fifteen minutes behind schedule. No matter what she did, the morning drowsiness only got worse. She grabbed her phone and fumbled over the keys to call her manager at Roasters, her heart sinking at the realization that this time there were no missed calls from work, dialing correctly the second time. *What is happening to me?* She knew. Her obsession with finding her father was, once again, interfering with her life. From experience she knew she wouldn't be able to move on until she saw it through, or until she hit a dead end she could not move past and then forced herself to move on for a time.

"Hey! Sorry Anne, I overslept. I'll be —" Sarah stammered. "But Anne, I promise I won't be late tomorrow, it's just I've got this new story... I know, but...listen, if you just— I see. Okay. Fine. I... I understand. Bye."

The phone rang again. Sarah threw it forcefully across the bed then plopped down belly first on the bed to pick it up again.

"Hello?! Joey this is really not a good time."

"You've been saying that all week. I'm beginning to think that you don't want to see me anymore."

"Joey, come on, you know that's not true. I've just been ... Drano! God, he peed on the carpet! Crap, I have to go, I'll call you later. I promise."

"Can I come over after you get off work, maybe we can go to that Italian place you like?"

"Joey, I just got fired and I've got this new story I'm working on."

"What? What happened?"

"I'll talk to you about it later, okay? You know what an asshole Anne can be."

"Okay, fine. Call me later."

Sarah stared in disillusionment at Drano, who stood by the sliding glass door, head cocked, producing a concerned whimper. She cleaned up his mess, thinking how ungrateful he seemed to have a live-in maid mopping up his pee, and threw herself face down on the bed. She rolled over and popped open the pocket watch. She watched her tears blow up the picture of her and her father's faces like a magnifying glass.

4. Dream Life: Canoeing before Dawn

For once, Sam woke up way before the alarm clock went off. The sun wasn't even up. She sat up in the pitch-black room, staring out at the motionless trees through the bedroom window. She thought it was funny how when she used to go camping with her parents, they would never let her sleep in. She would be rudely awakened at the crack of dawn so they could fit as many activities as they could, into their "vacation."

She looked over at Elijah who looked strangely like a crime scene cutout: head to one side, mouth gaping open, arms and legs splayed out. She covered her mouth to suppress a giggle. She quietly wiggled out of bed and tiptoed to the other room where her bags lay, still unpacked, as she had firmly decided not to do any form of work on this vacation. She would be back in an hour, hoping that Elijah would still be asleep when she returned. He was one of those deep sleepers and wouldn't wake, even if a tornado was tearing through the yard. However, come 8:00 a.m., and he would spring out of bed, wide awake, on his fine-tuned internal clock. He promised her that he would let her sleep in this morning though, and she was counting on that.

Yawning quietly, she slipped into her fuzzy boots and pulled her heavy sweatshirt over her head. She tucked her hair into a messy bun, then closed the back door gingerly behind her as she stepped out onto the dewy grass.

The cabin was behind the old creek where she used to go craw-fishing with her father and brother. There was a spot there she loved, where the creek met the river mouth. It was surrounded with low-hanging willows where you could just float in a canoe and sit under them, completely shaded in your own world. It was beautiful.

As Sam approached the creek, she noticed a couple of old canoes lined up on the bank. They looked abandoned and were covered in cobwebs, their insides green with moss and rot. After a quick once over, she decided they were sturdy enough. *Who in the world would just leave these here for anyone to take?* It was only a passing thought. Sam's keen desire for adventure quickly took over. This was an opportunity she could not pass up.

She picked up one of the paddles and threw it inside a canoe. She pushed off the bank and hopped in just like her father had shown her when she was a kid. It was just like she remembered. *Why haven't I been here in so long?*

Her life in the city had become a whirlwind of meetings, presentations, and projects. She loved it but missed the outdoors terribly. She oversaw a team of over forty people. She got to project her creative vision and see it come to life, just like when she was a little girl, making and selling handwoven wicker baskets to the local residents and visitors of Bear Creek. Except now, she was all grown up and her work became exceedingly more complicated. She conducted competitor analysis, market research and design, and sales strategy. She must have made at least seventy-five dollars off those baskets each vacation; enough Starburst and Tic Tacs to last her all year. But what she remembered loving most, was just being outside with her father, swimming in the lake, stumbling over the slimy moss stones in her socks, trying to scare a crawfish into her bucket.

She had not felt so alive in a long time. Excited by the scent of wisteria in the air, the cool breeze blowing across her face, the sounds of bugs and birds chirping away in noisy unison, she paddled on. It was sensational! Sam put her hand up to shield her eyes from the rising sun, in the gleam she caught a glimpse of an old grandfatherly tree, leaning slightly to its side.

Sam's heart raced with excitement, "This is it!" she said aloud to no one. She could not believe that after all this time, she had found the exact tree. She had to row harder to pass under its thick green canopy. Once through, she grabbed onto the trunk to steady herself and the canoe. As she ran her hand over the bark, she saw it, the engraved letters from over sixteen years ago, reading: *Sam and Benjamin were here.*

Sam passed her hand over the letters and smiled. They had grown like a keloid scar into the old bark. She would call her father when she got back into town, maybe take him out for lunch and a movie. It had been over three months since she'd seen him and her mother.

~~~

Sam crawled back into bed around 7:30 a.m., wrapped one arm around the snoozing Elijah and nestled face down into his neck, blissfully exhausted. At 11:30 a.m. they were out the door, headed to Silver Falls.

"Did you get enough sleep? You seem tired." Elijah asked.

"Yeah... I am. I woke up too early and couldn't go back to sleep."

She didn't know why she was omitting information. Something about her experience just seemed too precious to share, as if talking about it would violate the sacredness of her and her father's secret hiding spot.

~~~

The waterfall was a twenty-foot drop into the warm, bubbling hot spring below. Staring down at the plummeting water, she realized she had forgotten how high up it really was and how much braver she was when she was twelve. The business world had made her savvy and quick witted, but this, this, she was not prepared for. She climbed tenuously up the rope on the side of the rock face, and waited her turn in line behind a crazy, middle-aged man, who slid in head-first and upside-down. Sam's heart raced.

"Ahhh!" Sam let out a vicious scream, squeezing her eyes shut as she slid, stiff as a wooden plank, off the slippery surface and plunged into the water below. She felt the water bubbles rising up all around her, tickling her sides. She had cut down deep below the surface and was sinking still further down, feeling so comfortable as the silent stillness of the water cradled her. As she felt the pressure in her chest increasing, from lack of oxygen, a blurry vision came into focus in her mind's eye. It was her, sitting in a coffee shop, talking with another girl who was now coming more clearly into view. She had long, straight blonde hair and cherry lipstick.

She looks familiar, Sam thought. And just like that, the image was gone. Sam remembered where she was and began to struggle for air. The feeling of relaxation suddenly gone. She broke the surface of the noisy, foaming water, coughing and gasping for air. No one around her seemed to notice. Elijah slid in head first from above and popped out beside her, grabbing her up in his arms.

"Hi, gorgeous," he said, kissing her face and smiling at her.

He's really enjoying this.

"Hi," she replied, bewildered, wrapping her arms and legs around him like a spider monkey and giving him a half-hearted smile. "Sorry, I just got a little disoriented."

"Let's go home," Elijah said scooping Sam up into his arms and carrying her out of the water, like a gladiator carrying his maiden. He even puffed his chest out a bit, making Sam burst into laughter.

~~~

Dinner that night was refreshingly simple and satisfying; fresh caught trout they fished from the river, grilled over hickory smoked wood chips from the local mini mart. Sam sat on the wooden bench, munching on salad and talking over the adventures of the day.

"I still can't believe you slid off that waterfall upside-down," Sam said taking a big gulp of sweet tea.

"Yeah, you know it's been a while since I've cut loose like that," Elijah replied. "The practice has been killing me lately; working on all those stupid medical claims... and that one guy with the arthritis, you remember?"

"Uh-huh," replied Sam, dryly.

"Well, I'm convinced that it's all in his head. Maybe I can refer him to Dr. Shandi?"

"Ha. Ha."

"No, I'm serious! There's nothing wrong with that man's joints. In fact, I saw him jogging around Lake Jennie last week."

"Elijah!" Sam rolled her eyes at him, incredulously.

"No, really!" Elijah grinned.

Elijah was a good lawyer. He had his clients' best interests at heart and loved to take on cases that made a positive difference, even though most of his clients were big firms. He told Sam that his motivation came from a feeling. He loved the feeling of helping someone turn their life around; the feeling of seeing peace come over someone who deserved to get their affairs in order; the ones that got the money they deserved to feed and clothe their kids; the ones who salvaged some dignity in their final days. This, however, was not a feeling he got from his big clients, but they were the ones who put bread on the table, so to speak... at Le Gordon.

Suddenly the room was spinning. Sam held her head in her hands. "Jeez, I feel like I'm going to pass out."

"You can't be tired already, it's only 8:00 p.m. You never fall asleep this early..."

"I'm not tired... I'm dizzy."

Elijah came to her side and guided her to the bedroom. "Here, lie down."

Sam sat down on the bed and pulled the covers up around her.

"Did you maybe hit your head when you slid off the waterfall?"

"Yeah, that could be it, or maybe it's because I was underwater for too long and got disoriented. I think I'm just going to lay down for a while."

"Okay, you rest, and I'll come check on you soon. Do you want me to stay?"

"No, it's okay. I actually don't feel as dizzy now, just tired. Goodnight. I love you."

"I love you too. I guess we can get that early start tomorrow morning!" Elijah clapped his hands together in enthusiasm.

"Yeah, I guess so." Sam shook her head at him. "Ouch!"

"Careful with that noggin of yours."

Sam flashed him a devilish look.

After Elijah turned off the lights, Sam sat there and stared into the darkness. It felt good to be alone for a while. She wanted to process what she saw earlier. Was it oxygen deprivation? A hallucination? Sam had no history of that. Then she remembered something. She turned on a lamp and crouched by her duffle bag, digging through the main compartment, until she pulled them out, Balixa. She turned the bottle over to read the side effects: Changes in appetite, Constipation, Diarrhea, Dizziness, Daytime drowsiness, Dry mouth or throat, Vivid dreams. *Okay, but vivid dreams are not the same as what happened to me.* She crawled back into bed, placing the pills on the nightstand and turned on the T.V.

After an hour of reality television and some ice cream in bed with Elijah she decided that yet again, she was not going to fall asleep naturally. She swallowed a pill and turned out the lights. Not long after, she was asleep.

~~~

Sam could see herself inside a rising fog.

"Who's there?" She called out, knowing that she was not alone. She heard a murmur, a faint whisper and then a thud, like someone falling to the ground. She rushed into the fog, forgetting her fear.

The fog was not clearing, and the thudding continued, growing louder.

Suddenly, the mist parted in a neatly divided white curtain. Behind it stood a young girl. Her face was a blur. Sam frowned. *Something is not right.* Sam shuddered. The girl's face was blurred, like the snow of a television set. The girl held out her hand.

"My daddy fell, can you help me pick him up? Mommy says he's dead, but I think he's just sleeping."

"Can you show me where he is?" she heard herself say, in third person.

"I don't know. I don't know where he is, but he keeps on falling. I can't see him! I can't see him!" The little girl shouted and ran off as the fog began closing in around Sam again.

She caught a glimpse of the girl's hair and skirt billowing in a strange wind that seemed to come from nowhere, before she disappeared. The thudding grew louder still.

Gasping for air, she sprang up from the nightmare. This time jumping out of her bed and making it to the doorway before realizing where she was. *The dreams are getting worse,* Sam thought, warm tears running down her face. She had never cried over a dream before, not one like this, where the characters had no relationship to her. *What the hell is wrong with me?* Suddenly, Sam felt silly and angry at herself for getting so emotional over a dream that meant nothing, a side effect of a medication.

She looked over at Elijah and laughed, then walked over to him and laughed again, a little louder and closer to his ear, in a kind of petulant way. *Figures, he wouldn't wake up, even to the sound of my screaming.* Then came a terrifying thought: *maybe it's not the medication.* This was the first time she had experienced a dream like this, and she had been taking Balixa for over a month now.

Sam wrapped the thin fleece blanket around herself and tiptoed to the backyard.

There was a wooden swing beneath a large weeping willow. She made her way to it gingerly, trying not to step on a rock or twig. The night was cold and silent. Sam sat down on the swing, wrapping a fleece blanket around herself, and leaned her head back, the willow cascading around her body in wispy green streamers. That same deep calm came over her, as it did underwater at Silver Falls. She closed her eyes and rocked back and forth. In her mind's eye, an image began to come into focus. It was the little girl sitting on a swing, notebook and crayon in hand, staring out at the fireflies. Sam opened her eyes, looking up at the stars and the intermittent yellow gleams of fireflies. *I must have fallen asleep. What a strange day.* Sam went back inside and fell into a deep, dreamless sleep.

5. Waking Life: The Hospital

T hirteen unheard voicemails flashed in neurotic red on Sarah's answering machine. Her cell phone's voice mailbox was full too, as she never remembered to clear it. Bri had come by numerous times, leaving her latest boyfriend's "authentic Italian lasagna" on the doorstep, going through her usual caregiver rituals. Sarah was too busy for the world to bother her with their concerns.

This wasn't the first time Sarah had barricaded herself inside her house for days. No, this was the third or fourth time. Bri and her mother thought it was bipolar disorder and a psychiatrist confirmed it. Sarah was diagnosed two years ago when she had gone through what was described as a hypomanic episode. But she believed all the psychiatrist saw were her symptoms: rapid speech, insomnia, high energy, flight of ideas. Yes, Sarah had experienced all those things, and going by the book, it sounded like a pretty valid diagnosis, but he was not seeing the full picture. Sarah knew it wasn't a chemical imbalance that drove her to this state, but the glimmer of hope that her father was alive and coming back to her, and this time hope had appeared in the shape of a pocket watch.

After exhausting all the usual avenues: online searches, obituaries, police reports; all of which had once again turned out to be fruitless, Sarah decided it was time to pull out the secret stash. She had been keeping a box of her father's things, mostly notebooks, but also keepsakes, a few of his shirts, a pair of old glasses, as well as various patents and awards he had received throughout his lifetime. She had gone through everything at least three dozen times, but some of his writings still held mysteries, secrets only his mind could decipher.

Sarah pulled her hair back into a messy bun and tucked the loose strands behind her ears. She reached down and touched her growling stomach, moving her hand up to her protruding ribs. Sarah had always been skinny, mostly because her insatiable mind would suck her into her work for hours at a time. She would forget to eat when she was in these modes, sipping on cold coffee she had set aside and forgotten about, reheated and forgotten about again.

Sarah got up from the basement table and opened the mini fridge: a pack of baloney, some American cheese slices and a jar of pickles. "What, no bread?" Sarah muttered to herself as she put everything on the counter before her. *God, I sound just like Dad*, she thought. Sarah flipped open one of his notebooks, as she munched on a pickle wrapped in baloney. She laughed softly, as her eyes fell on a page with a ketchup stain. *Typical*, she thought, *never putting down his work, even to eat...*

Sarah's father had spent a lot of time at her apartment after she got her own place, mostly to get out of the house when Sarah's mother would become infuriated with him. Hurston and Addelyn were married for only two years when his obsessions began kicking in: the incessant writing, late nights and quality time lost with family. Being kicked out was almost a weekly occurrence.

The browned ketchup stain was from their picnic at the lake. She was eight, her father must have been forty-one. He was drenched in sweat, overdressed for the warm weather. They were at a picnic table with the lunch mom had packed them: hot dogs, a ketchup bottle (they loved their ketchup), potato chips, chocolate chip cookies, and lemonade.

Her father had wandered off somewhere down the trail as Sarah began eating a ketchup drenched hot dog. He told her he would be back before she was done, muttering to himself in his way. It was at least an hour before he came back. Sarah sat there by herself, feeling uncomfortable as families at the surrounding picnic tables ate and laughed together, whispering to each other, some even coming over to the table to ask where her parents were.

Her parents had been separated for one year at that point and Sarah had become exceptionally crafty at covering up her father's neglectful behaviors, which occurred more often than she liked to admit. She heard about kids being taken away from their parents, so she wised up quickly. Even her mother had no idea what her father was doing at that point, and Addelyn still believed that her husband's obsessions did not interfere with his ability to parent, or maybe she couldn't handle the guilt of not letting Sarah spend time with him.

The writing on the page was sloppy and large, the letters falling off the lines. She suddenly remembered that the writing was hers from many years ago. And the writing above it was her father's. It was a game they played sometimes, making up riddles to keep the mind sharp, as he would say. This one was particularly interesting.

What is the name of something small, something young, whose mind has no walls? It runs and leaps all day in light and then awakes to play at night. But beware! It's watched at day, and late at night keen eyes do prey. When all the owls convene to hoot and poke and prod at Lizard's Foot, they play in whistles on night's flute. Their stories tell of dreams turned dark, of dark turned light, where sleep is stark. For there is only sleep in dreams and dreams are only life's blue screens.

And her crabby and defeated response underneath: Daddy you are crazy. This is too hard. I give up!

Sarah laughed aloud. Sometimes, even though her father was a brilliant chemist and neurobiologist, he forgot about basic things, like her developmental level: the fact that her young mind could not possibly wrap itself around something so complicated and obscure.

Still, it was interesting that her father was somewhat of a poet. She studied the writing for a moment, trying to make sense of the words. *Okay so it's something that's not sleeping day or night, it's young and it's being studied by owls?* This was strange, nothing in this riddle seemed cohesive to Sarah, like her father's other riddles used to be. Sarah suddenly remembered her father talking about a sleep study he conducted when she was younger. It went on for a couple of years. *Maybe the riddle has something to do with his research at the time?*

The next day, Sarah put on her most expensive dark blue blazer and pencil skirt, a silk white blouse, a pair of black pumps, and her green framed glasses. She smoothed and pinned up her loose hair. She looked professional, and not the least bit the crazy, neurotic person she felt like. And she needed that today. She would be scoping out the psychiatric hospital.

She had already run the usual searches, checked the archives of all the local news sources, including her own. Apparently, *Resonance Weekly* wrote a tiny story on the hospital renovation about a month ago. It was more of an aside really, and it didn't provide much detail into what was happening. There was no information available other than inconclusive banter about hospital remodeling.

~~~

When Sarah walked up to the hospital's front desk, the receptionist was on the phone talking in an irritated tone to someone clearly in disagreement with her. The woman smiled politely at Sarah and hung up the phone without saying goodbye.

"Hi! Can I help you?" The receptionist chirped, in a Jekyll and Hyde change in demeanor.

Sarah stared at her for a moment before responding.

"Yes, my name's Sarah Davis. I'm a reporter from *Resonance Weekly*. I was hoping to speak to the director about the hospital renovations."

"Is there a particular reason *Resonance Weekly* is interested in hospital renovations? I thought you people were here last month."

"I'm writing a small piece on city development and I figured it was worth looking into in greater depth. After all, this is the only psychiatric hospital around and a large fixture and resource for the community."

"I see... hold on a minute." The receptionist dialed and after a minute or so someone picked up.

"Dr. Neely, there's someone here from *Resonance Weekly* here to talk to you about hospital renovations. Uh-huh... okay, I'll let her know. Thank you. Bye." She hung up the phone.

"Miss uh?"

"Davis, Sarah Davis."

"Ms. Davis, Ms. Neely will be down in just a few minutes. You can wait over there." The receptionist pointed at the right side of the room, which was tightly packed with small wooden tables, blue chairs and a kiddie sofa.

Sarah sat down, looking around the room. A lot had changed since she was here four years ago, visiting her father. The walls were no longer stark hospital white, but a more pleasant shade of sky blue. She stared at a picture on the wall to her left. It was an oil painting of an older white man, his mustache curled on the ends, a look of indignant stoicism on his face. The portrait seemed ancient.

"That's the founder of the hospital," said the receptionist. "He founded the hospital one hundred and twelve years ago."

"Wow. I thought this hospital's only been around for thirty-five years."

"Yes, well this location has. The first hospital opened over a century ago."

"Oh, I didn't know that!" Sarah flipped open her notebook and quickly jotted down the information. "Where's the first one located?"

"Oh, in some obscure desert valley in Texas called Lizard's Foot."

"Lizard's Foot?" Sarah asked inquisitively, putting her pen down and looking at the receptionist.

"Yeah, that's the one. Lizard's Foot. Lord I know, that was my reaction too. People have some strange names for places."

"Yes, they do," Sarah said in a monotone voice.

So, Dad has some connection to the psychiatric hospital in Lizard's Foot, the original hospital. Wait, isn't that where those sleep studies were conducted?

Sarah's train of thought was abruptly interrupted by the pitchy clacking of heels on linoleum. A very official and serious looking woman approached from the back hallway, cell phone glued to one ear, a blue file in the other. Sarah glanced back at the painting. *Oh, you've got nothing on her.* She exuded confidence in her swift strut, despite her four-inch pumps and the skin-tight skirt restricting her leg movement to very small and calculated steps. Her wavy, dark brown hair was pinned back smartly, not a strand out of place.

The woman stared directly at Sarah with darkly lined, gray eyes, that had no softness in them. She had a pronounced yet elegant nose, which somehow added to her commanding presence. She was not smiling. Quickly she ended her phone conversation and outstretched her hand. "Hello, how may I help you?" Dr. Neely shook Sarah's hand firmly.

"Hi Dr. Neely, my name is Sarah Davis. I wanted to ask you a few questions about hospital renovations... I believe this hospital is a vital community resource and the public should be informed of any new developments to further the treatment and well-being of its residents."

"Oh, I see. Well, Ms. Davis—"

"Sarah."

"Sarah, I will be happy to answer your questions and show you around, but I doubt you'll find these renovations newsworthy. We're simply remodeling a few rooms to make them more spacious and functional. Here, follow me and I'll show you." Dr. Neely turned on a dime and began walking back down the hallway before Sarah had a chance to respond. "Here is where the first renovations took place. This is the recreation room. We put in new sofas, a pool table and extended the walls to make a larger television viewing area."

"I see. I'm sure the residents are enjoying that."

"They sure are." Dr. Neely picked up the pace again. "Over here is the laboratory, where we check vitals, administer medication, do weekly checkups, etc. There was too little space in here, so we extended the space to fit more equipment."

"I see. And what sort of equipment did you add to this room?"

"Let's see... a state-of-the-art blood pressure reader and scale for our clients with eating disorders and other health issues."

"Okay."

"Now let me show you the last room, the one with the most renovations. They actually haven't finished this one yet."

Sarah followed Dr. Neely down a long hallway to two double metal doors.

"Now this... this is our sleep lab. We have installed new EEGs, MRIs and beds."

Sleep lab.

"Well this *is* interesting. Are you conducting some research here?"

"Well that is our hope for this lab." Dr. Neely slightly narrowed her eyes. "For now, it's really more for monitoring patients after medical procedures as well as for monitoring medications for effectiveness and side effects. Our old equipment was outdated."

After a careful scan of the room, Sarah's eyes fell upon the closet door, obstructed by a heart monitor. The door was slightly ajar. There was light shining through it, casting a bright blue incandescent glow onto the floor.

"Okay. Well thank you for showing me around... Dr. Neely, is there another room back there?" Sarah pointed to the closet. "I didn't see a door for it from the outside."

"You're very welcome. And, that? That's just the equipment storage room. It's pretty large, but no, there is no additional room beyond that one. Someone must have left a machine on. I'll have someone see to it. Now if you don't mind, Ms. Davis, I do have an important meeting starting in fifteen minutes." Dr. Neely began walking towards the door.

Weird.

"Thank you for your time. I do have some additional questions for my story."

"Story? You still want to write a story? Right, well fax your questions to Wanda at the front desk and I'll get back to you as soon as I can. Thank you, Ms. Davis."

Dr. Neely left the room abruptly and turned off the lights, leaving Sarah standing in the dark and awkwardly running to catch up to her. Sarah turned her head one last time to look at the light. The blueish glow flickered brighter for a moment. *There is definitely more than a utility closet back there.*

6. DREAM LIFE: DREAM JOURNAL

A cloud of dust filled the air, making Sam cough violently.

"Mom, how long has it been since you've cleaned out the attic?!" Sam yelled down the stairwell, choking on the scratchy particles caught in her throat.

"Oh, you know...." Connie Brennan responded from downstairs.

Never, Sam thought.

"Come on down, honey. I made your favorite!"

"One minute!" Sam called down as she pulled an old book from a cardboard box. "My dream journal," Sam said aloud.

She pulled the large, dusty, leather-bound book onto her lap. Her childhood journal was filled with drawings, little poems and her dream descriptions. She had forgotten all about it. Her mom must have thought it precious and stowed it away. Sam sat cross-legged on the floorboards and opened up the book down the middle, the way she always did as a kid. "She wanted to surprise herself," she would tell her mother, when told to start from the beginning.

Her breath caught in her throat. There it was. The picture. A little girl sitting on a swing, a crayon colored blue/black night sky filled with small yellow and white dots, *fireflies and stars*, she thought. A large willow loomed overhead, and there was a cabin in the background. She must have been at that cabin before, as a little girl. *Wait a minute, this is my dream journal, stuff of pure imagination.* Sam remembered a couple of the dreams in this book, depicted as illustrations. But, how could this have been a dream, if it was a real place? *Maybe I went there and then dreamed about it or maybe I didn't just record dreams.* Sam grabbed the journal and headed downstairs.

"Hey mom, do you remember this journal?"

"Let me see," said Connie, adjusting her reading glasses. "Oh sure, your dream journal! You were a very creative child."

"Yeah, I guess I was… mom do you remember a place called Bear Creek?"

"Of course I do, why?"

"I think this picture was based on a cabin we visited when I was younger," Sam said pointing at the childish, but highly detailed crayon drawing.

"Let me see," Connie said frowning over the picture scrupulously. "No, I can't say that we've ever been there. Remember, we always went camping. We never could afford those fancy cabins with those porch swings."

"That's what I thought, too."

"Oh look, your father's home. You can ask him."

"Hi Dad! How'd the trial go?" Sam smiled at her father from the kitchen doorway as he hung up his coat.

"Wiped the floor with those guys, he grinned and shook his head. But more importantly, how are you? Is Elijah treating you well, or do I get to try out my new twelve gauge on him?"

"Ha-ha." Sam grinned at her father. He was always cracking jokes.

They were corny, dirty or just downright obscene at times, but with him there was never a dull moment. Sam's father, Benjamin Brennan was one on the best criminal prosecutors in New York. His reputation preceded him. Benjamin worked for the district attorney and was known for working hard, putting in overtime and doing whatever necessary to get a conviction. As a result, he almost never lost a case.

"Connie, do I smell pot roast?"

"Yes, you do."

"It smells sublime."

"Why thank you," Connie smiled and gave him a little wink. Benjamin promptly gave her a little slap on the butt.

Sam rolled her eyes. Her parents acted like they were still teenagers. They kept their love going strong by reenacting their early dating years. Benjamin would leave the house and come knock on the front door to pick Connie up for dates. She insisted he do this every time.

Connie even wrote a self-help book for women in troubled marriages. She was convinced that she knew how to keep a marriage spicy, and well, it was working for them, even after twenty-three years.

"Dad, do you remember taking us camping at Bear Creek?"

"Yes, I do. And I remember you getting eaten alive by mosquitoes every night, wandering around the campsite with Michael. You were their favorite meal, speaking of which..." Benjamin said eyeing the meat ravenously and sitting down at the table.

"Do you remember a place with willows and a porch swing behind a cabin?" Sam put the picture in front of the carnivore.

"I can't say that I do," reflected Benjamin, as he helped himself to his usual, extra-large portion of pot roast and mashed potatoes.

"Pass the gravy, hun," he said licking his saucy thumb and reaching across the table.

"You were a great artist," he continued as he smothered the large helping of roast on his plate, "but who knows, maybe you wandered around in the campground at night and found a swing."

"Maybe, but this drawing is very specific. You know how I focused in on details, and the place I was at last week with Elijah looked just like this drawing, almost to a T. I don't know, it's just strange. I haven't been there before, but at the same time, I feel like I have. I don't know, maybe I'll show the journal to Dr. Shandi tomorrow."

"Great idea, honey. Let her psychoanalyze that!" Benjamin said with a grin.

"Oh, be quiet!" Sam laughed.

~~~

Sam pulled up to Dr. Shandi's office the following afternoon, wondering what she would make of all this, and somewhat anxious to bring it up.

"Hi Sam, how are you this week?" Dr. Shandi smiled up from the lime green couch, her long curly hair spilling around her circular, purple glasses.

"Good. I went to the mountains with Elijah last week."

Sam was holding back. She was an expert when it came to putting on appearances, a natural talent. She could even fool Dr. Shandi, sometimes. This was not one of those times.

"Great. How was the trip?" Dr. Shandi crossed her arms and raised one sharply lined brow.

"Wonderful. It was a much-needed break."

"Well, you definitely needed to unwind after all the hours you've put in on that project."

"Yes."

"What's that in your hand?"

"Oh this? This is my dream journal, from when I was a kid," Sam said as she contemplated how to tell Dr. Shandi about the drawing without sounding insane. She bounced up and down in her chair nervously.

"Wow, what a wonderful artifact! So, you kept one back then too. May I take a look?" Dr. Shandi asked with an outstretched hand.

Dr. Shandi was a very vocal and colorful woman. She was opinionated, but not overbearing in her delivery. That's why Sam loved coming. She could vent away, knowing that Dr. Shandi would always shoot straight with her, without coming down on her.

Today, Dr. Shandi wore a wizard-sleeve butterfly shirt and bell bottom high-waist jeans. She grew up in the 60s and it definitely left a lasting impression on her, not only on her fashion sense, but in her liberal political views and even in the way she practiced therapy, Sam thought.

"Sure," Sam sat down slowly on the sofa and handed the book over. "Well, that's why I brought it. It's been driving me crazy."

"How so?"

"Well, I found it last night and was just flipping through it, you know? Then I found this picture and it weirded me out. I just... I don't know... it felt like I had drawn a place I visited before, but when I asked my family, no one could remember going to a place like that."

"Hmm... do you think you dreamed it up? It is a dream journal after all."

"Well, I thought that initially, but no, I don't know how to explain it, but I feel like I've actually been there before, like it was a memory. I just can't shake that feeling."

"Hmmm, interesting," muttered Dr. Shandi as she leafed through the journal. "You know Sam, the information you're seeking is probably already stored somewhere in your memory. There's probably something to that feeling, you just can't consciously remember it."

"Well that's frustrating."

"I know."

"Is there something you think I can do to, I don't know, jog my memory?"

"Well... yes, there are several things we could try... I'm wondering if hypnosis might be the best route here. Have you heard of hypnosis for memory recall?"

This type of therapy was right up Dr. Shandi's alley. Sam could tell Dr. Shandi was trying to suppress the excitement in her voice.

Finally, she could use that hypnotherapy training she painstakingly learned at the two-month mindfulness retreat in Tibet.

"Yes, I've heard of that... you would be controlling my mind or something, right? Guiding my thoughts? How do you know it will work?"

"No, not really controlling. It's more like a guided, deep relaxation. And I don't know if it will work on you... for sure."

"I'd be willing to try it, if anything, just out of curiosity," Sam said.

"Yes. You know your willingness will be a big factor in determining whether you will be a good candidate for hypnosis. If your subconscious is nagging you about something, then that's good reason to explore it."

Sam chuckled, thinking of her father's words from the night before.

"Oh, I assure you it's a lot less cheesy than you think. We can try a short session today if you would like, we just need to go over some rules and precautions first. I will need you to sign a couple forms."

"Okay, that's fine."

"Also, I don't want to derail anything else you planned to talk to me about today," Dr. Shandi said, throwing Sam the proverbial bone.

"No, I'm fine with moving forward with hypnosis today."

"Okay, great!"

After a thorough explanation and introduction to hypnosis and some minor paperwork, Dr. Shandi spent a few minutes rearranging furniture and dimming the lights. They were finally ready to begin, with only about twenty-five minutes left in their session.

"Okay, first thing is relaxation. I want you to get into a comfortable position and uncross your arms and legs... there... good, just lay them at your sides. Now, I want you to close your eyes, relax and just listen to the sound of my voice." Dr. Shandi shuffled around the room, looking through her nature sounds CDs. "Ah, this will work perfectly."

Seconds later, Sam was listening to the noisy chirping of crickets filling the room. It felt like she was back there, at the campsite again. Sam sighed audibly.

"That's right, release all of your tension. This will help create the necessary atmosphere, the white noise, if you will," Dr. Shandi continued.

She sunk back into the couch, allowing her arms to rest limply at her sides. She could hear Dr. Shandi's voice growing softer and softer. In her mind's eye, a blurry form began coming into view. It was a little girl. Yes, she had seen her before, long brown hair, white dress. It was the girl from her dream, looking for her father.

"Sam. Sam." Dr. Shandi's voice broke through from overhead, as if through a muffled speakerphone at a baseball game. "Sam, what do you see?"

What is that? This is so strange.

"I see a girl in a white dress. She's walking through a field. No wait, it's a yard." *This is so weird.* "There's a small green house and white fence and... oh wait she's walking towards a tree now. It's a willow..." *What's with all the willows?* Sam thought to herself, though her awareness of thinking to herself now seemed like a very abstract and foreign concept. "There is a shed in the yard. The girl is running towards it and trying to open the doors. They're locked. She's turning around now. The sun is hitting her face. I can't see her face."

"Think Sam. Who is this girl? There's a reason your subconscious isn't letting you see her face. Just concentrate. See if you can will her face to come into view, it is *your* mind's vision after all."

Sam jumped. She was not used to Dr. Shandi's voice speaking to her in this manner. It was as though she was in her own narrated movie.

"Ok. It's nighttime," Sam continued. "There are lights on in the living room, but she's sitting outside on a swing. There's a notebook in her hands and she's writing something. I can't see the writing."

"Ok Sam, come back to me now. Just listen to the sound of my voice. You're becoming more and more awake."

Wait, why am I... leaving?

"Because you're going too deep for a first session. You need to come back and regroup."

She felt a jolt of terror shoot through her. *Oh god, can she hear my thoughts now!?* Sam opened her eyes and saw Dr. Shandi's office coming into focus. Dr. Shandi was sitting cross-legged with a notebook in her lap, leaning forward in anticipation.

"Sam, you were just talking to me. You didn't notice? I can't hear your thoughts, but sometimes you actually speak your thoughts out loud as you dream, you know, like when you wake up from a nightmare screaming out loud. Sam, honey, it's okay." Dr. Shandi stroked Sam's arm reassuringly. Sam stared at her wide-eyed, breathing heavily. "You did great Sam, you're a natural at hypnosis! It didn't take much to get you there, either. I took some notes down for you. Now I don't know think we have the answers you're looking for just yet, but I think they have something to do with this girl you were describing."

"That was so... strange. I mean, it felt like I was inside of a dream or something, except I was completely aware of everything that was going on, everything, except speaking my thoughts aloud. Can I get control of that?" Sam finally responded, disregarding what Dr. Shandi just said.

"Exactly. That's hypnosis. And yes, you can get a handle on your thoughts, once you get used to the dreamlike state. We're going to figure out what's going on, Sam. I promise."

"Okay. Thank you for stopping it. Things were getting kind of strange."

"No problem. It's what I'm here for. Now... before we end today, was there anything else you wanted to talk about?" Dr. Shandi asked.

Sam could tell Dr. Shandi was proud, not just of Sam, but of herself for conducting such a quickly successful hypnosis session. It was one for the books.

"No, I think I'm fine for this week. I just want to process everything." *Wow, that was incredible!* Sam walked outside shaking her head. *How am I so susceptible to this stuff?*

7. WAKING LIFE: CRAWFISH

B ri put a bottle of sleeping pills called Somulex into Sarah's hand and closed her fingers over hers. "Listen, take one each night, thirty minutes before bed. They work and they'll help you, I promise.

Sarah rolled her eyes in annoyance.

"Please take them," she implored, squeezing Sarah's hand more firmly. "You look really tired and you have bags under your eyes... I got these from The Green Place. They're amazing— all natural, no side effects, and honey... you can't go on like this. You need to sleep!" Bri rubbed Sarah's back and gave her the same look of concern mom always gave her. Bri was the spitting image of their mother, Sarah thought.

Oh, god. Suck it up Sarah and just accept the pills. Sarah sighed and smiled at Bri.

"Of course, I'll try them. You're right. I can't lose any more sleep over this hospital case. I'll take it easy," Sarah said in her most convincing voice.

"Oh, thank god! Now, you're going out with Joey tomorrow night, right?"

"Yeah…"

"Good and please don't bail on him again. You really take him for granted, you know."

Says the gold digger.

"Bri, you make me sound like a terrible girlfriend. Look, you know I've been stressed with work lately."

"More like obsessed," Bri snorted.

Sarah rolled her eyes again. *Just let it go.*

The following night, Sarah stood in front of her full-length mirror, smoothing her knee length, royal blue dress. The black eye liner, pink lipstick and mascara was an unusual addition. Sarah stared at her reflection and smiled at the transformation. *This is good. I need to enjoy myself for once.* The thought surprised her, like maybe Bri's advice was finally starting to sink in.

~~~

The movie that night was deliciously frightening. Sarah screamed and covered Joey's arm with nervous pinches and bruises. Sarah could tell he loved every minute of it. It had been a month since they were out together. Both left the movie that night buzzing with energy.

Dinner was an equally delightful surprise. They sat around a large round table with a pit in the middle, labeled: fish bones. Sarah was a fan of seafood, but she'd never tried creole cooking before. Joey spent the night convincing her that she would love it and needed to give it a try.

"Let's get the Private Captain's Platter. It's huge and comes with all the seafood."

"Ok, let's do it. Let's live dangerously," Sarah smiled mischievously and rubbed her hands together. She was having a genuinely good time. For the past couple of hours, she had forgotten all about her father and the hospital. She was finally living in the moment.

The platter came out steaming, with crawfish, mussels, shrimp, catfish, corn on the cob, and boiled potatoes.

"Wow!" Sarah gushed, her eyes bugging out of her head.

"Well someone needs to make sure you eat," Joey smiled.

"Clearly, you and my sister are on a mission."

"Yes, we are. We're going to fatten you up," said Joey, tucking a napkin into his shirt collar.

Sarah snorted.

"What?"

"Nothing," she smiled and shook her head, as she picked up one of the crawfish, turning it over and looking at its beady black eyes. "How are we supposed to eat these things? You know," Sarah frowned, "I like to think my meat grows from the ground."

"Here, let me show you." Joey picked up a crawfish and delicately twisted it at the waist until the tail came out in one smooth piece. "Here try it. It tastes sweet." Joey fed Sarah the crawfish.

"It *is* sweet. Kind of like lobster, but chewier."

"Exactly. It's called poor fisherman's lobster, very tasty and way cheaper."

Sarah sat back in her chair and stared off into the distance. This crawfish reminded her of something. The taste was so familiar, but she knew she never had it before.

"Sarah, are you okay?"

Joey's voice trailed off as a river came into focus in her mind's eye. The edges of her vision were blurry, but clear as day she could see a river flowing into a small creek. It was surrounded by large rocks, the water rushing around them in roaring white foam. She could see her feet balancing on a large rock underwater. She was wearing white socks. That water felt so cool, so refreshing. She saw her hand reaching down...

"Sarah!" Joey's voice pierced her daydream like a bullet.

Sarah snapped out her reverie, jumped up and blinked at him. "Wha... what?"

"Are you feeling okay? You just turned into a zombie for a minute. I kept calling your name, but it's like you couldn't even hear me."

"Oh, I don't know, this crawfish just reminded me... ugh, my stomach really hurts. This crawfish must have been a bad one."

"There's no way you could have reacted so quickly to it."

"Maybe I'm allergic or it mixed with something it wasn't suppo—"

"What?" Joey got up from his seat and came to her side.

"The sleeping meds!" Sarah grabbed onto his arm for stability as she got out of her seat. "I think there was a warning on the label that said something about not combining them with shellfish. I just didn't think they would still be in my system at this point. Wow." Sarah held her stomach. "I have to go," she yelped, running for the bathroom in the back of the restaurant, almost knocking over a waiter in the process. She threw open the stall door and fell on her knees in front of the toilet seat.

"Sarah, are you okay?" Joey burst into the bathroom after her.

"Joey, get out of the women's bathroom! I'll be okay."

"Okay, do you want me to get you a glass of water or something?"

"No, I'll be out in a minute. Just wait outside." She heaved into the toilet bowl. Ten minutes later, she was washing her face in the sink, staring at her haggard reflection in the mirror. *One night,* she thought. *Just one night off, and this happens.* What in the world just happened to her? She was prone to daydreaming, but this came on so abruptly, in the middle of a conversation, and it felt more like a memory than a dream. Sarah patted her face dry with a paper towel and left the bathroom.

~~~

Early the next morning, Sarah sat munching on a buttered roll from the restaurant that Joey had thoughtfully grabbed for her, right before her embarrassing departure. She had called in sick today and told Joey she had a stomach bug. However, the only bug she had now was the one that bit her the day Bri gave her their father's pocket watch. What happened to her last night was only a sign that she needed to keep digging deeper and not take too much time out for herself. Sure, she wished she could enjoy herself, but she knew she wouldn't really be able to until she had some answers.

Sarah's eyes fell upon an old newspaper clipping of the hotel where her father was last seen. She stood before the bulletin board again, studying a new amalgamation of pictures she had assembled. It was the last lead she had on her father, and it turned out to be fruitless. *That PI was not worth the money.*

She sat down in front her old laptop and began web-searching Private Investigators. She clicked on a link. The profile page read: *Lucas Bremmer, Private Investigator.* There was a mission statement underneath a rather awkward picture of a young man dressed like someone's grandfather, which read, "Private Investigation with integrity, where we put you first." Sarah scoffed at the words. *Sure you do.*

She scanned his picture. He was young, probably fresh out of the academy and in his mid-to-late twenties. He didn't look like he had much life experience, let alone professional experience, though his website advertised otherwise. Still, there was a look of hunger in his eyes that Sarah recognized, a kind of restless drive. She picked up the phone.

"Hi. May I speak to Lucas Bremmer? Hi Lucas, my name is Sarah Davis. I was wondering if you could help me with something. But first, what are your rates? Oh, really... well that's very much out of my price range. Well, ok. I guess I can come in today, just to talk. Yes, 2:00 p.m. works for me. See you then."

The guy really seemed desperate for work. His voice was laced with nervous energy and his prices were on a sliding scale that seemed to have no set formula. His inexperience was glaring. Still, she thought he might be worth a shot; she had nothing to lose at this point.

~~~

The small office smelled of mildew and old books. The place was cluttered with antiques, more of a history museum than an office. *He must have inherited this place or I'm in a time warp.* Sarah looked around, unsure of where the front desk was, until she realized she was standing directly in front of it. It was a tiny brown oak desk, topped with a small green desk lamp, and stacked high with legal volumes, newspapers, and loose documents.

"Hello? Anyone there? I'm here for my 2:00 p.m. appointment," Sarah called out to the seemingly empty room.

"Oh, hi!" A tall, thin man popped out from behind a bookcase, making Sarah jump.

"Don't scare me like that!" Sarah put her hand over her racing heart.

"I'm sorry, there's a lot of places to hide around here, as you can see. Sorry I frightened you."

"It's alright," Sarah said, putting out her hand for a handshake.

Lucas looked as if he had been teleported from another century with his Ivy League sweater vest, tucked neatly into brown corduroy pants held up by green suspenders. His longish hair was curly and wild. He held a brown leather-bound book in his hand.

"Sit down," Lucas said, motioning to a chair covered in newspapers. "Oh." Lucas quickly grabbed them off the chair and pulled it out for Sarah.

"Thank you."

Sarah looked at the certificates on the wall, above the desk. One was a certificate of graduation from Brown. The other was a Private Investigator certificate of Licensure.

"I apologize for the heat. The A.C. is under repair. Here..." Lucas scooted the fan from behind his desk and aimed it at Sarah.

"Thank you, that's much better."

"Not a problem. Now then! How may I help you, Sarah or Ms. Davis... which do you prefer?" Lucas stammered.

"Sarah's fine. So, have you heard about the hospital remodeling at Forrester Care Psychiatric?"

"Yes, I've read about, but I haven't seen much information."

"Exactly! I'm actually a reporter for *Resonance Weekly*."

"Oh, are you?" Lucas sat back in his chair, arms folded, splaying an oddly attractive, interested smile.

"Yes. I've been investigating the hospital remodeling for a few weeks now. I think there's more going on than the director's letting on, at least from my experiences with her. I was hoping you could assist me."

"Yes, I believe I can. You see, my specialties are multi-faceted... investigation, surveillance, finding missing people."

"That... is actually the second reason why I'm here."

"Oh?" Lucas raised an eyebrow and dropped his jaw slightly. He was ripe with anticipation. It was clear that business was slow, and the sound of a double-dip case gave him more excitement than he could conceal.

"Yes," she continued, "I'm looking for my father. He's actually been missing for four years now, and the previous PI gave up looking pretty quickly."

Sarah sat there, wringing her hands and looking into his eyes, a lost puppy.

The detective moved his jaw up and down nervously before responding. "Ma'am, I can assure you that at Lucas Bremmer Investigations, I work tirelessly, and will not stop until the customer is satisfied."

What an odd response. This guy does not get out much.

"I appreciate that. I really do," Sarah said looking down at her hands. *Well at least he cares.*

Sarah's last PI was a much older and more experienced detective. In fact, he had over thirty years of experience under his belt. But he was burnt out and had long been hardened to the "lost causes" he had encountered over the years. When Sarah came to him it was like he had made up his mind right from the beginning.

A sense of invigoration was beginning to set in as Sarah left Detective Bremmer's office that afternoon. The payment plan they came up with was one she could afford. She agreed to pay him a small monthly retainer indefinitely, in return for utilizing his

services on an as needed basis. Sarah had a good feeling about this
and was more determined than ever to find her father.

The hospital case would be the perfect cover for looking for her
father. It would keep everyone off her back, plus, the idea of double
case made the reporter in her giddy. It could not be a coincidence
that her father wrote a riddle about the birthplace of the hospital he
had spent so much time in. Her head was swimming with plans,
which in her mind seemed to be coalescing into real, tangible,
productive leads. She called Joey as she started her dumpy Toyota,
thinking it would need some major tune-ups very soon.

"Hey! You want to go on a road trip?"

8. DREAM LIFE: JUMPING OFF A CLIFF

S am's ponytail whipped over her face in the strong breeze. She moved it out of her way and took a careful sip of her piping hot cappuccino. She and her father sat outside a local café enjoying a lunch break together. She frowned and looked into the distance as a taxi whizzed by, nearly hitting a pedestrian.

"How are you feeling today, kiddo? You seem tired." Her father sat back in his chair and crossed his arms. "Did you see that giraffe riding a unicycle? He was juggling apples."

"Uh-huh." Sam replied in a drone, eyes vacantly staring ahead.

Benjamin slapped his head and ran his hand down his face in exasperation. He leaned forward. "Honey!"

"Huh? Yes! Why are you yelling at me?"

"Because, you're on autopilot."

"Oh, sorry, I was just thinking about how noisy this city is. Dad, don't you ever get sick of this place?"

"Oh yeah, the croissants here do start tasting like cardboard after a while..."

"Dad! Seriously, don't you miss camping, or spending summers with grandma at the farm? I miss that."

"Yeah, I miss it too... But hey, I thought you liked being a city big shot."

"I do, I mean, I love what I do."

"Well honey, the job comes with the territory. Otherwise, you'd still be making wicker baskets. Hell! You could have had your own wicker basket factory. Just think of the all the missed opportunities!" Benjamin exclaimed, waving his hands dramatically.

"Dad!"

"I know, but still, how nice is this? I get to have lunch with my daughter on a Tuesday afternoon."

"You're right, that's a big perk of living here."

Sam smiled at her father. Ever since she could remember, Sam had always been a daddy's girl. She was close with her mother, too, but preferred the company of her father. He was less neurotic. He understood her, and despite his frequently obnoxious sense of humor, she felt like she could talk to him about anything.

She used to be close to her brother Michael, too, but he had long since moved out of the city to pursue his passion for the rugged life. She was jealous that he had latched onto everything their grandmother taught them as kids about wilderness survival and growing their own food. She couldn't even keep a cactus alive. Michael was living a quiet life in some remote location, away from cars and traffic and deadlines. She envied him.

Benjamin put his coffee down and looked at Sarah sympathetically.

"You know honey, I really miss the mountains too. Why don't we take a trip out there? We can visit Bear Creek again, if you want."

"I'd like that."

~~~

That afternoon, Sam would have her second attempt at hypnosis with Dr. Shandi, and for some reason she was feeling more nervous than usual. Her hands were shaking on the steering wheel as she pulled into the parking lot. She inhaled deeply a couple times to steady her rattling breath before walking inside.

"Hi Sam! How are you today?" Dr. Shandi asked energetically, eager to see what results this next hypnosis session would yield.

"I'm fine," Sam said halfheartedly, setting her purse on the sofa.

"What's wrong?"

"Nothing. I've just been reminiscing a lot about the past, being in the country with my grandma. I think that vacation showed me something I was missing in my life."

"I know how much you miss her. Maybe you could take another trip out there soon?"

"Yeah, my father and I are already planning one."

"Well, that's wonderful."

"Dr. Shandi, are we going to try another hypnosis session today? I'm a bit nervous, but I feel like I'm ready to continue, that is, if you think I'm ready..."

"It's okay to feel nervous. You had a pretty intense experience last time. But, if you think you're ready, then yes, I think you are too. Also, I wanted to try something a little bit different today. This is called a Hypnograph." Dr. Shandi reached over and picked up a flat rectangular machine off the side table and flipped on a bright blue screen. "It measures brain wave activity. I wanted to see if we could get you into an even deeper state today, so we can really get to the bottom of this mystery girl business."

"So, you'll be using this Hypnograph to track my brain activity? It'll let you know when I'm in that state?"

"Exactly. I'll be asking you questions and giving you commands or suggestions, rather, to help you navigate. At some points, you may not be able to hear my voice, but rather experience it on a subconscious level. Also, I don't want you to be alarmed when you find your visions suddenly... changing."

"Okay. But can you give me the commands now?"

"No... I don't think that would be such a good idea. I don't want to influence your subconscious in any way before you are in that deep state. It might affect the outcome. But I promise you, these suggestions are nothing to be afraid of. You can think of them as checkpoints on a map, guiding you towards what you're trying to understand."

Sam let out a deep sigh, trying to rid herself of her apprehension. "Alright. I'm ready," she said with conviction.

She wasn't sure why her dream life had flourished so much in the past week, or why she suddenly felt like she was on some kind of mission. Originally, she came to therapy to deal with her chronic anxiety and insomnia, but now it was as if those were just blips on the radar, pointing to something bigger.

She closed her eyes and began breathing deeply like Dr. Shandi had shown her, listening to her melodic, soothing voice, guiding her towards relaxation. After several minutes, she began to fully relax, and her black field of vision began vibrating with energy. In her mind's eye, a picture began to form.

The cool, salty ocean air nipped at her arms as she stood at the precipice of a towering cliff, looking down a steep drop to bright, almost transparent green water. Waves broke off into foam against large, grey boulders. The sun was shining high above her, and large white clouds drifted around an open, blue sky in vaguely familiar shapes. The faint smell of wisteria was in the air. She closed her eyes and smiled. This must have been her mind's idea of paradise.

"Sam," Dr. Shandi's voice came through abruptly, shattering Sam's sense of peace. Then annoyance seeped in. For a moment Sam had completely forgotten she was in an office.

"Sam, now that you're picturing a peaceful place in your mind, I want you to think about that girl. Try to find her. She will come to you."

Sam looked around. The air was dry and the land around her arid, with haphazard patches of tall dune grass.

"Try calling out to her," Dr. Shandi's voice commanded from above.

Ok.

"Little girl! Kid? Are you out here?" Sam yelled out, with uncertainty. Sam walked away from the cliff and down a long dirt road, the red dusty earth cracking beneath her feet. Something blue caught her eye. A periwinkle ribbon whirled around in the air in front of her, then snagged on a piece of tall, dune grass. Sam went over to the ribbon and plucked it up.

"That's my ribbon," a soft voice popped up from behind her.

Sam jumped up and gasped. She turned around to find the same little girl, in the white, flowing dress. Her face was covered by a blue scarf tied strangely around her head, concealing everything but her eyes. *Those eyes. They look so familiar...* She took the ribbon from Sam's hands, and before Sam could say anything, she swiftly turned and ran towards the cliff's edge and jumped.

"No!" Sam screamed and ran after her, stopping abruptly at the cliff's edge, arms flailing, to keep herself from falling off.

"It's okay," Dr. Shandi said, "you can go after her, this is a vision after all, not real life."

"But... I'm afraid to jump."

"You won't get hurt, you can't die in a vision."

But this stuff feels too real.

"Sam," a little voice came from below. Sam looked down and saw the girl standing on a rock, jutting out of the water, completely unharmed. "Come on Sam, I want to show you something."

She waved her arms, motioning for Sam to follow her, and then turned again, to run.

"Here goes nothing," Sam said aloud and jumped off the side of the cliff. She fell in slow motion, as if she were floating. *Like Alice in Wonderland falling down the rabbit hole.* Suddenly, things around her got quiet, except for the faint murmur of voices, deep male voices, which gradually grew louder. They sounded angry, like they were in the middle of a heated debate.

Sam touched down on the same rock the girl was standing on, except the girl was now bounding far ahead on a rock path, in the direction of a cave. She followed. After what seemed like only a matter of seconds, she was inside. The cavern was dark, but the little girl handed Sam a glowing torch, that seemed to appear out of thin air. *I'm gonna have to get used to this,* Sam thought to herself, her mind still wrestling with the absurdity of everything happening around her.

Sam and the girl took a right turn in the cave. There were more torches lining the walls. The girl pulled out a book of matches.

Ok, now the burning torch makes more sense. Is my brain auto-correcting the environment to make things more realistic?

Again, Dr. Shandi's voice pierced the silence, causing Sam to once again jump out of her skin like a petrified cat.

"Stay focused on what's happening, Sam. Don't try to over-analyze."

God, this is really going to take some getting used to.

Sam and the girl split up and began lighting the torches, one by one, each time, illuminating a new section of the cavern. When they finished, the girl took off again, hold a glowing torch before her. Again, Sam bounded after her, almost running into her seconds later, as the girl abruptly stopped.

"Look," she motioned at the wall in front of them.

"What?" Sam asked. "I don't see anything."

"You *do* see some things," the little girl replied. "You just can't see everything right now. Look again."

Sam looked at the door and it opened to reveal a room full of hospital equipment: MRIs, EEGs, heart monitors, IV bags, and a Hypnograph.

"I don't know how these things work, Sam, but I think you do."

"No, I'm not a doctor."

"Can you help me save my dad? I think he's sick. This is a hospital. Isn't this a hospital?" Distress began permeating her voice.

"I... I don't know. I don't think so..." Sam put her hands on the girl's shoulders and knelt down on one knee in front of her. "Why can't I see your face?"

Sam felt more disturbed by the fact that she couldn't see this girl's face, than the fact that she was standing in a cave full of hospital equipment.

"Because you can't. You can't, even if you tried."

Sam began to lift the scarf off the girl's face.

The girl vanished into thin air, leaving Sam standing in the dimly lit room full of hospital equipment. On a whim, she lay down inside an MRI machine.

"So... who's going to start this thing?" As if by command, the machine hummed on and Sam began sliding into its brightly lit, tube-like enclosure. After a few minutes of lying there, she decided she would go look at the computer monitor. "Okay, I want to come out now," she said aloud. Again, the machine obeyed, letting her out. Sam got up and walked over to the monitor, no longer worrying about the absurdity of what was happening, but relishing with utter curiosity all that she was doing. The monitor displayed a three-dimensional picture of her brain.

She had never seen her brain before, but could tell there was something odd and out of place. At the center of the brain she could see an image. She zoomed in closer with the cursor. It was a picture of an owl. Sam frowned and backed away from the computer. *An owl? In my brain?* A sense of foreboding came over her. She somehow knew that if she remained calm, then nothing would hurt her. She didn't know how she knew this. The knowledge seemed to appear from nowhere. But it was too late. Sam could hear the deep angry murmur of voices again. They were coming from all around her, reverberating off the walls of the cave.

She began running back toward the entrance, towards the light, at the end of the curving, dark tunnel. She had not realized how far back she had wandered. As she reached the entrance, a flock of birds flew out of the cave around her, knocking her to the ground with their heavy bodies and great wings. Looking up to the sky, she saw a flock of great, white owls flying into the distance. She closed her eyes and breathed in deeply. Then again, she could hear Dr. Shandi's, familiar and now comforting voice.

"You are becoming more and more awake," she heard her say.

She could feel her feet on the carpet again. She opened her eyes and touched the top of her head. Her forehead was dripping with sweat.

"You're incredible," Dr. Shandi said. "I've never had a patient so adept at hypnosis. Here, look at the monitor." Dr. Shandi put the machine in Sam's lap and pointed to the large, widely-spaced waves. "This is where you were during most of the past hour."

Past hour?

"This is the slowest brainwave state, and you only reach it when you're in the deepest stage of sleep. Sam, you were there for the majority of the time! See, look here. This is when you woke up." Dr. Shandi pointed to the short, tightly-packed waves at the end of the image.

"It felt so real." Sam panted, digging her fingers into the arms of the couch.

"That's why I pulled you out. You weren't calming down and I didn't want you to ruin the experience for yourself."

"Thank you. I don't know why all those things happened: the owls, the machines, the scarf over the girl's face. Wait a minute. That was you, talking to me, telling me to calm down, wasn't it?"

"Yes, you remember what I said about not hearing my suggestions consciously when in deep hypnosis. You experienced them at that moment, more as a feeling of knowing, as intuition."

"Yes, I did! I knew that if I calmed down, then nothing could hurt me. But I panicked anyway."

"Yes, unfortunately you did, but it's okay. Nothing can hurt you physically in those visions. Also, all those things you saw were symbols, Sam. All metaphors your subconscious created to tell you something important, something you need to know, something perhaps, you already know."

"Something I already know?" Sam asked in confusion. "That little girl said I can see some things, but not others. It's weird that my own mind feels like a stranger to me."

"That's because our minds are not our own. What I mean is, they are not things we are in control of or can fathom the depths of. We can study the brain, the images on an MRI machine, and the corresponding areas that light up. When certain brain activity occurs, we see the lights, but we don't really know where this activity is coming from. Our minds are endless caverns, and we have to keep lighting the torches, to see further into ourselves."

"Did you gather all that from my vision? I didn't even think I was talking out loud."

"Oh, that's because you were somewhere else in your mind. You and I were talking the entire time, Sam. That's the power of the mind under hypnosis, and yours is truly remarkable."

Sam left Dr. Shandi's office completely dumbstruck. *This all has to mean something.* She could feel it in her bones. A shiver ran down her spine in a chilling affirmation.

9. Waking life: Road Trip

Perfectly formed white clouds flew overhead as Sarah headed out of town. Joey was sipping on an old-fashioned vanilla coke beside her, out of a small, glass bottle. It was their first road trip in a long time, and she had a solid plan. Joey would come along for the companionship, while she worked both cases. In her mind, she would be killing three birds with one stone. The newspaper had already given her the green light, and she was officially on assignment, investigating the hospital.

Of course, she had to justify this trip as more than just a hunch to Mr. Chesterfield. She bent the truth slightly, talking about credible sources in the original hospital, who knew more about the renovations. She also told him that the flash of light she saw was definitely new technology, and something that the hospital was covering up.

She suspected that Mr. Chesterfield didn't believe much in the story, but wanted her to take a break, or maybe he pitied for her for believing so much in what he thought was a pipe dream. Either way, Sarah was heading west, now eighty-five miles outside of Raleigh, NC and well on her way to Lizard's Foot, Texas. It would be a long twenty-hour drive, and she planned to go as far as she could without stopping. It was a hot day for a road trip. Sweat was running down her face, and her legs were sticking to the leather seats in her green Toyota. The air conditioner was working but Sarah loved riding with the windows down anyway, the breeze hitting her face. Joey was asleep next to her.

Only two hours into the trip, Sarah thought, shaking her head. How am I supposed to stay awake with him snoring away next to me? Joey's head rested against the passenger window.

He had worked late last night, and Sarah wanted to leave early in the morning. But she really didn't mind the solitude of the open road, it gave her time to think.

Three hours later, they finally reached a gas station with a twenty-minutes past empty gas tank, blaring red. Black birds sat around a water spigot, their beaks open, panting in the heat, when Sarah and Joey pulled up to the remote two pump station, at the end of a town.

A bird perched on top of the spigot, reached his beak inside the spout and gurgled down the coveted liquid. Sarah parked in front of a pump and went inside to get drinks as Joey put gas in the car.

The gas station attendant was nowhere to be found. Sarah walked to the small fridge in the back. The selection was sparse: orange juice, cranberry cocktail, a few types of soda, and water. Sarah grabbed two waters, then walked through the other aisles, in search of potato chips and gummy bears.

She put her snacks on the counter and waited, looking around her. The store was small, only three aisles and one small fridge. *They don't even sell beer? Must be a dry county.* There was a large jar of red picked eggs on the counter and an odd collection of bobble head hula dolls. "Hello?" Sarah called out. No answer. "Hello, I need to pay for this stuff." Still no answer. Sarah began looking around nervously. *Maybe they're using the bathroom.*

She decided to wait to a few minutes longer before leaving. Five minutes later, no one was coming out of the bathroom and Sarah was getting tired of waiting. The thought crossed her mind, to just take the stuff and go. Besides, it was completely unprofessional of them to not be manning the counter. She was hot and needed a drink. She twisted open a water bottle and took a few large gulps. *This is getting ridiculous.*

Sarah grabbed her things and left six dollars on the counter. As she pushed open the door, she heard footsteps behind her. She froze. Quickly, she tried thinking of something to say: an apology, a complaint, something. She turned around.

A short man in a red, plaid shirt stood before her. He shook his head at her, as if to say, "No, you shouldn't have done that."

Is he going to call the police? I left the money on the counter. Wait. What is he doing!?

The man had suddenly broken into a full-speed run, headed directly towards her. Before she could even think to scream, she felt a hard strike to her head, and then everything went black.

~~~

The beeping grew louder and sharper. Slowly, Sarah opened her eyes and the room came into focus. The noise she heard was a heart monitor. She turned her pounding head to the right to find Joey slumped over in a chair, sleeping.

Typical, she thought and then chided herself for being so cynical. *What is happening to me? To my relationship? I'm literally falling apart.*

"Joey?" she croaked. Her voice was abrasive, breaking the silence like a creaky door.

Joey startled awake and came to her side, looking into her eyes with concern and leaning over to kiss her gently on the forehead.

"What happened to your eye?" Sarah reached her hand up to gently touch his swollen, black and blue face. Joey winced a little.

"It's nothing. How are you feeling?"

Sarah reached up to touch her head and cringed in pain. Her eyes began to water.

"I have a terrible headache. What happened?"

"Well…" Joey started, fidgeting with his watch, "I was waiting for you at the car and then I started walking towards the bathrooms in the back of the building. This guy was coming out the back door…. with you slung over his shoulder, so I went after him."

"What?! I was being kidnapped? Ouch!" Sarah clutched her head – apparently getting upset was not a good idea right now.

"I know, I'm freaked out too. But try to take it easy."

She sighed and closed her eyes for a second, trying to quell the fear and confusion boiling up. She looked up at Joey, who was visibly upset, clearly beating himself up. "Joey, it's okay," she said. "He got away, but you stopped him and that's what matters."

"That asshole was fast."

"He was. I mean, I couldn't get a word out before he knocked me out." Sarah rifled through her purse and pulled out her green, leather wallet. "Well everything's in there."

"We need to call the police back. They told me to call back when you woke up."

Sarah closed her eyes and tried picturing the man's face: his short blonde hair, buzzed close to his head, his short beard and mustache and a diamond stud earring in his right ear. He also had a distinctive scar on the left side of his forehead, which looked like a knife slash. Maybe Sarah needed to talk to the police after all. She seemed to remember him in detail and knew that she could give the police an accurate description of the asshole.

What if this attack was premeditated? Sarah shrugged off the thought, thinking there was no way. She had no real enemies that she knew of. Still, the way he shook his head at her, made her feel as if he knew something about her.

After about fifteen minutes, the police were knocking on her room door.

That was fast.

"Hi ma'am, I'm Officer Matthew Bergeron." The officer slowly approached the bed. "I hate to disturb you while you're resting, but I was hoping you could answer some questions for me about what happened earlier this afternoon at the gas station."

"Sure." Sarah sat up in the bed and tucked her hair behind her ears, to make herself more presentable. "I'm Sarah Davis." She extended her hand.

Office Bergeron shook her hand, gently.

"Please, don't worry about sitting up, stay comfortable."

"I'm fine, officer," she said, convincing no one.

The cop gave her a pitying look.

"Okay. So, the man that knocked you out, what did he look like?"

"He was a very short, Caucasian male, couldn't have been taller than 5'5" maybe 5' 7" at the most. He had short blonde buzz cut, and a closely trimmed beard and mustache. He also had a horizontal slash, a scar on the left... yes, the left side of his forehead." Sarah traced the line on her own forehead.

"I see. You remember quite a bit of detail about him, in the short time you saw him. But this is a normal response when you encounter a rather traumat— well anyways. To cut to the chase Sarah, we believe the man that assaulted you is Rocky Henson. This is not his first offense. Still, it's the first time he's committed this type of crime."

"What was he charged with before?" Sarah asked nervously, suddenly dreading the response.

"Look, that's not important. What is important is that we are going to catch him. We will do everything we can and will keep you updated."

"Well okay, but why can't you just tell me."

"What charges of his are public record, you can read online, I'll give you the link, but worrying about that is not going to help you any. They are smaller scale crimes, nothing to write home about.

Still, it's important for us to understand his motivations. Do you have any idea why he would come after you?"

"I have no idea. All I know is that it's been a really weird day. I don't have any enemies, as far as I know."

"Sometimes, the way these criminals operate, is by going after someone's kin. You know, hitting them where it hurts, in order to send a message. Sarah, is there anyone in your family that might interest this man in any way, maybe someone who has set him off, wronged him in the past?"

"No. Not that I know of. Wait, are you saying he might come after my family next?!"

"No, I don't think so. We just need as much information as possible, to figure out why he targeted you."

"I understand. Well, my father was involved in some confidential research."

"Confidential? Where is your father?"

"Well, he's been missing for four years. I haven't heard anything from him." Could someone be after Dad? All those experiments, all that information, maybe he finally figured out something remarkable, something a criminal would want to get their hands on.

Sarah's brain was teeming with ideas, painful, headache-inducing ideas, swirling around her like hungry mosquitos in summertime. Her mother was never involved in anything too interesting, or out of the ordinary. Bri was much too involved in her love affairs, shopping, travel, and beauty rituals to even think about getting involved in something like this. Her father, however, was always full of mystery, always looking for the next puzzle to solve. *But why would this guy be after me?*

Officer Bergeron spent several hours gathering information about her, her father, and her whereabouts. They figured out a few scenarios that could explain what happened. A: Rocky knew she was going on this trip, in which case he has been following her and planning this kidnapping for a while. B: he had stumbled upon her at the gas station by happenstance and already had plans to kidnap her, or C: he had no idea of who she was, and she had averted an attempted rape, a disturbing thought. None of these scenarios really made sense to Sarah or the officer, but he promised he would be in touch.

Sarah spent the rest of the evening in a transient state, hopped up on pain meds, and caught in a frightening kaleidoscope of sleeping, dreaming and replaying the horrific events of that day.

10. DREAM LIFE: UNCOMFORTABLE CONVERSATIONS

The sun beat down on Sam's face, lulling her to sleep. She had been dozing in her parents' backyard hammock for the past couple of hours, an open book lying across her lap. She was tired from the week and had nothing to do, nowhere to go. It was just the warm sun, a good book, and her mother's bacon wrapped meatloaf and homemade strawberry lemonade.

Elijah was away on business. He had flown out Friday to see a client in California. It was one of those high-profile cases, and an opportunity he could not pass up.

Although Sam was thoroughly appreciative of her time off, she could not shake the sick feeling in the pit of her stomach, from everything that had happened to her, over the past month.

She had been having relentless, vivid dreams, and strange flashback-like daydreams, of herself doing things she did not remember doing. She wasn't sure if what she was seeing was a memory, or a creation of her imagination. It was happening with increasing frequency, and it was starting to scare her. Her parents didn't know what to think of it. Their advice was to take it easy, come home and take some time off work.

Trying to take it easy wasn't helping. Dr. Shandi thought it was a side effect of her subconscious attempting to reveal important information, aided by the nightly and much needed use of Balixa. They even began exploring the possibility of dissociative amnesia in therapy, since Sam felt like what she was seeing was more like memories of people she had not met before.

Additionally, Sam had begun thinking about searching for her birth parents. She never had an interest in it before, because she felt satisfied with her family. But now, she felt an increasing possibility that there was a biological component to what she was going through. She wondered if this was some form of mental illness that had been passed down to her. It was time to ask again about her birth parents, even if the conversation was going to be uncomfortable. She had done so once before, as a kid, and received a short answer, curtailed to a child's understanding, that left her sufficiently satisfied. She decided to have the talk with her parents tonight over dinner.

~~~

Connie made her famous bacon-wrapped, ketchup-smothered meatloaf. Sam was in a great mood and so were her parents. It was the perfect opportunity. Her father was back from another courtroom battle, a victory he described as equivalent to the pairing of a pigeon and a lion in the Roman Gladiatorial arena. Needless to say, he was the lion. Benjamin laughed and spoke in his expansive, loud voice, waving his arms to really get his point across, and accidentally flinging some mashed potatoes onto the carpet in the process.

"Really, Benjamin! For heaven's sake put the spoon down when you're talking. You're getting mashed potatoes everywhere."

Sam and Benjamin simultaneously burst out laughing, as her mother yanked the spoon out of his hand and shook it at him threateningly, splattering mashed potatoes on his nose. Her parents really acted like children sometimes.

When things quieted down a bit, Sam began.

"Hey, so… I wanted to talk to you guys about something. Please don't be alarmed. It's actually something I've been thinking about doing for a while," said Sam moving the mashed potatoes around her plate, waiting for a response before continuing. The silence stretched on.

After a moment, she continued, "And I think it would be helpful for me at this point in my life…"

"Oh my god, she's finally having a baby!" Sam's mother blurted out, clapping her hands together.

"No, that's not it," said Sam looking at her father, who was sitting quietly, with his arms crossed in front of him, eyes squinted.

"She wants to find her birth parents, Connie," Benjamin said calmly.

"What?" both Sam and her mother exclaimed simultaneously.

"Dad, how did you know?"

"Oh, I knew when you began rifling through our file drawers yesterday. You had moved everything around, plus the birth certificates were out of place."

"Wow. How do you always do that? I can't get anything past you."

"Not with your organizational skills, you can't… well, if you want to look for your birth parents, you can. You don't need our permission," Benjamin continued. "And I can give you the name of the attorney we used to finalize the adoption, if you want."

This is too easy…

"But… why now?" Connie finally said, her voice, laden with concern, or maybe it was hurt, Sam thought.

"Mom, I know we don't have any medical records from my birth parents," Sam continued, treading lightly with her words, "and I just think that maybe talking to them and finding out more information, might provide some answers as to what's... what's happening to me right now."

"Oh honey, like I said, it's just stress. But if you really want to do this... I have the papers upstairs."

Sam's mother got up suddenly, picking up the half-eaten plates of food, grabbing up Benjamin's plate as he reached for a bite of meatloaf.

Oh no.

Connie was clearly in distress.

"Who wants dessert?" She said in her worst, fake-happy voice.

"Mom, let me help you with that."

"And I'll take that!" Benjamin whisked his plate out of Connie's hand to finish his coveted meal.

Sam tentatively followed her mother into the kitchen.

"Now Sam, I'm not trying to be dramatic, I just know that your birth parents, well your mother was quite ill. I don't know if it was from drugs or from disease. Who knows if they're even alive? I just want to prepare you. You know, you may not like what you find."

"I understand, Mom. And believe me, I'm going to be careful about this whole thing. I promise. Please don't worry about me. I can take care of myself," said Sam wrapping her arms around her mother's waist and leaning her head against her back as she scraped the food off the plates into the trashcan.

The tension abated the rest of the evening, thanks to her father changing the conversation, and she was grateful.

~~~

The attorney at Tessler, Tessler, and Tessler was a gruff, older man, who reeked of whiskey and a musty suit. He was apparently the latter of the three. His father had long retired from the business – his father, being the one that finalized the adoption. Still, the records were there and after a lengthy phone conversation, and a visit to the office to confirm Sam's identity, names were produced, along with an address.

Maybe I had a home birth with one of those traditional midwives, Sam thought as she left the office. She did not want to consider the scary alternatives, like a bloody, unhygienic birth, somewhere in the back of a car, or worse, inside a truck-stop bathroom. She envisioned her mother, lying on a dirty floor, screaming in the throes of labor, withdrawing from heroin. She shook away the terrible thought. *Mom's getting to me again.*

Within 15 minutes, Sam was sitting in the back booth of a local diner. She had no intention of opening this envelope at home. Gingerly, she peeled open the manila envelope and pulled out the contents. Their names were Charles and Clara Hoffer of Allenwood, New Jersey. It was a little less than an hour away from Middlesex Borough, New Jersey, where her parents lived, and about an hour and a half away from her and Elijah's studio apartment in Manhattan.

How strange. All this time, my parents were living practically next door.

11. WAKING LIFE: THE DINER

J oey pulled into the dusty, gravel parking lot of a small diner called Fatty Joe's. They had made it to Alabama and were more than halfway there. Joey volunteered to drive this leg of the journey, much to Sarah's relief. Bright blue, neon lights were strung up around the rail-car shaped restaurant with stainless steel siding. A colorful jukebox flashed through the large glass window.

She was released from the hospital after just one night. She had convinced the doctors that she was feeling much better, at least physically. The blaring headache was almost gone now.

Walking inside, she immediately felt more comfortable. It was like a little piece of home, despite reminding her of her recent job loss. She was determined to continue this trip, regardless of Joey pleading with her to go home. A middle-aged waitress, wearing a light blue, button-down dress approached the table, a pot of steaming coffee in her hand. Her name tag read *Rosie*.

"Hi there! How ya'll doing? I'm Rosie and I'll be taking care of you today. Would you like to start off with some coffee?"

"Black tea, please," Sarah replied. "Oh, and I'll have a BLT with fries as well."

"Okay, sure thing. What about you honey, are you ready to order?"

"Yes. I'll have a coffee and a cheeseburger, please, with whatever comes on it and fries." Joey responded.

"Okay! Easy crowd," the waitress smiled and walked off. She returned promptly with tea, coffee, and a handful of creamers.

As Sarah sat sipping her tea, her eyes wandered over to the booth in the left corner of the restaurant. There was a considerably handsome man sitting there, with black hair, green eyes, an olive complexion, and a clean shaven face. Sarah guessed he was in his late thirties. He was dressed casually, in a white, V-neck T-shirt and jeans. He glanced in her direction and for a moment their eyes met. She looked away and then back again. He was still staring at her. A chill ran down her spine. This was not a good stare.

She immediately felt paranoid. *Who is this guy? Maybe he's working with the guy who attacked me. Two coincidences back to back, cannot be a coincidence.* Her heart began to race. *God, what is happening to me? Am I really going crazy?* Her nervous soliloquy was momentarily interrupted, as a man entered the diner and walked to where the eerie, handsome stranger was sitting. He sat down across from him and the two began talking.

"Joey," Sarah whispered, leaning in close to him, across the table. "That man behind you is staring at me. Don't turn around, but he is definitely staring. It's freaking me out!"

"He probably thinks you're hot," Joey leaned in and whispered back, a smirk on his face.

"Joey, don't mock me! I'm serious. He was looking at me in a really creepy way, like that guy in the gas station."

"Sarah, I know you were shaken up. I was too, I still am. But I think you're being a little paranoid, you know understandably..."

"You know, I could be, but why would someone want to kidnap me? What if there are more people working with Rocky? How could you be so nonchalant about this?"

"I'm not trying to be nonchalant, I just think... you're right, I'm sorry. I have your back."

Sarah and Joey quickly finished their meals and walked over to the counter to pay the bill. As Joey was paying, again Sarah turned her head in the direction of the two men. Again, her spine sent its warning signals down her back. He was staring right at her, with the same expressionless look on his face. Sarah's heart jumped into high gear, but she did not want to appear frightened. She decided to hold his gaze, to prove to herself, she was not crazy. He turned away and resumed his conversation. She kept staring. Nothing. *Okay, I need to calm down.* Slowly, methodically she turned toward the front door.

~~~

They arrived at Lizard's Foot hours past sundown, so there would not be any hospital tours happening that day. Still, she wanted to see the place, at least from the outside. They followed the long, winding dirt road off the highway. The stars were shining fiercely against the ebony sky.

There is something larger than life about this place, Sarah thought. There were no man-made lights along the road, so the sky expanded endlessly around them. Sarah felt like a speck floating in the middle of space, in a comforting kind of way.

The road opened up to a large clearing. Sarah could see the hospital looming in the distance. It was a gargantuan, multistory building. It was also pitch black, except for a few lampposts, which cast small pools of light over the surrounding garden. It gave her an eerie feeling, as if she were riding into a former era. Things seemed to be left untouched here.

Sarah looked over at Joey, half expecting to find herself in a horse and buggy. He grabbed her hand suddenly.

"What?" She half whispered, in a startled voice.

"It's eerie," Joey said. "This place looks ancient."

"I know, that's what I was thinking too... let's go outside for a few minutes. I want to look at the sky."

"Okay," Joey replied.

They left the car parked unseen, behind the lofty metal gates. Sarah jumped up on the hood and patted the space beside her, inviting Joey to sit. She laid down, her hands behind her head, and sighed loudly. She felt swallowed up by the sky, like during those nights at the planetarium with her father. She would get lost in the sky simulation, completely forgetting where she was, or that she had a body of her own. It was like magic. Her breathing slowed as she gazed at the layers of constellations and galaxies, more stars appearing the longer she looked, as if by her command. She closed her eyes for a second and a picture came into focus. She was on a lake, rowing an old canoe through the water. Willow trees jutted out of the water, waving their leafy branches around her, enclosing her.

What just happened? Was that a memory or did I just fall asleep? She looked over at Joey and frowned.

"Hey, have you ever taken me canoeing?"

"Yeah, remember we went canoeing on the lake near your apartment. I think that was last year. Why?"

"I remember that, but I'm remembering a totally different location. And I was in my own canoe, surrounded by willow trees. You remember a place like that?"

"No, that doesn't sound familiar. Maybe you went with one of your friends?"

"Maybe."

Between the attack, the creepy, handsome stranger, and this out-of-place vision, this trip was turning out to be filled with a ridiculous amount of unexpected surprises. Sarah could not help but feel that her father was somehow steering her here. Otherwise, why else would all these things be happening now, after she took up the search again?

Her cellphone rang. After fumbling for it for a few seconds in her uselessly-tight, jean pocket, she pushed the talk button. The caller I.D. read: Lucas Bremmer.

"Sarah, sorry to be calling you so late. But I think I've found something you need to hear."

12. DREAM LIFE: THE DYING AND THE IMBIBING

"Charles and Clara Hoffer, let's see..." Sam thumbed through the phoned book until she landed on the right page. "Arnold Hoffer, Betsy Hoffer, Cla...got it!" Enthusiastically, she ripped the page out. In fact, it was the only Clara Hoffer in the phone book. There was an address too. *It has to be her.* 1399 Callenwood Drive. She decided she would make the trip immediately. *Or maybe I should call first,* she went back and forth in her head, as these two looming and largely non-discussed figures from her past, became increasingly real to her. *What if I'm not ready for this? No, mom. Get out of my head! I can do this. I'm just going to show up. It'll be easier that way. If they aren't home, I'll just leave them a note. Yeah.*

Flinging her teal "just-in-case" travel bag into her trunk, Sam set her GPS for 1399 Callenwood Drive, Allenwood, New Jersey. *Will she be home? Most people are home at 11:00 am on a Saturday. Or maybe she's Jewish and at Synagogue? Here I go again.*

~~~

The New Jersey traffic was heavy and running over a nail and deflating her tire didn't help. These events added about an hour and a half onto her trip. She arrived late that afternoon, tired, largely discouraged, and sweating through her dress. The sweat stains showed darkly on the small of her back and under her armpits.

A small, one story, white house sat sweetly on a neatly trimmed lawn of young grass. It was covered in simple white vinyl siding and preceded by a plastic white mailbox. *Middle class suburbia.*

Sam smiled, the house exceeding her expectations. She was half expecting to find herself in front of a dilapidated trailer, with rusty lawn furniture and those ridiculous pink flamingos adorning the front yard. She had also imagined a vicious looking Pitbull or Doberman, angered with hunger and neglect, tied to a tree by a metal-link chain.

Sam addressed her smudged eyeliner in the sun-visor mirror and smoothed out her frizzy, windblown hair. She frowned at her reflection and quickly closed the mirror, thinking of what to say to her. *Hello, my name is Sam, I'm your Daughter. Hi, I'm Samantha Rosie Brennan, your long-lost... the daughter you gave up... no.* She grabbed her purse and exited the vehicle. She would just say whatever came to mind. She was a pro at this after all, coming up with the right thing to say on the fly.

All inspiration left her the moment the door opened. The person standing before her was definitely not Clara Hoffer. The white haired, hunchback old man, dressed in a blue bathrobe, squinted suspiciously at her. His face looked tired, creased with worry lines, and his beard and mustache were unkempt.

"Can I help you?"

"Maybe. I'm looking for Clara Hoffer, the phone book said this was her home address."

Sam backed away slightly, as the man had a particularly strong, alcoholic musk to him and looked like wasn't wearing much underneath his thin bathrobe.

"And what business do you have with her?"

His abrupt and rude demeanor threw her off.

"I... I don't know exactly how to say this, but, I'm her daughter."

"Daughter? But Clara doesn't have a... oh," the man's voice trailed off. "That daughter."

That daughter? What in the world does that mean?!

"Well, come on in, then, I guess," said the man. "I'll put on some coffee, or maybe you prefer something stronger?" The man motioned for her to come inside.

"Coffee sounds good."

"Suit yourself."

The man left for a few minutes, then returned to the living room in much more presentable attire: slacks and a button down, plaid shirt. He handed her the coffee and poured himself an extra-large glass of scotch.

"My name's Sherman Hoffer and I guess that makes me your grandfather."

"I'm Sam Brennan."

"I gotta say, this is a surprise. But, why didn't you call first?" The wrinkles on Sherman's face converged into a multi-tiered frown, shrinking his face inward.

Sam paused for a moment before responding. "I guess I thought I would just drop by. It seemed like an odd conversation to have over the phone after not seeing my mother all these years. I never met either one of my birth parents and I'd really like to know more about them."

"Uh-huh... well, I can tell you this much," Sherman began, "Clara is a wonderful woman, would go out of her way for anybody, even a complete stranger, has a heart of gold. As for your father... well he's a different story altogether; abandoned your mother when she needed him most."

"What do you mean?"

"Well, I don't know how to break this to you, but... Clara's sick."

"What do you mean she's sick, like with a cold?" Sara immediately regretted her question, knowing this was not the type of sick he was talking about.

"No." Sherman blinked at her. "I mean, she's very sick," he said gravely.

"Oh."

"Your mother suffers from a rare form of blood cancer, a type of Leukemia, and the chemo's not working for her anymore." The man stopped talking abruptly, his eyes welling up with tears. "She went into remission twelve years ago and was doing fine. She got better, but then the cancer came back, so we tried chemo again, but she just wasn't responding to it. Then we tried other treatments, but they weren't working either. So, she refused treatment about a year ago, said she was sick and tired of being poked and prodded. I can't say that I blame her."

She's dying?! My god, I really am too late.

"I'm so sorry. My father hasn't been around to help at all?"

"That son-of-a-bitch left, excuse my language, when Clara got sick, not right away, mind you, but when he saw that she was getting worse. The coward couldn't handle it, I guess."

"Are they still married?"

"Yes. They'd been in love since the god forsaken day they met. You know, I tried reasoning with her, told her to slow down, but of course she wouldn't listen."

Sherman shook his head and sunk it down low, below his shoulders. Something like a smile came and went, like he was remembering another time.

He continued, "She just plunged full speed ahead into the relationship. She was twenty-three when she had you, and she was in no shape to raise a kid. You see, Clara was a sickly girl from the beginning, and well... I didn't have the means at the time." His eyes darted uncomfortably around the room.

"I see," Sam smiled awkwardly. "Look you don't need to be sorry. I've had a great life with the parents who raised me and I'm sure you did all you could... Do you know where my father is now?"

"No idea. He's been AWOL about four years now. I haven't been able to find him, and believe me I've tried," Sherman said in a deeply agitated voice. "You know, it was the strangest thing; he was an educated man, went to college, got some fancy science degree, nothing seemed to faze him. But then this happened and he just... disappeared."

"I guess he didn't give anyone any warning?"

"None."

"I see...that's ridiculous. So, you really have no idea why he would do something like that?"

"No clue."

"That doesn't make any sense."

"You're preaching to the choir, honey."

Sam sat in silence for a while, trying to digest this information. After a couple minutes, she spoke.

"Do you think that I could see Clara? I mean, do you think she would want to meet me?"

"I don't know. I can talk to her. But I don't want to put any more stress on her, especially now."

"Now?"

Sherman looked at her, his eyes deep with anguish. "I'll give her a call."

~~~

The hospital had a sickly, clean smell to it. It reminded Sam of dying people and sent a feeling of nausea into the pit of her stomach. Never having had a bad experience at a hospital herself, she couldn't understand why she always felt that way upon entering one.

Get a grip, Sam! Stay positive. This will be a good visit, an important visit.

"She's sleeping, Sam, I don't want to wake her. Maybe we can come back later." Sherman stopped abruptly in front of his daughter's hospital room and looked around, wringing his hands.

It was clear to Sam, that Sherman was having cold feet about the situation.

"Dad, is that you?" A weak raspy voice drifted from inside the small room.

"Yes honey, it's me. Wait right here," Sherman whispered to Sam, then turned and walked into the room.

After a couple minutes, Sherman said, "Clara, there's someone here that wants to meet you."

"Who... who is it?" The shaky voice croaked.

Sam began shaking with anticipation herself. She didn't expect any of this, to be meeting in this way.

"It's Sam... your daughter," Sherman said hesitantly.

"Oh my god."

Sam peeked her head into the doorway.

"May I come in?" she asked timidly, trembling all over, like a nervous Chihuahua.

"Yes, please."

Sam was the spitting image of her mother. It was like looking into a mirror or a time portal, at an older version of herself, a sick, balding, wiry version.

"Sam, I don't know what to say." Clara's skin was thin, her veins visibly protruding from her white arms, which were covered with IVs and bluish-green bruises. She was wearing a pink knit cap and her large brown eyes had a glassy, watery appearance. She had the same seagull shaped curve to her lips as Sam, and the same high cheekbones. Yes, this was indeed, her mother.

"Come here honey, I want to get a closer look at you."

Sam moved forward slowly, to her paper-thin mother's side, holding back all the new-found emotions welling up inside of her.

"You are so beautiful. You are definitely my daughter." She smiled. "Chip always said you were the most beautiful thing, we ever made. You know, he told me he was coming back."

Sam's eyes grew large as she turned to look at her grandfather.

He shrugged his shoulders. "Some half-assed promise he made. Clara's held on to it all these years, but as far as I'm concerned..." his voice trailed off. He knew that he had said too much.

I thought he gave no warning of leaving?

Clara reached a shaky arm out and grasped Sam's wrist, with her cold, bony hand. She gently pulled Sam down to her side. Then, she whispered into her ear: "Listen Sam... your father was always... a man of his word. Don't listen to my father. Your father... he loved us both... very much, believe me... he's watched over you from afar. There is more to the story, but as for me... I don't have much time left." Clara breathed in deeply for a few moments, struggling to catch her breath before continuing. "Trust him. Your father has kept secrets in order to keep us safe... he can trust no one. Please believe me when I say, he has always been steadfast... and you will meet him one day." Clara held Sam's wrist tightly for a moment, almost hurting her, and then let go, closed her eyes and drifted off to sleep.

13. WAKING LIFE: LIZARD'S FOOT, TEXAS

The air was hot and dry. But Sarah wasn't just sweating from the heat. She had called Lucas after getting out of the hospital and shared all that had happened. Officer Bergeron had called the next day too, but more so to check up on her. In no time, Lucas had dug up some information on Rocky Henson. She could not believe the amount of information he was able to extract with the little data she had provided him. Rocky had been working on this year's presidential campaign for North Carolina senator, Thomas Remmer, a complete shock to Sarah. Rocky had been sighted in Raleigh at some of Remmer's campaign events, handing out flyers. Some local businesses had seen him dropping by as well, with promotional handouts.

She tried to set her thoughts on the monstrosity of a building looming ahead as she rumbled her grumpy old 97' Toyota Corolla to a halt. Despite Sarah's disapproval, Joey insisted that he come along, just to keep an eye on things. He promised to be quiet and out of the way. Sarah relented, realizing how hard the events of the previous day must have been on him. Besides, he just needed the assurance that she was safe. The hospital looked no less barren and abandoned in the light of day. Sarah turned off the engine and took in the vacant surroundings, a stark difference from the hospital in Raleigh, which was closely embedded into the surrounding community.

The steep sides of the valley towered hundreds of meters above her in all directions. The valley was a few miles wide and completely barren, apart from the hospital's gardens and an enormous oak tree.

According to the website's picture, the head of the hospital was an elderly, white-haired man with an austere expression. Sarah, of course, had done her research and dressed accordingly, in her most conservative button-down white collared blouse and her brown, tweed skirt. Her hair was pinned up into a neat bun, and she wore contacts this time. Her *Resonance Weekly* badge was pinned symmetrically to her dark blue blazer. Joey put on a casual, button-down plaid shirt and jeans. It was the best he had.

After a short chat with the receptionist Sarah and Joey made their way down a long white hallway towards the hospital CEO's office. The hall extended out endlessly before them. It was eerily quiet. Patients were not wandering around like they did in Raleigh.

"Ah, Ms. Davis!" A short-statured man in a smart brown suit, emerged from a hall door and made his way towards Sarah with a quick step, his hand already outstretched for a handshake.

Sarah instinctively reached her hand out as well and stood there, an awkward statue.

He took her hand in both of his and squeezed firmly, standing quite close to her and looking directly into her eyes.

"Welcome to West Forrester Care. I'm Dr. Rainer Blanch. It's a pleasure to meet you."

Sarah could smell scotch and cigars on his breath.

"I'm Sarah Davis. It's good to meet you as well, Dr. Blanch."

"I've been expecting you, Sarah." He shifted his gaze to Joey and smiled warmly, "And who might this be?"

"I'm Joseph Beck, sir, Sarah's boyfriend. It's nice to meet you. Please don't mind me, Sarah was kind enough to let me come along, but I will be out of the way today."

"Oh, nonsense! Both of you come along now to my office and we'll have some tea."

This was not the reception Sarah was expecting from this prestigious looking man.

"Okay," said Sarah, and they both followed the friendly man into his office.

Sarah sat down on one of the brown leather chairs positioned around a striking, stone fireplace. Surprisingly, the hearth was covered in old black and white family pictures. The large room had an ancient feel, an ornate red, Persian rug stretched across the expanse of the room. Antique oil paintings of dignified looking men and a few women covered the walls.

A fat and very expensive looking cigar rested on a glass ashtray, in the center of a round table between the two chairs. A mahogany hutch in the back of the room was filled to the brim with crystal bottles containing amber liquors.

This place is like something out of a movie. A rich old warden sitting back in his ornate office with his bottles of scotch and expensive cigars.

A cold chill ran through her as she remembered how most of those creepy, psychological thrillers ended, the patients turning on the staff, or the warden turning out to be a raving madman. *He even looks the part!* His bald head and perfectly round bifocals made him look like an old owl. He also had a seriously Freudian white beard and mustache. He reminded her of the Monopoly man.

"So, you're looking for a story, are you?" He smiled at Sarah, handing a crystal tumbler filled with scotch to both her and Joey. *I guess we're not having tea.* Before Sarah could answer, the man continued, as if the question was rhetorical. "Well, we definitely have stories; this place is filled with history. You know, a lot of famous names have wandered these halls: writers, movie stars, CEOs for fortune 500's, you name it."

She took a small sip, remembering she was on the job. "Is this hospital undergoing renovations, like the one in Raleigh?"

"Oh, no... well, I would say we're always improving, but as far as renovations go, things have stayed largely the same around here over the years, hence the historic feel."

"I've noticed! This place reminds of the old psychological thrillers I used to watch."

Wait, why did I just say that?

"Ha! Yes, we get that a lot. But I assure you, our practices are modern and up-to-date. In fact, we've always had best and brightest minds on staff. Did you know we were originally founded as a research institution?"

"Oh, yes. I've done my research."

"That's right, you're a reporter, after all. Then, let me show you something really interesting." Dr. Blanch stood up and motioned for Sarah and Joey to follow him into the connecting room.

He opened the door for her to reveal a modern, state of the art facility. Everything shined, the floors, the walls, the pristine equipment, even the ceiling. It was as if they had entered a different hospital altogether.

"This is the research facility. I know, everyone has that same look on their face when they see it. I told you we may be historic, but we are not antiquated. All the men and women you see on these walls, are the brightest minds the country has ever seen. They came from various backgrounds: philosophers, biologists, psychologists, chemists. But what they all had in common was their passion for the pursuit of scientific progress. This is where we ran our famous sleep studies. Now, I'm sure you've heard of them."

"Oh yes, my father was one of the researchers."

"Yes, he was, Dr. Hurston Davis. His portrait is actually around the corner back there."

Sarah walked in the direction he was pointing and stopped before the large canvas. It was strange for her to see her father's likeness on a wall like some ancient, historic artifact. Her heart began to ache. He looked exactly how she remembered him as a little girl, with a full head of auburn hair, a bright twinkle in his eyes, and a crooked hint of a smile that wouldn't let the world in on his secret.

Sarah thought he must have had a brilliant day, when this picture was taken. Her field of vision began to blur, and she quickly turned away.

"Did you know that he's been missing for the past four years?" Sarah's voice wavered.

"Why, no. I just assumed the old chap was simply done with research and focusing on his family life."

Sarah stared at the old man in disbelief. "No, not at all."

"Oh, I'm terribly sorry to hear that, dear. Hurston was always one of my favorites, such passion for his work, such dedication."

"Do you happen to know anyone who worked closely with him? You know, a friend or a colleague that I could speak to about him?"

"Ms. Davis, I would be happy to help. Let me think. He did prefer to work mostly alone, but he had friends here. I..." He paused for a moment and looked at her squarely before continuing. "I'm sorry, I'm just not sure who would be a useful point of contact for you."

Sarah frowned. He was acting strange and she thought she heard a hint of fear in his voice and saw his eye twitch. *What is he not telling me?*

"Please Rainer, if there's anyone that you know that could help me, I would be so grateful. I don't really need this information for my story. It's just, I've been looking for my father all these years." Sarah stopped. She didn't know what to do. She wanted to burst into tears.

"Sarah," Rainer said slowly, she could definitely see fear in his eyes now.

No, he's not emotionally obtuse. There's something else going on here.

His eyes darted around the room and then quicker than a hawk scooping up an unassuming shrew from the forest floor, he grabbed her by the arm and pulled her close. Joey perked his head up and eyed him suspiciously from across the room.

"What are you doing!?" Sarah shrieked.

"Sarah!" Rainer whispered in a hushed, hurried voice. She could feel his hot breath on her ear. "Sarah, I should not be giving you this information, you understand? Do not speak of this to anyone. There is someone I think you should talk to about your father."

"Who?" Sarah's anxiety was turning into panic and beginning to consume her from the inside out.

"Leonard Fowler. He lives on 7836 Grovertown Ln., but you didn't hear it from me. Now go. Godspeed." Rainer let go of her arm and nudged her towards the door. Joey frowned at Rainer and followed closely behind.

Walking out of the office, Sarah tried to regain her composure, as much as she could.

"What was that all about?" Joey eyed Sarah with concern.

"I don't know. The man is scared of something and I don't think he was supposed to give me the information he did, but he gave me an address, someone I can talk to about my father."

She was playing a part in a script she did not understand and starting to feel like she was becoming involved in a terrible secret. She had an odd sense, that maybe Rainer wasn't the one she should be afraid of. She gave a polite nod to the receptionist on her way out, avoiding lengthy conversation and made a beeline to her car. When she got inside, she let out a huge sigh. She was rattled, but Dr. Blanch had provided her with an address, so she would follow that lead. After a few minutes of deep breathing to settle her nerves, she started the car and they were off.

~~~

Dr. Fowler's house was in a quaint, upper-middle class neighborhood only ten minutes away. She pulled up to a two-story colonial style, white brick home with a well-manicured front lawn lined with cypresses. As she approached the door, she gathered her thoughts. She wondered if she should mention her strange interaction with Dr. Blanch. She decided against it. Sarah knocked a few more times on the door, using her father's famous shave and a haircut pattern. She was surprised when her knock was answered with a two bits response on the other side of the door.

"Hurston? Is that you?"

Sarah stood paralyzed. Was this man really expecting her father to be at the door?

"No, it's his daughter, Sarah," she called out tentatively.

"Sarah!" The man swung the door open.

"My, my, I was wondering when this day would come, and you would come knocking. So many years have passed. So many." He looked over at Joey.

"Hi, Joseph Beck, Sarah's boyfriend. Everyone calls me Joey."

"Nice to meet you. Come on inside."

Joey began to cross the threshold, but Sarah stayed where she was.

"Excuse me? You've been expecting me? And why did you say my father's name when I knocked?"

"You and your father use the same knock. That's how he would always make his entrance, and as for expecting you... dear, I think you'd better come in and sit down."

The older man with the wispy, salt and pepper hair, thick, long beard, and black-framed glasses too large for his face, motioned her through the open door towards a white sectional. Sarah walked slowly across the living room, taking in the layout of the house. The room had a 70's feel, with its dark, wood-paneled walls, but was accented with more modern furnishings, including a glass coffee table and a white leather sectional and loveseat. The walls displayed a variety of colorful impressionist paintings. Sarah was particularly drawn to the pond scene hanging centered above the couch, where a great blue heron stood with its head bent towards the water, a pool of blues, greens, yellows, and ombres. Sarah sat down and Joey followed suit. Dr. Fowler plopped down in the chair across from her. His lips moving inaudibly, as he prepared to recite the script he had seemingly been rehearsing.

"Can I get you two something to drink?" He said suddenly, choosing small talk instead.

"No, thank you," Joey responded. Sarah just shook her head and continued to stare at the man.

"Sarah," he started and stopped, sitting back in his chair and staring back at her, a weary expression on his face.

She began to feel impatient.

"Look," she began, "I want you to know that I've spent a long time looking for my father. He's been missing for the past four years."

"I know."

Then came Sarah's long-withheld conniption. "What? You know where my father is? You knew that he was missing this whole time and didn't contact us? His family?"

"Sarah, please calm down and let me explain."

"No, you don't get to tell me what to do! I can't believe this." Sarah began laughing. "I knew it, I knew he was alive!" Her emotions were rolling into each other, fury into astonishment, astonishment into joy, joy into disillusionment.

"Sarah, I don't know where he is."

Silence.

"What?" Sarah's emotion-fueled tidal wave crashed, breaking onto a rocky shore.

"Let me explain. Your father and I worked together for a long time. About twenty years ago, we were working on a sleep study at West Forrester Care Psychiatric Hospital. Your father was – err– is a brilliant mind, too brilliant for his own good, you know. Sometimes he would take things too far. If he had a novel idea he got hooked on, he wouldn't stop until he saw it through."

Sarah was leaning forward, elbows resting on her thighs, listening intently.

"So, what happened?"

"Well, he kept journals, many journals."

Sarah pictured her father, with his stacks of journals, filling up the basement, a university, a hospital.

"The studies we were working on were classified. They involved a careful observation of dream states. It was experimental research that sometimes involved administering newly developed drugs and inducing various levels of consciousness."

"Dad was involved in cutting edge research... wait, dream states?"

"Yes. Your father believed he was onto something, something big. This research was not approved by the IRB nor by hospital administration. No one knows exactly what it entailed. I was his closest confidant, but even I was kept in the dark about most of it."

"What *do* you know then?"

"Well, what I do know is that your father strongly believed in the capabilities of the mind." The man chuckled, "Go figure, right? He became fixated on people's sleep states and the corresponding dreams they experienced during those states. I believe he began to see some sort of pattern. We had some special equipment that could map visual images of the dreams people experienced."

"Wait, you mean, he could actually see into their minds?" Sarah responded incredulously.

"Exactly. The images were black and white, and not always very clear, and, of course, there was no sound."

"But still, that's incredible."

"Yes, it is. And your father became obsessed. Well you must know how he gets from time to time. I went without seeing him for a month, which was unusual, he was so absorbed in his work. Then, one day, he showed up at my door, with his old shave and a haircut knock, and I was absolutely stunned. He looked distraught, a complete mess, like he hadn't showered or slept in days. He told me that there were people after him, that he had to leave, and that no one could know where he was going, not even me. However, he did give me instructions to give to you, if one day you came looking for him, and he said you would."

"He did? God...."

It felt like she was speaking to her father now, silently thanking him for believing in her and in the strong connection they shared. *He knew I was coming. I knew he was guiding me here.*

"Where are these instructions?"

"Hold on, I'll be right back." Dr. Fowler pulled himself out of the chair and made his way to a little chestnut cabinet near the entrance to the kitchen.

He returned with a yellowing envelope in his hand, with no markings on it. Gingerly, Sarah peeled open the envelope. Inside was a necklace. A piece of glass dangled from what looked like a silver chain. There was also a letter. It read:

Dear reader,

The piece of glass that hangs from you, sides of a mirror, there are two. Look through one and you will find, that you can see clearly to the other side. But look through the other and you will see, yourself staring back. So, darling, don't forget the mirror is a glass and the glass is a mirror.

If you have found this letter, then you are one step closer. Don't give up hope, your intuition and intelligence have guided you here. Burn this when you find it. And don't forget, the owls are watching, so follow them to where they sleep.

Yours Truly

Here's that owl reference again!

"Do you know what this means?" Sarah asked.

Dr. Fowler sat pensively in his chair, scratching his chin through his thick beard. "I've never opened this letter. You know your father and I had a long and loyal friendship, so I honored his wish to not open it, to this day. The owls... I'm not sure who or what he's referring to. It might have something to do with the people that run the hospital, they were always meddling with and trying to control his research. He seems to use owls in a negative connotation here."

"Right, it does. That hospital CEO Dr. Blanch kind of looks like an owl."

"Ha! Yes, he does."

"He's actually the one who sent me to talk to you, but he didn't seem to know anything."

"Ah, I was wondering how you found me. Yes, he was the one who initially disapproved Hurston's newest research, but I'm not sure how much he knew about it."

"Well, where did my father conduct his research after it was disapproved? Was it somewhere in the hospital?"

"You know, I don't think so. I never saw him in there."

"Hmmm... is there anything else you can think, that has to do with owls and my father?"

The letter seemed impersonal to her, but she also realized that her father probably needed to remain cryptic, in case it fell into the wrong hands. She also noticed that the riddle was uncharacteristically unmelodic, the rhyme and rhythm were broken up awkwardly. *Dad must have really been in a hurry writing this.*

"Wait!" Dr. Fowler slapped his knee and smiled up at Sarah, "There are barn owls that nest in the caves of Lizard's Foot. You could scope those out."

"There are caves here?"

"Oh yes, large, beautiful, deep caves, that are home to many a bat and barn owl. As you can imagine, not many people venture into them. It's likely your father wasn't talking about them. But then again, he is a man of mystery, isn't he?"

"Yes, yes he is." Sarah replied while thinking, *that's the understatement of the decade.*

Sarah liked that this man talked about her father in present tense, unlike her family who referred to him as the deceased, or as if he might as well be, as far as they were concerned. She knew in her heart that her family missed him too, but their dismissiveness infuriated her.

"Thank you. You know what? I have the time, and this is the best lead I've got, but... would you be willing to come with us?" Sarah asked, sensing that this would probably be a smart move, considering the man's knowledge of the caves.

"Absolutely. You could easily get lost without a guide. It would be my pleasure."

14. DREAM LIFE: PLAYING SPY

Sam was heartbroken. She stood beside her car, thinking the entire trip might have been a mistake. There was nothing she could do now. Her father was missing, and her mother was dying. Sam had learned nothing about herself, and the meager information that her grandfather was able to muster up, did not even begin to explain any of the freakish dreams and visions she was now experiencing on a weekly basis. *At least I got to meet my grandfather.* It was only a mildly reassuring thought, since the old man, who might have been only rough around the edges, was in the midst of a bitter grief, probably aggravated by what looked to Sam like alcoholic tendencies.

Sam drove him to the hospital herself because she was worried he might get a DUI. Regardless, it just felt wrong to enter their lives like this, her grandfather unraveling, her mother dying, and her father nowhere to be found. Nothing made sense anymore. Sam slammed her hand into the hood of her innocent BMW. It felt like her life was nosediving. She was feeling less and less in control every day. The visions were happening all the time. They made no sense and Sam felt that something was missing. *Could my father know something about this? What was my mom talking about anyway? I can't believe she's dying, and I just met her.*

Sam leaned against the side of the car and sighed heavily, her voice shaking on the exhale. Pitifully, she choked back the tears, which were now flowing from her eyes like leaks in a dam on its way to collapsing.

She envisioned her grandfather drinking himself into an oblivion. He did not offer to let her stay longer. He simply told her goodbye and that he was tired after the visit. Sam understood that he was suffering, and that she was not welcome to partake in his grief. Honestly, Sam didn't want to interfere.

"What am I supposed to do now?" She said to no one. There was no response except for a car that happened to be driving by at that moment, with one of the windows rolled down. The smell of coffee hit Sam's nostrils as it drove by. *That sounds good right now.*

~~~

"That'll be four seventy-three, please" the cashier rang up Sam. She had decided to stop for coffee at a trendy cafe downtown, catering to high-school and college students. Sam handed the young woman a ten and looked around at the modern décor, which included a dark gray wooden-paneled floor, with rustic looking tables and chairs, and a corner with a neatly arranged, crisp-white bookshelf and beanbags large enough for a giant.

"Five twenty-seven is your change."

"Thank you." The woman handed her the bills and fumbled the change into her hand. After putting her coins away, Sam began arranging her dollars by smoothing them and flipping them right-side up and facing forward as she always did.

"Huh," she said, turning over and inspecting one of the dollar bills. On the front there was some scribbling in blue ink. Sam squinted at the chicken scratch. The writing was messy, but definitely not a child's. It was a grocery list of sorts: baloney, milk, plant food, and then something almost indiscernible. *Wait... does that say what I think it says?* In slanted cursive, the sentence read: "Send Larry email about Balixa side effect ASAP." *Balixa?* Sam could not believe her eyes. Her thoughts began their races, whizzing past each other in a blur. *Where in the world did this bill come from? Blakely Pharmaceuticals is miles away from here. Why is this person using a dollar bill as a day planner?*

Larry was Vice President at Blakely Pharmaceuticals and in charge of internal research and development. Sam reported to him directly.

"Thank you." Sam looked up to the sky and told herself that she would pray more from now on. Whatever was happening to her, seemed too strange to be coincidence. It came to her, in a time of desperation, like a nonsensical answer to a prayer, something you hear from time to time in an episode of Oprah. Whatever this was, Sam saw it as an omen.

Sam snorted disdainfully, shaken out of her depressive thoughts for a moment. "And how is money going to make this any better?" She asked out loud again, to the sender of the green, speaking to God, or maybe to the universe, she wasn't really sure who at this point.

~~~

Sam strolled into Larry's office the next day with a large vanilla latte. This was about the time he would send out one of his ridiculously good-looking assistants or interns for his afternoon latte. He would then spend the next hour, pensively staring out of his fifteenth-story window at the Manhattan skyline, or watch wrestling matches on his large, flat-screen.

Although Reeves had a low threshold for anger and some questionable personal behaviors, Sam still liked him. She knew that his overall intentions were good; she wouldn't have worked with him for this long if they weren't.

There was nothing Larry enjoyed more than his latte hour, and Sam whole-heartedly planned on monopolizing this time. This was too important. Sam waited until the young, barely out of high school intern with the high-waisted pencil skirt stepped out of his office. Sam shook her head at her and lifted up the latte, motioning towards the office door. The intern understood, sighed, and walked off, probably to attend to one of her other nondescript duties, which usually involved nervously hovering around meeting and workrooms and making copious amounts of coffee, as Blakely employees were known for being a highly caffeinated bunch. Sam laughed quietly and swung the large wooden door open.

"Hi Mr. Reeves, I brought you your usual." Sam strolled inside. She didn't earn this position without a great deal of audacity and risk-taking, essential in this field.

"Sam, I wasn't expecting you. Come on in. I have a few free minutes to talk."

Sam laughed to herself. A few free minutes. This guy.

"Mr. Reeves," Sam began, "I was visiting family this weekend, about an hour away from here, when the strangest thing happened. This one-dollar bill," Sam held the bill in front of her, "was handed to me at a coffee shop."

Sam placed the bill on Mr. Reeves' desk. He lifted it and examined the chicken scratch, meticulously, forming his mouth into the upside-down u-shape he made when he was deep in thought.

"Ah, I guess I have to call the old hermit up then," Mr. Reeves mused.

"Call who up? Wait, you actually know the guy who wrote that?"

Reeves stared at Sam blankly for a moment, before continuing, "Yeah... um, he's no one important, never mind. Thank you for this, Sam. Now if you don't mind, I need to make a phone call."

"Okay sure... no problem." Sam lifted an eyebrow and eyed him for a moment. *Something fishy is going on here.*

"Oh, don't worry Sam, everything is fine. Thank you for bringing this to my attention. Now if you'll excuse me..."

"Okay." Sam turned to leave. *Am I the only one who thinks this dollar bill thing is insanely serendipitous?* She lingered outside the office door for a minute, listening to find out who this mystery person was on the other end of this phone call. She had to know who he was, if not because of this insanely un-happenstance occurrence, then out of sheer curiosity. She continued waiting quietly outside Mr. Reeves' door. Silence. He knew she was there. She could feel it.

Sam tiptoed away towards the elevators, waited a few minutes, awkwardly rearranging the vase of white lilies, as people passed by. A couple minutes later, Sam made her way back to his door, like she did as a child, when she snuck up on her brother Michael, when he watched reality television. The irony was that he would loudly critique it as the bane of existence when anyone entered the room and caught him in the act, stating he was just channel surfing. She would throw herself on him, in a fit of giggles, and playfully grab him around the neck, making him scream like a frightened cockatoo.

Of course, this was a different situation. Sneaking up on her boss was no laughing matter, but she felt like she had no choice. She had to know who this mystery hermit was. She checked to make sure no one was around and pressed her ear to the door.

"I know I'm not supposed to contact you like this. But listen, I will meet you at our usual spot. Yes, I'll be there in thirty minutes. Look, this better not be something serious. We are due to release Balixa next month. How did I find out? Well, our Marketing Manager found your expensive grocery list... yes, yes, the dollar bill. She brought it to me. Look, I'm heading out now."

Sam ducked into the next hallway and threw herself into the bathroom around the corner, crashing into Rosa, another one of the young interns on Mr. Reeves' payroll. She apologized awkwardly, lingering in the bathroom doorway for a minute, then making her way to the elevators. She was not going to miss this chance. This aching drive that had emerged in her recently, was consuming her, and she would not let up. She would not stop until she found whatever it was she was looking for.

Sam took the next elevator down and quickly ordered a taxi. The map indicated that it was scheduled to arrive in exactly four minutes. *Hopefully, Mr. Reeves' taxi won't arrive at the same time and see me getting in.*

Following Mr. Reeves in Manhattan in a taxi was going to be difficult. Sam didn't care right now, she had a one-track mind.

She quickly ducked into the back seat of the taxi and looked around.

"Hey there. Where you headed?" A friendly sounding man turned around to look at Sam.

"Give me just a minute, I'm waiting for someone."

"Okay, no problem. Your dime."

Less than a minute passed before an equally one-track-minded and oblivious Mr. Reeves emerged from the building and made his way to a cab about thirty feet ahead. Sam ducked. "There! Follow that cab."

"Great! Is this some kind of stakeout?" The young driver responded eagerly, looking for some action in a job that clearly did not deliver the adrenaline rush he craved.

"Not exactly. Just follow him at a good distance... Don't lose him. I'm going wherever he's going."

"Ok, I got this!" The animated redhead rubbed pumped his fists in the air and pulled off.

There was series of abrupt twists and turns as they lost sight of the car a few times. About twenty minutes later, Mr. Reeves exited the taxi near an old, abandoned building. There was a pond nearby, overgrown with reeds and knee-high grass.

"Park over on this street, so he doesn't see us," Sam motioned to the driver. Without another word, she slipped out of the vehicle, nodded to him politely and gave him a good tip.

Wow. That was a lot easier than in the movies. Now for the hard part.

Sam waited behind a bush. She could not believe she was doing this. She watched, shaking her head at the ridiculousness of her current situation. After a few minutes, Sam watched as a middle-aged man with fluffy white hair, a short beard and rectangular glasses, wearing a long-sleeved blue shirt, approached the door of the building. A feeling came over her, like he was watching her. *Can he see me behind the bush? No, impossible. It's too far away.*

Mr. Reeves entered the building, and after spending some time looking around in a paranoid fashion, the mystery man followed suit. Sam, quite paranoid herself, at this point, was not entirely convinced that the man did not lock his eyes on the bush again. Then the doors closed, and Sam was back to square one.

After about five minutes, Sam sensed that no one was going to be coming or going for a while, so she quietly made her way to the entrance. She took a deep breath and said a silent prayer that this was not one of those squeaky hinged doors, and cracked one open, just slightly. She could hear voices coming from somewhere deep inside the warehouse. She opened the door a bit more and slipped inside. The place had high ceilings and rows of fluorescent lights overhead. It was filled with row upon row of massive, metal shelves. *This must be some kind of storage facility.*

As Sam moved deeper into the warehouse as stealthily as possible, she could hear the voices growing louder. Her heart pounded at the idea of being discovered. Suddenly, the implication of what that would mean began pouring over her in a heated torrent. *What if I get fired? What if they have to kill me, because I know too much?* Sam shook her head at her own ridiculousness and made a note to herself to stop watching so many crime dramas. She took a deep breath to steady her rattling breath and walked quietly along, staying close to the shelves in case she needed to duck out of view. The voices grew louder.

She could hear Mr. Reeves now. "Look, we talked about this numerous times. Why am I hearing about this again? And on dollar bill for that matter?"

"I just wanted to talk to you again, to see if you were completely sure about releasing Balixa."

"Why would I not be sure?"

"There are potential repercussions, as I said before. Maybe they will come looking for me or come after you or the corporation for answers."

"Perhaps, but it's a stretch. How else do you propose that we handle this, Chip?"

What the hell are they talking about?

"Patiently."

"Listen," Reeves' voice grew louder with frustration, "Balixa will be released either way, it has to be. We've been working on this for ten years. The research is sound, it's the best sleeping drug on the market, you know this, I know this, and the board knows this. We've come too far." Mr. Reeves knocked his chair over accidentally, clumsy in his moment of irritation. The chair reverberated on the ground with a loud clamor.

Sam stumbled back, startled, and banged against a stack of metal chairs. Then came the dreaded moment.

"What was that? Reeves, is someone else here?!"

Sam bolted, kicking off her heels and scooping them up as she scrambled for all her life was worth, down the hallway.

"Hey you! Come back here!" The mystery man screamed in a frenzy of footfall.

Sam didn't turn back around, she ran faster, seventh grade track races flashing through her mind, her legs like Jell-O, her nerves electrified. She ran like her feet had wings, and eventually, she lost them. Cars, passersby, and shops whizzed by her, like she was on a moving train. She took a sharp right and flew through the open doorway of an old-fashioned drug store.

Hunched over, hands on her knees, she heaved, trying to catch her breath and ignore the inquisitive stares of customers. She felt the long-forgotten ache in the back of her throat, tinged with the taste of iron. She sat down at the lunch counter and wiped the sweat from her brow with her shirt sleeve. *I probably broke my old track record.* Her head was swirling, literally and figuratively, as she tried to process what just happened. Then came the old familiar line of logic that had escaped her for the past hour: *what the hell am I doing?*

"Hi!" The startling voice came out of nowhere, like the mysterious dollar bill. Sam realized it was the waiter standing in front of her. "Can I get you something to drink? You look thirsty."

"Two coke floats," came an equally startling and familiar voice from behind her.

Sam slowly turned around, half expecting a loaded gun to be pointed at her face. The man seating himself next to her was indeed the mystery man from the warehouse. But surprisingly, he did not look angry.

15. WAKING LIFE: THE OWLS

The flashlight beam illuminated the dust particles floating around the ceiling of the dark cave, stirring the bats. Sarah quickly pointed the light beam to the path ahead of her, as she, Dr. Fowler, and Joey made their way deeper into the recesses of the winding cavern. The scene reminded her of old horror films, where a serial killer, or perhaps a demonic creature was lying in wait in some abandoned house or cave, just waiting for some unassuming idiots to come wandering inside.

They had entered the cave at approximately 11:15 a.m. after meeting at Dr. Fowler's for breakfast and to assemble supplies, including a backpack containing sweatshirts, light snacks, water, and three flashlights. They had been wandering for about fifteen minutes at that point.

It was pitch black, except for the beam of light cutting through the darkness, illuminating the dust particles. She moved her light from side to side. From the corner of her eye she saw something that looked like movement. Sarah whipped her head around, shining the beam in the direction of the movement. The edge of the beam caught something that looked like the hem of someone's skirt, stopping Sarah dead in her tracks. She looked around, but there was nothing there. Joey and Dr. Fowler stopped as well.

"What? What is it?" stammered Joey, obviously spooked.

Meandering through a cold, dark cave was not exactly his idea of a good time, and his claustrophobia did not make things any better. However, he refused to let Sarah go at it alone, and with a stranger, none the less. But the bats and increasingly narrowing walls were getting to him.

"Nothing. It was nothing."

"You know, in these situations, where there is extreme sensory deprivation, the mind can play tricks on you," Dr. Fowler remarked in a detached and scholarly manner.

The blackness of the cave reminded her of the passing shadows when she would lie in bed at night as a child, staring intently into the blackness. It was like dreaming with her eyes open, watching the colorful dots of pixilated light swim through the black ocean around her.

The dark was bringing her inwards and it was an eerie feeling, being transported back to those nights, her father out somewhere working, her mother drinking vodka tonics in the bedroom, attempting to kill the loneliness.

Suddenly, the skirt appeared again, but this time, it was clear as day, a little girl running away, illuminated by the light beam of Sarah's flashlight, her white dress swaying to and fro, almost in slow motion. Sarah watched silently, too awestruck and terrified to speak. The girl turned a corner and was gone.

"Did you guys see that?" Sarah asked.

"See what?" Joey asked.

"You didn't see anyone running ahead of us?"

"Maybe we should turn around," Dr. Fowler suggested, his boyish humor suddenly maturing into fatherly concern.

"No. Let's keep going."

"Are you sure? It's okay if we turn back," Joey said.

"My father wanted me here for a reason and right now this is where my intuition is guiding me. I want to follow it."

"If you're sure, Sarah," Dr. Fowler continued in a concerned tone. "Remember though, if you become afraid, we are right here beside you and we can turn back at any time."

"Thanks."

Sarah was freaking out, but she couldn't let anyone know. They would surely turn back around. She had to keep going, despite her heart beating inside her ears and beads of sweat collecting at the top of her forehead. *I have to calm down. I can't let this get to me. Besides, it's probably a sign that I'm moving in the right direction.* She steadied her breathing, filling up her belly with air and exhaling it slowly and silently.

Sarah thought of Dr. Fowler and Joey. They would surely be paying attention to her. She turned her attention on other thoughts. She liked Dr. Fowler, he was odd, but she liked him none the less. She imagined him for a moment with her father. Her father fumbling over his words with all the nervous energy of his latest idea. He would exclaim, "Fowler, my man, I've found it!" And Fowler, would excitedly chime in, being his most loyal and enthusiastic supporter, "How wonderful!" Sarah laughed out loud at the thought of this dynamic duo. A giggle escaped her like a bubble rising to the top of a body of water.

"What's so funny?" Joey was clearly not in a joking mood.

"Oh, nothing," replied Sarah, shaking her hand loose of Joey's ever tightening, death grip.

Sarah sighed loudly and stirred the owls, bats, vampires, and whatever other creature of the night she suspected resided in creepy, pitch-black caves. *What time is it?* Sarah had completely forgotten it was still early afternoon. The darkness threw her off and she was beginning to lose her sense of time and orientation. Apart from occasionally tripping over a rock and feeling her feet hit the ground, she had no idea if she was heading north, south, or in circles.

The blackness of the cave turned her mind into a movie reel and the memories began to flood in, one by one, in a picture slideshow with no particular order: Sarah's brother Michael digging to China in the back yard, Sarah stuck in the five foot hole, yelling for him to help her out for twenty minutes, while Michael laughed hysterically above her, staring at herself in the mirror as a kid and dissociating, working herself up to think that a different little girl, an alien, who had inhabited her body, was staring back at her, and again as a college student standing in front of the dorm bathroom mirror, after learning in her Neuropsychology class that the mind can mistake a carefully positioned reflection of a limb, for an actual limb.

Sarah could see an office with colorful posters exclaiming motivational euphemisms, like "Dream Big!" There was a woman wearing purple-rimmed glasses reclining in a love-seat. She had curly hair and colorful, bohemian clothing. She had a notepad in her lap. *Maybe she's a therapist?* Sarah didn't recognize her and was abruptly pulled from her reverie, by Joey whispering in her ear. Sarah jumped, stirring the bats again, and from the sound of it, owls, as well.

"Hey, are you doing okay? Looked like you were daydreaming." He put a hand around her waist and drew her close to him.

Sarah closed her eyes and smiled as his touch brought her back to the present. Suddenly she remembered that she was not the only one in that cave. She had been traveling deeper and deeper into it, like the recesses of her mind.

"Joey," she began hesitantly.

"Yes?" He whispered in her ear, not daring to disturb the sleeping beasts.

"Do you remember me ever seeing an eccentric looking therapist, with curly hair, who dressed in sort of retro, boho clothes?"

"No, you never saw anyone like that. Your last therapist was pretty standard looking from what I remember."

"That's what I thought, but I'm remembering a different woman. I must have seen her at some point."

"If you say so, but Sarah you've been remembering a lot of things lately that don't seem to have happened to you. Are you sure these are memories? You're really starting to freak me out."

"What else would they be? I mean they feel like memories, I'm not hallucinating or making this stuff up." Sarah clutched her necklace for comfort, rubbing her thumb over the glass surface, like she did with the pocket watch. *Dad, where are you leading us?*

THUMP!

And just like that, Sarah ran into a wall.

"Ouch!"

The vampires stirred in their ceiling caskets, and a few of them suddenly flew past Sarah's face. She covered her mouth to keep from screaming. Everyone ducked down and waited in silence until they settled back into their places. When Sarah carefully stood back up, she realized that she was standing in front of a dead end. Unbelievably, it was still not the end of the cave, which veered sharply to the left. This was a rather large wall.

"We can keep going this way," said Dr. Fowler, motioning to the left.

"No, wait a minute," said Sarah touching the oddly smooth surface of the wall in front of her. "This wall is so smooth. I think it's the same material as the other walls, but the texture is so different, like it's been smoothed out or something."

"You're right," Joey walked over and pressed both hands against the wall firmly. "There's something strange about this wall. It feels like it's giving way a little, like it's not part of the rest of the cave."

"Curious," Dr. Fowler said as he examined the wall for any sign of fissure. He frowned. "Sarah, you know your father hinted at something like this once, a place where no one could interfere with his work. Maybe this is something."

Sarah stood in front of the wall frowning, one hand on the flashlight, the other rubbing the glass necklace pensively. *Wait a minute...two-sided. This wall is two-sided.*

"Joey, Dr. Fowler, this wall could be two-sided, I mean, there could be something on the other side of it. Look for some kind of crack or opening."

"My dear, that's what I was doing," said Dr. Fowler, "but there's nothing here that indicates a separation from the rest of the cave wall."

"No, you're wrong," Sarah said, "Just keep looking. There's something off about this wall." Sarah rubbed her hands down the length of the door, until she reached the ground. It was an odd feeling. "Look down at the bottom of the wall."

She knelt on the ground with her flashlight as everyone hovered over her: moths around a lantern. She brushed the rocks and pebbles delicately away from where the wall met the ground. "See this? The wall of the cave is too perpendicular to the ground, too perfect, like the way a man-made wall rests on a floor, or a door" Sarah trailed off and began fervently digging into the ground around the wall, the soil jamming underneath her fingernails. She did not care. She just felt like she had to keep digging. Dr. Fowler and Joey watched her, perplexed.

She turned her head and stared at them "Well, is someone going to help me?" She kept digging, extracting the dirt from the ground like the memories of her father; piece by piece she was getting closer to him. Sarah breathed heavily as she scooped out the dirt with more and more vigor, fueled by rage, joy, and the feeling that finally after years of fruitless searching, something was happening.

"What are you doing?" Joey knelt down next to her.

"I think this wall connects to something...if it is man-made, it has to be. Is there anything in that backpack that can help us?"

"Well you can use this." Dr. Fowler pulled a swiss army knife out of his pocket and opened up the blade, extending it down to Sarah.

"Thanks."

Joey took out an old plastic rewards card from his wallet and began digging too.

After several minutes of digging along the length of the wall she felt something hard poking out of the ground. She pried it out of the dirt. "A shovel!"

"Wow. Ok, so someone clearly wants us to keep digging," Joey laughed in astonishment, despite his fear. Even he couldn't help being amused at this point.

"This is something your father would do," Dr. Fowler said.

"Yep, this is just like him."

The soil was much softer and looser the further down she dug, like it was prepped for them. It did not take long before there were two large piles on either side, and she hit something hard. "A floor!" After several minutes of everyone clearing the area around the wall and floor, they stepped back to look at their work. There was a small opening, where the ground and wall separated, she reached her hand through and turned to look at Joey and Dr. Fowler on either side of her.

She gasped, "It *is* a door!"

Sarah paced back and forth as Joey and Dr. Fowler scoured and searched for a way to open this mystery door. *So, there's a door in a cave and Dad's letter helped me figure it out. What did that letter say? Look through the glass and you will see clearly to the other side, look through the other side and you will see... yourself. What does that even mean? Oh, come on Dad, stop being so cryptic. Okay, focus Sarah. The mirror is a glass, the glass is a mirror, the mirror... is a glass, the glass... is a mirror.*

Sarah walked over to the opening again and laid down on her stomach, pulling the glass necklace from her pocket and shining the weak flashlight through it. She rested her head on the ground, to get a better view underneath the door, squinting her eye to look through the glass in front of her.

"What are you doing?" Joey looked at her puzzled.

"Shhh... I think... I don't know, but there is definitely some functional purpose for this necklace. My father is not all riddles and no substance, there's usually... some kind... of meaning... behind his words," Sarah stammered, carefully positioning her glass and cocking her head in various angles. "I think... I see something. It looks like..."

A beam of light showed to the left of her, the glow grew brighter the longer Sarah aimed her flashlight at it through the glass. A quiet buzzing sound became audible from the same direction.

"Do you guys hear that?" Sarah asked.

"No, I don't hear anything," replied Dr. Fowler.

"It sounds almost like a... oh!" Sarah gasped and covered her mouth immediately to prevent another critter from swooping down, maliciously.

The light had intensified to the point that a light beam sling-shot itself into the glass, then back to its source and then directly into the door, in a zigzag fashion. Then came a click. The door started moving up in a garage style fashion. Sarah had activated some kind of laser-beam, latch-opening mechanism.

This time everyone let out a gasp.

"Genius, Sarah! You're just like your father. Incredible!" Dr. Fowler marveled at the door.

Everyone's excitement was abruptly interrupted by an angered barn owl, screeching and swooping down towards them, like a demon from the depths of hell, black eyes searing out of its ghostly, cratered face, talons outstretched, ready to maim. Everybody stumbled inside the room, falling over their feet in panic. Sarah landed on the ground, with Joey on top of her like dominoes. Dr. Fowler reached up and pulled the door down, barely missing the owl. She picked up her head and pointed the weak flashlight beam into the room. It was all she could do not to faint.

16. DREAM LIFE: FATHER DEAREST

"**A**re you going to kill me?" Sam whispered in a small voice, although somehow she knew this was most likely not the case.

"No, Sam, of course not. I'm not going to hurt you. I could never hurt you."

"How do you know my name?" Sam was equal parts curious and afraid.

"Because... you are my daughter."

Sam spilled her glass of water, creating a little waterfall off the edge of the table.

"Excuse me?" She did not bother to stand the glass back up. The man knelt beside her and began mopping up the water with a wad of napkins.

Looking up at her he said, "Sam, I know that this is a strange way for us to meet. But there is a very important reason that you and I are coming back into each other's lives again."

"Again? And what reason would that be? Wait a minute, did you know that I would be at that warehouse?"

He did see me behind that bush!

Sam made another quick mental note to work on her not-so-stealth-ninja hiding skills.

Words poured out of her in a torrent that had finally bridged the gap between her brain and mouth. The dam was broken. She could see that this man was clearly going to answer at his own pace and could not possibly comprehend the word vomit spewing out of her. Regardless, she could not stop herself.

"After Reeves told me that one of his employees found the dollar bill, I had a feeling."

"A feeling? Did you know that I work for Blakeley Pharmaceuticals? Why did you not contact me after all these years? And why did you abandon mom?"

Sam could not make up her mind about this man. He was either a stalker or a crazy man. The implications of that thought were sinking their claws into Sam's gut.

The man, who was apparently Sam's father, opened his mouth to speak.

"No, you don't get to talk now. This is ridiculous. Why did you run after me like that? Why did you abandon your wife? And me?"

"Look... I'll explain everything. Can we just get a booth over there?" He motioned for a booth at the back corner of the restaurant.

Sam narrowed her eyes at him, then sighed and dropped her arms down at her sides in exasperation.

"Fine." She followed the man in a dumbfounded stupor to the open booth at the back of the store, near the bathrooms. It was around 3:00 p.m., and the place was oddly full of people. Only a few booths were empty.

"Popular place," the man claiming to be her father said, reading her mind. "Gives us the right degree of privacy, but please keep your voice down, okay?"

"So— Chip is it?"

"Yes. Chip Hoffer."

"Chip... is there someone after you or are you just a paranoid schizophrenic?" Sam did not blink. She was beyond niceties.

"I know this is difficult for you to understand, but there is a reason why you and I are meeting now," Chip continued, ignoring her comment, "Do you think it's coincidence that you followed your boss right to me?"

This is true. Wait, how did he know that I was looking for him? Oh my god, he IS a stalker!

"I did look for you, as any curious adopted child growing up without her biological parents would.... but Clara — my mother, said you were in hiding. That you were keeping secrets and you were coming back. What did she mean? She's dying now, you know." She stared at the man, as if she were looking at a child, a child who did not know right from wrong. There was no reason, in her mind, that a husband would stay away from his sick wife for years. No excuse.

"Your mother is right, and she knows things that I will reveal to you, in time. It just has to be done... delicately."

Did he really just disregard the fact that she is dying?

"Stop being so cryptic, Chip."

"Sam, my intention is not to be cryptic. Let me see..." Chip leaned in close and spoke in a hushed voice. "Well as you know, I am the developer of the Balixa formula, and the fact that you, my daughter, got a job at this company is no coincidence."

"Excuse me? Are you insinuating that I didn't earn this job on my own? Did you do something?"

"Shhh."

Sam rolled her eyes.

"Not at all, you did earn this job, it's just..."

"What?"

"I might have put in a word for you."

"Unbelievable! So, you *have* been stalking me!"

"Sam please, what I need to tell you is highly sensitive information... and I wouldn't call it that. I would call it, watching closely... from afar."

Sam grabbed her purse and stood up abruptly. Enough was enough.

Chip reached out his hand as if to grab her and then thought better and retracted it, "Wait. Please, wait."

Sam sat back down but remained unconvinced.

"Talk."

"Okay. I developed Balixa for two reasons, the first reason was to help with insomnia, which you know about, the second... is what Reeves is afraid of... You see, a side effect of this drug is vivid dreams."

"I am well aware."

"Yes, of course you are."

The waiter came back over.

"Sir," Chip began, "We would appreciate some privacy here."

Creepy AND tactless.

"Look, if you're going to be sitting here, you need to order something, sir."

"Okay, I ordered two coke floats at the counter earlier, please bring those over."

The waiter rolled his eyes and walked off.

Chip nervously tapped his fingers on the counter, as if playing out a melody on a miniature piano.

"Sam, let me show you something," he reached into his pocket. He put a quarter down on the table. "This coin has two sides." He held it up in the air, turning it this way and that, as the waiter set the coke floats down on the table. "Each side is looking outward and is seeing only what is ahead. You see, Washington does not see the eagle, and the eagle does not see Washington."

Okay, definitely a nut job.

Still, Sam stayed and listened, against her better judgement. Oddly enough, she wanted to hear where this wayward riddle was going. Was this guy really her father? She was not fully convinced. Sure, he seemed to look like her, his almond-shaped, brown eyes, his defined jawline, but could her father really be this crazy?

"Sam, are you listening?" He seemed to sense how transfixed she was with her thoughts.

"Yes. Go on, but cut to the chase, please," said Sam with growing irritation.

Her father continued.

"This coin has two sides, but neither the eagle, nor the president, know the other exists. But that does not mean that they don't exist. Each one is very much real. Sam," Chip lowered his voice even more, so that she had to lean in close across the table to hear. He continued holding her gaze, "Those vivid dreams you've been having, the ones that seem like memories from another life, those are real as well. In fact, they are just as real as you and me, sitting and talking in this store."

"What do you mean, they're *real*?"

"I mean, *they exist*. You have another self, Sam, that exists in that world, we all do. I know how all this sounds, and, no, I'm not schizophrenic or delusional. I can prove it to you if you'll let me."

And that's my cue! Sam grabbed her purse and this time did not sit back down. She ran towards the door, not turning around.

17. WAKING LIFE: THE SECRET ROOM

The room they stepped into was a bigger surprise than anything Sarah could have imagined. The room was actually *a room*, complete with chairs, tables and faint and flickering overhead lights. There were also two huge generators to power the lights that softly hummed on when they came inside, as well as several pieces of hospital equipment.

Joey walked over to the generators and whistled. "This setup is incredible. He's got the exhaust pipes running through the walls. I wonder where it all goes?"

"This is just too weird," Sarah said aloud.

Her flashlight flickered. She turned it off to save power.

"Hey guys, my flashlight's dying, how are yours?"

"Mine is barely visible, not even enough to illuminate a small space," Dr. Fowler answered, slapping his flashlight on the side a few times, as if it would fix things.

"Yeah, mine too," Joey answered.

"I'm so sorry," Dr. Fowler shook his head, "I thought the batteries would last longer. I was sorely mistaken."

"There have got to be some batteries around here somewhere," said Joey.

After a couple minutes of looking around he located several stacks of batteries, up on a shelf.

"Look! D batteries. Let's hope these are still good!" Joey began fumbling with his flashlight and inserting the batteries.

"Shit, they don't work!" Joey yelled, a bit too loud, stirring the flying hell-birds outside.

"Shh!" Sarah hushed him in irritation. "Keep trying."

After a couple minutes, it was becoming clear that they would not have working flashlights much longer.

"None of these are working, Sarah. You know what this means," Joey said, "Batteries don't last more than three to five years, which means there's probably not been anyone down here for a long time."

"Some can last as long as ten years," Dr. Fowler encouraged. "Keep looking."

Sarah sighed.

Joey fumbled through the packs, tearing them open and trying the batteries on by one.

Finally, after what seemed like an eternity, Joey's flashlight responded with a brighter new beam.

"Yes! So, there is a newer pack in here."

Fowler and Sarah fitted the last four batteries into their flashlights and pushed their switches. Sarah and Dr. Fowler's flashlights glowed in a soft, barely perceptible light.

She looked over to Dr. Fowler who shrugged his shoulders and gave her an apologetic look.

Joey sighed.

"Looks like we'll have one strong flashlight for the way back. Everyone turn them off to save power."

"Well let's stay here and look around a while," said Sarah.

"Sarah, your father was right for entrusting you with that letter." Dr. Fowler chimed in. "This lab must be where he began working when his latest sleep study was not approved by the IRB. He didn't have the funding, so I helped him out. All he really needed was willing participants and space. What an odd location though."

"Yes, it's just like my dad to think outside the box. So, you knew about this study all along?" Sarah asked.

"No, not exactly. You see Hurston never really explained this new study to me, in detail. He was very cryptic, as you might imagine. We really should be going soon. We don't want to get stuck feeling our way out of this cave in the dark."

"Well, let's at least look around first. I mean, we got this far," said Joey, with a new-found air of confidence, probably compensating for not taking on a more valiant role on the trek through the cave, Sarah thought. "Maybe we'll find another light source we can use and take with us."

They continued walking around the abandoned room, scouring the corners.

A large pile of composition notebooks lay on the floor in the back of the room. The pile was stacked waist-high. Smiling, Sarah picked up the black and white journal on top, figuring it would be his most recent, and opened the cover to the first page to look at the date. February 21, 2020, four years ago. Sarah tossed the journal down on the floor. The thought that her father had been here and let her family believe he was dead, made her furious and sad.

Sarah felt a hand on her shoulder, surprisingly, it was Dr. Fowler's.

"Sarah," he began, reading her thoughts. "You know your father would have contacted you if he could. He loves you very much. There has to be a reason he abandoned this place."

"And there must be a reason he didn't want to be found," she said, finishing his thought. "But there has to be some kind of clue, somewhere. He wouldn't have led me here for no reason. We have to keep looking."

"Look at this," said Joey, marveling at a small black box near the front entrance. "It looks like some kind of reflective device." He looked in the direction it was aiming. "I think it's the device that opened the door. It intensified the light beam directed at it, until it shot the beam into the door latch," Joey turned and pointed at the latch on the inside of the door, unlatching it and pulling the door open slightly. "Your father is a genius, Sarah," he smiled.

The longer Sarah looked around, the more the place reminded her of her father. The floor and work spaces were covered in empty or partially downed Dr. Pepper cans, snickers wrappers, and potato chip bags, her father's foods of choice when he had to fend for himself. Sarah shuddered at the thought of how he had been feeding himself all this time.

She walked back to the stack of journals and began flipping through the pages for clues, while Dr. Fowler and Joey continued inspecting the equipment.

The top journal was filled with research observations, hypotheses, and what appeared to be, indiscriminate ramblings. Sarah sifted through it. Specific entries and themes began to catch her eye: drug induced dreams, slow wave Theta states, the use of white noise during somnolence to access information, and the strangest sounding of all to Sarah: guided group target finding through suggestive hypnosis. *What was Dad talking about?* These writings reminded Sarah of her father's hippie days, when he talked about dropping acid and astral projecting. *How far did he go with this sleep study?*

Sarah began impatiently flipping through the journals like a flip book, the pages dancing in front of her. And then... she saw it. About a third of the way in, something appeared at the top of the page, it looked like a picture of a little building, which moved and changed the faster Sarah turned the pages. Hurston had made a flipbook. It was one of the little games he played with Sarah as a child. The doors of the building began to open. Sarah picked up the next journal. Again, about halfway through, the little building reappeared and took her inside, which appeared to be some sort of warehouse.

The drawing grew more detailed. Sarah continued to pick up the journals, one by one.

By the time Sarah reached the last journal, she got a full view of the premises. The warehouse was at the end of a dirt road and looked abandoned. Further down, there was a busy street full of shops, in a city that Sarah did not recognize. There was a street name too. It had a pretty average sounding name, James Street, there could have been at least a million in the country. Sarah decided to take all seven of the journals containing the hidden flipbooks with her. She looked around for something to put them in and found a grocery bag lying on the ground next to the desk, a snickers bar still inside.

"Look at all this technology!" Dr. Fowler stood over a large machine, arms crossed in front of him, shaking his head. "These machines, right here," He pointed to the large, rectangular one. "This one measures brain waves, and this one... this one actually lets you see inside a person's mind, as they dream! You know, see what they are seeing. It's called, Pictographic Neuroimaging, and only a few machines exist in the entire world. How your father managed to get his hands on one is beyond me."

"Does it really work?" Joey asked.

"Presumably. This technology is very new, first manufactured in 2019."

"Well, only one way to find out, right?" Sarah walked up to the machine, laying herself down in the huge black tunnel. She was getting tired of being in dark, confined spaces, but what was one more? "Dr. Fowler, can you operate this?"

"Yes, I think so. That is, if the power source is still good."

Fowler flipped a series of switches. The machines hummed on, illuminating the rest of the room in a cool, blue light that was oddly familiar.

"Wow, I can't believe it still works," Joey's eyes bugged out in amazement.

"Now lie very still, Sarah," he pressed the button, sliding Sarah into the machine.

The sensory deprivation immediately sent Sarah down a heightened visual cortex memory spiral. In her mind, she saw the same, strange bohemian woman again, she was speaking to her this time, in a therapeutic fashion. Her vision changed. Sarah was inside a cave now, following the same little girl she saw earlier, except this time she was wearing some sort of scarf around her face. Then another abrupt change, and Sarah was running out of a building, a man's voice calling after her. And then she was inside a drug store with cherry-red booths, the sign outside read, Soda Pop Shoppe.

"Okay Sarah, I'm pulling you out." Dr. Fowler's voice drifted into her secluded cell, like the great and powerful Oz.

Sarah sat up, lightheaded, and walked over to where Dr. Fowler and Joey were sitting, studying the monitors.

"Let me play back the images for you."

Sarah watched in amazement, as all her very personal visions, played out before everyone's eyes, like a black and white movie reel.

"This is unreal," Joey said, equally stunned. "Are these supposed to be memories?"

"Hard to say exactly, but these are the visual images Sarah was seeing in her mind. The machine cannot decipher whether they were memories, dreams, or simply thoughts. However, if you match up Sarah's brain waves from this monitor to the images on that monitor, you can see that Sarah was not asleep, therefore these images were either memories or daydreams."

"They certainly feel like memories, but I don't remember being in any of these places. The building I'm running through seems familiar. Wait, what was that? Rewind it back a few seconds. There." Sarah pointed to the image of a small street sign, which had blinked by in less than a second, the letters barely legible.

"Sarah, are you okay?" Joey asked. Sarah had grown white as a ghostly barn owl.

"Joey...the street name. The street name, it says..."

"James Street, so what?"

Sarah's breath quickened. She could not wrap her head around this, it was all too much. What the hell was happening to her? How was she seeing these images in her head, so real and memory-like, with the same street name as the picture her father drew in the flipbook? Could her imagination really be that vivid? Sarah had never been a *visual* person. She did not think in pictures, not until the past couple of months. Not until this search began. Sarah wondered if there was something more to this, more than her brain, her father, was trying to tell her.

Sarah felt like she was going to faint. She needed to run, and fast. This all felt like a bad nightmare she had to wake up from. *Maybe this isn't real. Maybe none of this is really happening.*

"Joey, we need to get out of here, now."

"Sarah, are you okay?"

"No, I'm not. I just... I just have to go." Sarah picked up the bag of journals she had collected and took Joey's flashlight, which had the strongest beam at that point.

She walked towards the door and pulled the latch open, sliding the door up, she continued to move ahead.

"Come on, let's go!"

Joey and Dr. Fowler followed closely behind. The dark was playing games with Sarah's head, she felt dizzy, like her head was swimming. She did not feel real. She walked faster.

"Slow down!" Joey yelled after her. His voice, which did not seem real either, sounded distant, like it was filtered through the static of a radio, in between stations. "Sarah!"

She moved forward, her legs moving faster, with a sense of urgency. She couldn't breathe. She needed to get out. Panic. She was having a panic attack, and there was no stopping it. She needed to get out.

The little girl appeared before her again, more real than Joey's distant voice. She was glowing like a beacon, guiding her out of the cave. She could see her dress and brown hair whipping ahead of her.

Sarah finally reached the cave entrance and fell to the ground. An enormous group of white owls flew out all around her. She looked up into the pale blue sky, filled with great beating wings, flying into the clouds.

Joey ran out behind her a minute later, followed by Dr. Fowler, a few minutes after that. Dr. Fowler heaved over, coughing and trying to catch his breath.

The strongest sense of Déjà vu Sarah had ever experienced abruptly came over her. *Why am I still here? Why can't I wake up?*

"Wake up! Wake up! Wake up!" Sarah yelled at the top of her lungs, her voice quaking. She beat her head against the ground repeatedly, trying to break the spell. "Wake up, wake up, wake up, wake up, WAKE UUUUUP!"

"Sarah!" Joey ran to her and held her head in his arms, creating a barrier between her and the ground. "Sarah! Sarah, please calm down, what's happening?! Dr. Fowler, call 911!"

18. Dream Life: Dr. N

S am submerged herself in the warm, bubbly water. She was back where she started, soaking in her parent's bathtub, feeling utterly disillusioned. She was now awaiting the only outcome that seemed to make sense to her, her drastic decline into mental illness, because clearly the rest of her family was delusional.

After almost an hour, the water had cooled off and Sam refilled the tub. She did not feel like leaving any time soon. Technically, she was on vacation. There was a lot of opportunity for paid leave during the down times, a huge job perk she did not take for granted.

The scent of lavender essential oils filled the room and softened the edges of Sam's burdened mind. She closed her eyes and submerged herself again, a familiar wave of calm washed over her, like it did at Silver Falls.

She held her breath. It felt so good, she held it even longer. The tightness in her chest started, and then she was gone. In her mind's eye she saw an open road and a welcome to Raleigh, North Carolina sign. A miserable reflection of herself reflecting off a car window startled her, changing the channel of her vision swiftly.

She now saw the outside of a gray, high rise building with glass windows. Suddenly, she was walking down a white hallway. There was a door, opening to a room of medical equipment, like a doctor's office. *What is this place? Am I in a hospital?* In response to her question, her vision cut to the front of the building again, she could make out one word: Psychiatric.

The tightness in her chest spiked and sent Sam popping out of the water, gasping and splashing water all over the floor.

"Honey, are you okay in there?" Her mother called from the hallway.

"I'm fine, mom!" Sam yelled back through the closed door, quelling the shaking in her voice. "I just slipped and fell, but I'm not hurt."

"Okay honey, do you need some help?"

"No mom, I'm fine!"

"Okay."

Sam dried off and plopped down on the bed in her monkey and banana print pajamas with her computer in her lap. She began searching for psychiatric hospitals in Raleigh. Interestingly, after a few clicks, something turned up. Northern Weaver Psychiatric Hospital. It was the only standalone psychiatric hospital in the area.

Is there really something more to this dream thing? It's a long shot, but I have to find out.

~~~

Sam was shaking all over when she exited the plane in Raleigh International Airport. She had always had a fear of flying, something about being completely out of control and thousands of feet in the air. She prayed every time she felt turbulence, in an obsessive kind of way. It made her feel a little safer. However, flying was the quickest way to travel across the country. It was bad this time, the turbulence on the plane was intense. She thought any moment that the oxygen masks would drop down from their compartments and they would be plummeting to the ground. Luckily, they didn't. It was the worst flight she had ever been on.

~~~

Sam's taxi pulled up to Duke Street. She got out and stood in the parking lot, marveling. To a certain extent, the structure of the building was very similar to the one in her vision, a tall gray high rise, not that this style of building was unique, in fact there were many buildings like this all around the downtown area. She decided to put it to the test. She would step inside and see if the place matched the physical description in her vision, brief as it was.

Sam did not exactly have a plan for what she would do once she arrived. She just knew that she had to find out if all her visions meant something. Sam thought it through for a few minutes and then entered the building. She stopped at the empty front desk and looked around. Down the hallway she could hear the clack-clack of high heels approaching.

"Naomi, please make sure that Mr. Stevens doesn't go out wandering into the hallway unsupervised again. I already told you. This time it's a write up," said a tall, dark-haired woman.

The reprimanded woman stammered and slinked away.

The dark-haired woman seemed unaffected, standing there with her arms crossed.

Poor woman, Sam thought.

The woman of seemingly high status suddenly turned her head in Sam's direction and froze. A look of confusion came over her. Sam thought she could see a flash of fear in her eyes. The woman frowned and walked over.

"Hi, may I help you?"

"I hope so. My name is Sam Brennan."

Again, Sam noticed a brief look of confusion come over the woman's face at the mention of her name.

"I'm Dr. N."

"Hi! I read about you online, you're the director here."

"Yes," the woman raised an eyebrow at her.

"Listen," Sam continued, "I was wondering if I could get a tour of the facility. I'm a... psych major, and I'm doing a research paper on... um— psychiatric hospitals... in the U.S."

"I see," the woman looked at Sam incredulously.

She's not buying it.

"Why didn't you call ahead of time, Sam? We don't do unscheduled tours. You will have to make an appointment with Tanya at the front desk."

"Okay. Can I do that now?"

"Sure, go right ahead."

"Thank you. Is it possible that we could talk for just a few minutes? I would love to ask you some questions," Sam began.

"No, unfortunately I can't." She looked down at her watch. "I have a meeting starting in a few minutes and I have to get going. Call us please to set something up." Dr. N turned and made a quick exit.

"Okay, I'll do that." Sam said to the woman's back.

She expected this might happen, but it was not the start to her trip that she was hoping for. She resolved to get some lunch, check out the downtown area, and have a fresh start in the morning.

19. Waking Life: Mental Illness

The fuzzy, pale-yellow lights danced before Sarah's eyes, like fireflies signaling each other. The longer Sarah stared, the clearer and less firefly-like they got, until she realized that her eyes were adjusting to a set of ultra-bright ceiling lights and the soft murmur of what she thought was a brook, was actually the echoey voices of Joey, Bri and her mother calling out to her. She turned her head and blinked up at her mother, who she now felt gently stroking her head.

"What happened? Where am I?"

Her mother stroked her head gently.

"You're at the hospital, honey. Joey brought you here. They gave you a shot to calm your nerves. How are you feeling?"

"I feel... confused. I don't understand what's happening to me. I think Dad guided me to the cave and was trying to show me something about another reality."

Sarah's mother looked at Bri and Joey stoically.

"Well, *I'm* not going to tell her." Bri crossed her arms in front of her chest and stared back at her mother. "This is your idea, mom."

"Honey," her mother continued, "the family thinks... that you could use a rest. Things have been getting to you lately and we know that you are really stressed."

Oh, no...

"Baby..." Joey reached down to stroke Sarah's hair off her cheek.

"I won't go," Sarah said.

"It's not an option." Her mother's expression changed, her face hardening. "This is the best thing for you, and as your mother—"

"Sarah," Bri interrupted, obviously annoyed by her mother's impending monologue. "Mom went to the magistrate's office to file an involuntary commitment order. She's doing this to help you. You know that we love you. We just want you to get better."

"How is this going to make anything better, Bri? I was on to something. I was on my way to finding Dad. I had actual evidence, in my hands. We really did find some incredible things. Didn't Joey tell you? You told them, Joey, didn't you?"

Sarah did not like the way Joey grabbed her hand. She felt his pity and it disgusted her. *But he was there. Doesn't he realize the significance of what we found? What is wrong with everybody?*

"Sarah," Joey began. "I told them everything, but the fact of the matter is, you were not okay when you left that cave, in fact, you've been acting strangely for a while, confusing your dreams with reality. And when I saw you hitting your head on the ground..." His voice trailed off like a balloon losing air, tears collected in his eyes.

"Joey, I've been telling you things in confidence, because I thought you'd understand. It's no coincidence that I'm having these memories and visions. I think my father's trying to tell me something about them, about what's happening to me. Joey, I found that place in the cave, because he guided me there."

"That's true. But then, you were hallucinating in the cave. Don't deny it, please."

"Yes, true, but you know what Dr. Fowler said about sensory deprivation."

"It's not just that Sarah," her mother cut in. "I mean, going off on this wild goose chase," she eyed Joey sternly.

He looked down at the ground like a chastised child.

Sarah rolled her eyes and started praying for this spectacle to be over.

"And lying to your boss and family, telling us you were going on assignment for work. Sarah, this is just not normal behavior," Her mother covered her mouth, and produced a pained, gasping sound.

Oh, please god, just haul me off now. There is no arguing with these people.

"Fine. When do I go?"

"Today. As soon as you feel better," Bri said.

~~~

Being admitted to the same hospital she had just visited as a reporter was not a good feeling. She was embarrassed when the receptionist recognized her. Sarah did not acknowledge her. However, the worst embarrassment came when Dr. Neely strolled past her in the waiting room and causally said, "Ms. Davis." Her voice was laden with so much cavalier self-importance, it made Sarah's stomach turn.

Upon arrival to her room that first day, Sarah realized that her roommate Becky didn't speak, not a word, and mostly sat there, staring blankly ahead. As the hours dragged by, occasionally she rocked back and forth on her bed, moving her lips, inaudibly, like she was talking to someone no one else could see. Sarah did not attempt to make out her words. She was more focused on being invisible, at least for the first couple of days.

Sarah spoke to no one at first, except the therapist, psychiatrist and primary care doctor. She dared not speak of the dreams she was experiencing, no, then they would never let her out.

The best time of the day was when they let her go back to her room. She would lay awake as long as the meds permitted and think of everything that occurred in the past week, trying to piece together her experiences into some logical semblance of reality.

There were moments of despair, when Sarah would think that her family was right about her after all, that she was going crazy, just like they thought her father was. Several times she believed, that maybe, she had schizophrenia, and was not just an eccentric, free thinker.

Maybe she could not tell reality from what was in her head. But then she would remember what she had found, how her father guided her to that secret room, the journals that implied that her strange experiences might be shared by others. Maybe, just maybe, this wasn't mental illness.

Group therapy was easily the worst part of Sarah's day. Though at times, it provided her with some mild amusement. It consisted of an odd bunch: three women and two men. Her roommate was not in this group, as speaking was a necessity.

Rachel was an older woman, in her sixties, who suffered from severe depression. She would mostly talk about her children and how she failed them as a mother.

Raul was a twenty-four-year-old Mexican immigrant, his brother shot in front of him by the cartel, his father deported for raping his mother. He was suffering from extreme post-traumatic stress disorder. The other man was Frank, a forty-two-year-old failed businessman, diagnosed with bipolar disorder, like Sarah. He was prone to severe manic episodes, which repeatedly landed him in jail when he went off his meds. And then there was Kathy, the closest to Sarah in age. She was thirty-two, and a recovering heroin addict. Sarah often wondered why she was even in this hospital and not in a drug rehabilitation clinic somewhere.

The group was disjointed and could never stay focused on any particular subject for very long. The only consistent thing in this group was a banal warm-up exercise, which Sarah begrudgingly participated in.

Sarah was furious at her family and Joey for locking her away in here, she made up her mind that this time she was done with them all. Sarah thought them rash, for never properly evaluating to see if she was really a danger to herself, and honestly, she thought that at least Joey would have had more faith in her.

Lunch was a particularly disturbing part of her day. The food was comparable to prison rations, or so Sarah imagined, given that she had never spent time behind bars. The reprocessed patties of bland chicken and beef were hard enough to stomach, not to mention the browning, soggy salads, dehydrated, anemic corn and other such depressing vegetables. Not that Sarah had any appetite to speak of anyway. Sarah noticed that when she did not eat her food, one of the orderlies would scribble something down on their clipboard. So, she made sure to finish all the food on her tray from then on.

Her schedule was extremely regimented, almost every minute was accounted for. There was 7:00 a.m. wake up, then showering, and breakfast until 8:30 a.m., followed by a half hour of structured activities, and finally group therapy. After group there was exercise, lunch, and what they called healthful hobbies, which mostly consisted of music, art, journaling, or "gardening" (planting seeds in ceramic pots and watering plants around the facilities).

At 1:00 p.m. Sarah would meet with her therapist to talk. This time was exceedingly difficult for her, as she wanted to sound as sane as possible, but at the same time, not be seen as resistant to treatment or in denial.

Room time ran from 2:00 p.m. to 5:00 p.m. during which Sarah was to rest, relax and gather her thoughts. This gave Sarah much needed time to think and plan ahead, scribbling her thoughts onto napkins with a crayon.

At 6:00 p.m. there was dinner, followed by one more hour of free time. Everyone was to be in their rooms or bed by 8:00 p.m. At 9:00 p.m. it was lights out, and the whole thing would start over the next day.

After a week, Sarah was starting to feel terrible ennui. Those previously desired three-hour time blocks in her room began to feel like an eternity, and unlike the other patients, Sarah's roommate didn't talk. Sarah had also decided to not take phone calls and visits from her family.

Sarah began thinking about the strange blue light she saw in the "utility closet" of the hospital, and the machines inside the cave reflecting her flashlight, opening locks, taking pictures of her mind; things she could only imagine in some kind of Area 51, top secret, government lab. She wondered what secrets this hospital held.

Then came the day when an opportunity arose. It presented itself to her in the form of a change in routine. The normal three-hour block was broken up by a psychiatry visit, which happened once a week. Then something interesting happened. One of the orderlies who Sarah had particularly liked, because of her sweet and genuine demeanor, entrusted Sarah with a solitary task.

She was to fetch a coke from the soda machine in the staff break room and bring it back to her. Sarah could hardly believe this, this was definitely against protocol and the young, newly employed orderly was likely to lose her job if anyone found out Sarah was walking around the hospital alone.

Sarah grabbed the cold drink that tumbled to the bottom of the machine and headed out the door. Instead of turning right to go back, she turned left. The sleep lab was just a few doors down. As luck would have it, the room was unoccupied.

She walked tentatively into the room, remembering her rushed interaction with Dr. Neely earlier this month, in this very room. She walked over to what she was told, was a utility closet and looked inside. No glowing blue light. She turned on the lights and looked around.

Well, it looks like a utility closet, she thought, unconvinced.

Various machines were pushed against the perimeter of the closet, creating a bit of walking space. Sarah ran her hand across the back wall looking, for a doorknob. There was none. However, as Sarah was quickly learning, things were not always as they seemed.

She looked over her shoulder to make sure no one was coming and then quietly began moving the machines around. It turned out to be an easier task than she expected, since all the machines were supported by little, rolling wheels.

And then she saw it, a sign, in the form of a small keyhole against the back wall.

After that, things developed quickly. Sarah heard the pattering of footsteps down the hall. Pushing the machines clumsily back into place, she grabbed the coke and put on her best lost puppy expression.

The orderly was not fooled, but surprisingly did not look angry, either, maybe because she realized Sarah was her responsibility. She came over and grabbed Sarah by the top of her arm, leading her back to her room quickly. She did not say a word. It was clear to Sarah that they were both going to pretend this never happened.

20. DREAM LIFE: BEING FOLLOWED

*D*id she really call herself Dr. N? Maybe it's a nickname, or
maybe it's something foreign like, Enne? Sam sat gripping
the edge of her mattress in the cheap hotel she had rented
for the night. The dark blue comforter felt rough under her fingers
and musty smell of cigarettes poorly concealed by air freshener
wasn't helping her feel better. This place was real. It wasn't the exact
same building, but it was strikingly similar. How could she imagine
something like that? Chip's words began popping into her mind like
noxious little bullets, exploding in puffs of gunpowder, choking Sam.

Her lungs tightened; no, this was real anxiety. Her breaths
shallowed and quickened. *Oh no.* She had not experienced a panic
attack in months. Sarah laid down on the floor next to the bed and

put one hand on her belly and the other on the ground. She breathed in as deeply as she could, feeling the air inflate and deflate her stomach, focusing on her breathing for twenty counts. She ran her other hand along the carpet, feeling the rough fibers on her fingertips.

Could he be right? Sam asked herself, from the safety of the floor, staring up into the ceiling fan. *If he is, what does all this mean? Does it mean that the little girl was real too, or did I just imagine her?* The fact that she was asking herself these questions worried her. She could see how fragile her sanity was, like a fledgling on the verge of dropping out of its nest.

Rocking herself side to side on her back, she tried to steady her breath by focusing her attention on a fixed point on the ceiling. The fixed point was a moth. She followed its movements, the slight flutter of its wings. It was another one of the grounding exercises Dr. Shandi had shown her when they were working on her panic attacks. She remembered her words, "Every time a thought pops into your head, observe it and go back to your breathing, your fixed point. Don't follow that thought down the rabbit hole."

Sam stared at the cheap framed painting on the wall ahead. It was a cheap reproduction of a realistically painted flower vase. The bland pinks, greens and yellows reminded Sam of vomit. She focused back on her breathing and then turned her head to the side, shifting her gaze to the floor. The red swirling pattern of the carpet was dizzying. Sam turned on her side and focused on the twisted red fibers growing out the ground. She began to feel her heart slow down a little and realized how tired she was. She exhaled deeply and closed her eyes.

~~~

When she opened her eyes, she found herself looking at the little girl from her visions. She was standing on the edge of a cliff. Her face was blurry, but somehow Sam recognized her for who she was. The little girl flashed her a smile. As Sam came closer, her face became clearer. She was looking at an eight-year-old version of herself. The young girl smiled back knowingly, her cheeks dimpling. Sam shook her head, wondering why this didn't click with her before.

Suddenly, she remembered the white dress. She had insisted on wearing it on a hiking expedition, and after much pleading and begging, her parents agreed, as long as she wore hiking boots. Sam agreed, but had taken them off later that day when she stood under a trickling mountainside waterfall, laughing as the water poured over her.

She remembered now. But the funny thing was that in these memories her parents were her biological parents and not her adoptive parents. She didn't know how this was possible.

"You're almost there!" Her younger self giggled and grabbed her hand. In a flash, as if by teleportation, they were standing under a waterfall.

"Woah!" Sam instinctively put her arms above her head to shield her face.

Her younger version shrieked with glee as the water cascaded over her head, sticking a sheet of hair to her face.

Sam closed her eyes and listened to the sound of the roaring water. When she opened her eyes again, the blurry field of red fibers came back into focus, and the sound of the waterfall morphed into the din of a noisy air conditioning unit that had turned on to regulate the temperature in the room.

~~~

Sam called the next morning to schedule an interview. The receptionist told her once again, that she would have to wait, this time until Friday. She was pissed, but it was Tuesday and she didn't have to go back to work until Monday. She decided that she would make the most of the next three days.

Throughout the week, Sam experienced more dreams, all related to the hospital. Each day a noise from her dream would morph into another noise in her environment and wake her up: a heart monitor into a chirping fire detector, the din of patients chattering at lunch time into the sounds of morning traffic, the tap of heels on linoleum into a knock for housekeeping, and so on. She was almost becoming used to it.

Then one afternoon, Sam noticed someone new. She was sitting by the hotel pool, book in hand, when a strikingly handsome man with an olive complexion and dark hair emerged from the stairwell, walked silently past her, and crossed to the other side of the street. This would not have meant much to her, had she not seen him again, and again, and again.

Later that day, he was leaving the same coffee shop she had arrived at, wearing a baseball cap pulled low over his eyes, and then again, sitting in the parking lot of a pizza shop she was entering, with the engine and lights off. Again, his cap was low over his eyes. Sam couldn't help but feel like she was being followed. So, she decided to once again, give espionage a try. She was nowhere near having the spy routine solidified, but she needed to know who this guy was.

The past couple of days were spent fruitlessly scoping out the hospital, mainly through online research and questioning the locals. Her search did not turn up much. By the time Friday came, Sam received a phone call from the hospital denying her request to visit. The receptionist told her that Dr. N was yet again busy with meetings and no one had time to show her around.

Sam knew she wasn't wanted and thought it odd that they refused to reschedule her meeting that week. There was something fishy going on and she could not shake the feeling that the answers to her nagging questions, were lying somewhere behind the walls of that mental institution.

Hurrying her way back to the hotel, she called a taxi, giving the driver special instructions.

"Park at the side of the building. I will come through the emergency exit. Park close to the door. Let me know when the blue Pontiac has pulled off and then I'll get inside."

That afternoon Sam got into the taxi after watching the handsome stranger sitting in the parking lot a little over an hour. She slid inside, close to the side exit, as instructed, and they quietly pulled out. Following the man proved to be easier than expected. He wasn't trying to be stealthy, or maybe he was just not that cunning.

"Don't go too fast, I don't want him to figure out we're following him."

"All right, I'll follow him, but no funny business. This guy isn't dangerous, is he?"

"No, of course not," Sam lied. She had no idea who this guy was, but she wasn't going to blow this opportunity. "He's just my boyfriend... he's been acting suspicious lately, so I want to see where he's going."

"Oh! Well then, I can't say this is my first cheater's stakeout, but are you sure you really want to do this? You might not like what you find."

"I'm sure."

"Okay. Oh, look!" The taxi driver exclaimed. "He's parking over at Northern Weaver."

Now I know something's not right here. So, they didn't want me looking around, but now they're following me? Sam didn't have a plan for what she would do once she got here, and she certainly wasn't prepared for this scenario.

"What do you want to do?" The smell of cologne and aftershave wafted to the backseat as the driver craned his neck to look back at Sam.

"I don't know. Just, stay here for now."

"Sure thing, but the meter's running, and it doesn't look like he's up to anything, I mean, you think he's having an affair with a looney?"

"Well, that's kind of an insensitive thing to say, isn't it?"

"Hey, he's your man. Wait a minute, look, someone's coming through the back door to meet him. Oh man, she is definitely a looker. Sorry, looks like you were right. You want to confront him?"

Oh my god, it's Dr. N! What does that conniving woman have to do with this guy? Did she send him to follow me? Sam watched Mr. Tall, Dark and Handsome shrug his shoulders and shake his head in uncertainty. *Obviously, he had failed to complete his mission,* Sam thought. *Who do they think I am, anyway?* Sam could not make out all the words Dr. N was saying, as her voice drifted in and out in angry spurts.

"Why is... still here... knows nothing... is she sticking around... not good..."

She was missing something that fell in between the lines. Somehow, she felt like her subconscious and conscious were at battle to fill in the blanks. She could hear Dr. Shandi's voice in her head: *You are trying to tell yourself something you already know.*

~~~

That night Sam sat on her hotel room bed with the details she had gathered, written out on sheets of notepad she got from the front desk. She spread the pages across the bedspread and tried to make sense of everything that had occurred in the past two weeks: Chip's words about an alternate reality, Chip and Dr. Reeves fighting in the warehouse about releasing Balixa, the little girl in her visions who was actually herself, the visions from the hospital, the cold shoulder treatment from Dr. N, being followed, and finally, the conversation between Dr. N and the handsome stranger. *They must know that I work for Blakeley Pharmaceuticals. Could they know about Balixa and this dual world phenomenon? Do they know Chip? Could all of this be real?*

Once again, Sam was conflicted with the nagging question: how does one even tell dreams from reality? She knew there was a connection, a subtle thread that seemed to weave in and out, tying all the loose pieces of information she had gathered together. She couldn't see it right now, but she would find it.

21. WAKING LIFE: SNEAKING AROUND

Sarah had now been in the hospital for six long days and had figured out most of the schedules, not only for the patients, but the usual routes of orderlies, doctors, security guards, and families. So, it wasn't long before another opportunity came about, and she did not plan on squandering it. The staff that conducted nightly checks were supposed to be coming sporadically, but every night there was a thirty-minute window when no one came between 1:00 a.m. and 1:30 a.m.

It took her time to figure out where the keys to the rooms were, and who carried them. The third shift security guard would fall asleep watching his shows sometime between midnight and two in the morning.

Before she left her room that night, she bunched up her blankets and pillow, so it looked like there was someone lying there.

"Shhh," she hushed her roommate, knowing this was not necessary, still she didn't want to take any chances. "Don't tell anyone I left. I'm going to be right back, okay?"

Her first task would be taking the key. There was not a moment to spare as Sarah rifled through the bottom drawer and pulled out the spare set of scrubs the receptionist kept in the bottom drawer of the front desk. *This guy really should get fired.*

Sarah pulled on the scrubs quietly, then looked around to make sure the coast was clear. The security guard next to her began snoring loudly.

Keeping her head down, she walked softly down the hallway. As she rounded the corner, she turned her head the other direction, away from the security camera. Finally, she made it to the sleep lab. The door wasn't locked so she cracked it open and slipped inside. She made her way to the closet.

Things were as she'd left them, and Sarah quietly moved the machines around to locate the same keyhole she had found earlier. Surprisingly, the key she'd absconded with, which she had learned was a master key of sorts, turned and she was in.

Sarah's eyes widened as she took in the room. She wasn't sure what the bigger surprise was, this Lion, Witch and the Wardrobe entrance to a secret, embedded hospital room or the hidden lab in the cave. Her life just kept getting weirder and weirder.

Rectangular glass rooms lined the walls. Inside each cell was a person, lying on a hospital bed, hooked up to an IV and a heart monitor. Sarah recognized one of the men immediately. He was a young, African American man, in his twenties or maybe early thirties. She saw him visiting with his family last week. He was completely catatonic, like her roommate.

So, this is what those construction workers were talking about. Look at all these people. They must be drugged. Sarah continued looking around the room in disbelief. The walls facing the hallway were made of soft looking padded material. *To keep them from hurting themselves? Wait, no. These are insulated soundproof walls.* Images of recording studios flashed through her mind. *They are blocking out sound coming from this room, from the rest of the hospital.*

Sarah shook with fear. Her heart began to race, and the same panic she felt in the cave began to creep in; her stomach fluttered, she felt lightheaded. Her father's words were going in and out of her mind: *Sleep studies... drug induced dreams... guided target finding.* None of these things made sense at the moment. All she knew was she had to leave before she had another "episode" and was discovered, or worse, put on a more restrictive level of care, like these poor folks.

Sarah had been playing along with her therapist, saying that she was imagining things, that she could finally see her delusions were not reality, that her emotions were unhinged. This admission of guilt had worked with tremendous effectiveness on her therapist. She described it as a "breakthrough" in Sarah's level of insight into her illness. Of course, Sarah knew this was bullshit. When her father was here, he told them what they wanted to hear as well, so he could get out sooner.

Somehow sharing the same hospital experience as her father only validated her devotion to her cause. Her cause, however, was shifting, becoming much larger than she could have ever imagined. Sarah felt compelled to make sense of these experiences, knowing that her father was on the other side of the equation.

She made a fortuitous return back down the hall to the front desk where she had again silently removed the scrubs, neatly folding and tucking them away in the drawer. The security guard was still fast asleep. As she slid the drawer closed, he snorted loudly and startled himself awake for a second. Sarah froze. He drifted back into a noisy sleep.

That was too close.

Sarah made her way back to her room in her pajamas. The sound of heels around the corner sent Sarah scurrying and sliding, like she was stealing home plate into the next hallway. The staccato of heels stopped at the front desk. Dr. Neely was talking to Nisha, one of the nurses.

"Dr. Neely, excuse me," Nisha said. "I don't know how to tell you this, but it's important for you to know what going on. Jeremy is becoming more and more habituated to the meds. The last family visit was nearly a disaster."

"What do you mean?" Sarah could hear Dr. Neely's stoic voice spiking in irritation.

"I mean, he began to talk, during the visit."

"So, what did he say?"

"He said, well more like mumbled, a lot of things, including... hmm let me see, he said something like: too many drugs, sleep, need to get out. He repeated a lot of words like that. The parents were not pleased. They demanded an explanation."

"Well, was one provided?"

"Yes. Well of course, his therapist more or less explained it as a stress reaction caused by pervasive nightmares and lack of sleep. She showed them some of the client's brainwave charts. But I'm not sure..."

"What? What are you not sure of?"

"If the family was completely convinced."

After a brief pause, Dr. Neely responded.

"Well, first of all, let's get this under control, shall we? I'll call the family first thing tomorrow morning. And increase the dosages of Trilixol before these visits. We need to keep the family certain that these medications are helping him with his anxiety and panic attacks in the long run, that these catatonic states are a necessary evil. We can't have these moments of lucidity; it will only shake their faith in us."

"But, Dr. Neely, it's not really best practice to raise the dosages this quickly. It could lead to dangerous side effects, heart murmurs, seizures, sudden death."

"Then consult the psychiatrist and give him something for the side effects," Dr. Neely said in a harsh whisper, "because this cannot become a problem. We don't need anyone asking questions. Do you understand?"

"Yes, ma'am, but I just don't think this is going to work. What if more of them become cognizant during these visits?"

"Then we will stop the visits."

"Dr. Neely..."

"Nisha, you're on thin ice. This is an order, not a request. I have to think. Please calm yourself down, okay?"

"Yes, Dr. Neely. I understand."

The angry clatter of heels suddenly grew louder in Sarah's direction. She looked around. There was nowhere to duck and hide. Sarah bolted down the hallway, stopping in front of a door to a therapist's office. Fumbling with the knob, Sarah steadied her hand and slipped inside. It was mere seconds before Dr. Neely turned the corner, but Sarah was safe, at least for tonight.

22. DREAM LIFE: FAMILY FIRST

S am considered her options. She could stay and try to scope out the hospital more via the community, but her vacation days would be over Sunday, and she was still not making any progress. She could go back home and spend her last days of vacation actually relaxing. She laughed at the absurdity of the thought, knowing that the twisted ball of nerves in the pit of her stomach would only tangle itself tighter.

Then she remembered that there was another person she could talk to, one that possibly had some understanding of what she was experiencing: her birth mother.

Sam had hoped that she would see her again. Their last visit was awkward and heart-wrenching, but Clara of all people (with the exception of her deranged father) could potentially shed some light on some of these things for her.

Sam opted for option three. She quickly packed up her suitcase and plopped the half-drunk cup of coffee into the trashcan on her way out the door.

~~~

Okay. I can do this. Sam stood outside the hospital, pulling her cardigan tight around her waist against the cold breeze, conjuring up a pep-talk to prepare herself for the strange conversation she was about to have with this sick, stranger of a woman, who was her mother. *No one's even bothered to call me since the last visit.*

Abandoning the futile, positive self-talk, Sam let out a heavy sigh and walked through the hospital double doors to the front desk.

The receptionist looked at her with one heavily lined eyebrow raised.

"Hi. My name is Sam Brennan. I'm here to see my mother, Clara Hoffer."

"One minute honey, let me find out what room she's in."

The receptionist sucked her teeth and directed her attention to the computer monitor in front of her, her black eyebrows jumping around her forehead like frisky cats with their backs arched. After a couple minutes of clicking, her expression began to change. Her eyebrows congregated together, cats at war. She looked at Sam and then back down at the screen for a moment. She sighed heavily and gave Sam a pitying look that said: "bless your heart." She dialed a number.

That was all Sam needed to know. She was too late.

"Dr. Hersh, Clara Hoffer's daughter is here to see her. Would you come down for a moment please and talk to her? Yes. Okay, I'll let her know."

Before the doctor could even make it across the room to shake her hand, Sam had become painfully angered, enraged. No one had bothered to contact her. So, when the doctor had timidly took her hand, she had a biting response ready.

"No one told me. No one contacted me, not the hospital, not my grandfather, no one," Sam spat out, a failing attempt to conceal her pain. She only spoke in this curt manner when she was on the verge of crying. She met her mother one time. *One time.* Although this man did not deserve the brunt of her anger, Sam could not help it.

"I'm so sorry," the doctor stammered, disconcerted by Sam's response.

She imagined that this type of situation was usually handled by the hospital's social workers. Guilt sent its customary pang into her gut. Still, she did not relent.

"When did it happen?" she demanded, feeling slighted and past the brink of tears.

"Just this morning, about four hours ago."

Sam considered this new information for a moment. *Four hours.* She wondered if four hours was long enough for a grieving, alcoholic grandfather to gather his wits and start making the obligatory round of phone calls to family and friends. *No.*

~~~

She decided to call her grandfather after all and let him know she was at the hospital. He invited her over this time. Twenty minutes later, she sat nervously in his living room, spinning her coffee mug back and forth in her hands, thinking of something comforting she could say to the disheveled man, who was pacing the living room, hands on his hips, shaking his head. Every now and then he would mutter something to the likeness of "jackass" or "I knew he wouldn't show his face."

She wanted to tell him that it would be okay, that her father really did have a plan. But she couldn't say that with any certainty anyway. So, she spun the coffee cup back and forth and sighed into the black, bitter liquid.

After a few minutes she began to speak.

"Sherm... Mr. Hoffer, I spoke with my father a week ago. He said something abou—"

"You what?!" Sherman stopped in his tracks and stared at her in disbelief. She could see the anger, the disdain in his eyes that said, "Oh? And did you let him know his wife was dying?"

Sam knew this anger. She had felt this same resentment when she spoke to her father. She suspected that she had felt it unknowingly, for the greater part of her life, unseeded until their meeting. It lay hidden, deep in her subconscious, slowly digging through the recesses of her mind to get to the surface.

"I told him about Clar— my mother, that she was dying."

"Oh, and what did he say?"

"I don't know..." Sam's voice wavered, "he was rattling on about some weird stuff. He said that Clara knew about his secret plans."

Sherman stared at her wide-eyed for a moment, before saying an offbeat, "Oh, that bullshit again."

Sam felt terrible. She wished she had something more substantial to offer this grieving man, something to lessen his pain. She wondered what he must have thought of her father's absence all these years, what he must have thought of his own daughter, offering up lame excuses for her husband based on conspiracies: "Sorry Dad, Chip can't be here, he's trying to save the world from the evil forces blinding us to the reality of an alternate universe."

She knew how stupid it sounded, how it made him a poor excuse of a man, a father, a husband. An alternate universe was a lot less important to Sam in moments like this. Her mother just died without getting to spend her last moments with her husband, and it seemed like she still loved him from what her grandfather said. She thought back to that day in the coffee shop, when Chip chased her down and asked her to listen to his explanation.

How could he appear so aloof? Did he really not care about seeing his wife? The thought roller coaster had made its way to the precipice of her mind and was now hurtling at full speed down the drop. Sam could not stop wondering what this crazy man, that came out of hiding, wanted with her, a man who supposedly developed a drug that made people aware of an alternate reality.

Back at that coffee shop, Chip said that he and Sam were brought together for a purpose, and Sam had to admit the chain of events she had experienced thus far did not feel like coincidence. What made it all happen, whether it was the universe, God, or some other force, she did not know, and she still could not figure out why it was all happening. If there was a separate reality where everyone existed, did it really take precedence over this reality? She couldn't even see this place except in her visions and dreams, so what was the point? As far as Sam was concerned, her life was here, and Chip's life was here with his wife.

She stayed at Sherman's most of the day, he even heated up some chicken soup for her. They talked for the better part of the afternoon, and he actually started opening up, telling her stories about her mother, childhood memories. Sam began to see a glimpse of a different man, perhaps from a happier time. He became more animated, laughed even. But by the time the sun started setting, she could see him reverting back, his demeanor changing back to the angry and weary man she had seen earlier, and he went to make himself a drink. He was ready to be alone again, so Sam excused herself and made her way back home.

~~~

Trying to make sense of what she saw, Sam lay in bed staring into the blackness, puffs of black clouds, growing and shrinking before her eyes. It was late, and her body was exhausted. Her mind was relentless, pulling her along, in a losing tug-of-war battle, dragging her through the mud, face-first.

She didn't take her Balixa that night, and she didn't want to, come insomnia, come what may. She wanted her thoughts to expand, to rise higher and higher, like the black clouds floating around the room. She wanted insight and wisdom to rain down into her perplexed mind. These were the same clouds Sam watched as a child, playing guessing games in the dark, a nocturnal version of cloud watching. There were elephants, fish, faces, and ghostly creatures that only appeared when the lights were turned off.

She had never told anyone about what she saw but lying in bed that night she began to wonder. These were illusions, her eyes trying to make sense of the blackness, trying to find form, meaning out of nothing. Maybe that's all that reality really was, people trying to find form and describe what they saw to each other, when in fact, they were seeing different versions of the same thing.

I'll meet up with Chip again. Someone has to let him know his wife died and I need answers. Sam decided this against her better judgment, but knew that nothing else was working so far. She would find a way to get in contact with him.

23. Waking Life: Escape Plan

S arah stared at the liquid in the glass vial, shaking in her sweaty palm as she stood over the sleeping man. Her eyes darted around the room. She did not see a camera, but that didn't mean there wasn't one hidden somewhere. She tried to steady her shaky inhales and exhales. Never in her life had Sarah planned to do something so risky or illegal. If she was caught, she would be in serious trouble.

For a second time, Sarah had managed to get away from her room undetected, using the same technique as before. She was pretty sure no one suspected anything. The trickier task was managing to get the waking vial from the doctor's office without being discovered. Luckily, she discovered through eavesdropping on a conversation between her naïve nurse pal and another orderly, that the substance that awoke a sleeping patient quickly from a coma, was conveniently stored in the very room where the doctor performed weekly check-ups. After a quick, silent prayer that no one was watching the cameras, Sarah had swiped it from the cabinet, while the doctor stepped out of the room for a few minutes.

Plans of escape were teeming in the forefront of her mind. Sarah was tired of waiting and she needed answers. Her stay at the hospital had stretched out to almost two weeks now and had dragged on at a miserable pace. So, she had resolved to wake up one of the mysterious comatose subjects to get some answers.

At this point, for whatever reason, she had not been discharged. As far as she knew, she was cooperating with the treatments, both group and individual therapy. She was taking her medications and responding well to them. Additionally, she had not had any emotional outbursts, psychotic episodes, or suicidal thoughts since the beginning of her stay, but for some reason, she was still here.

The sleeping man seemed stressed. Deep wrinkles creased his forehead and his eyes twitched erratically behind his eyelids, like he was dreaming. Sarah had chosen him, specifically. He was the man she saw before, the one who was catatonic. She did not know why, but he stood out to her. Maybe it's because she remembered seeing him differently, when she first got to the hospital, before he became a living zombie. She remembered seeing him in the cafeteria on her first day. He seemed so happy, so nice, joking with one of the other patients over breakfast, slapping him on the back in the friendly way people do when they've known each other a while, a far cry from how he was now.

Sarah wondered what this man had done to deserve this disturbing twist of fate. She sensed that he had put up a fight before he was put to sleep. Sarah watched him, in his restless, nightmarish sleep, his nostrils flaring, his breathing quickening then slowing, non-rhythmically.

She wondered how he would react once she woke him up. Would he be disoriented or attack her? There was no plan B. If things went south, she would simply have to run, pretend to be lost in the hallway, endure an injection, a prolonged stay, or worse: a medically induced coma in the hidden room. She shuddered.

After taking a deep breath and shaking her head in her here-goes-nothing way, she carefully pulled the syringe from her scrub's pants pocket and slowly injected it into the IV. She wasn't a trained medical professional, but had seen this enough times that she was willing to take the risk. She pushed steadily, and the clear liquid made its way down the tube and into the crook of the man's arm. Sarah waited, holding her breath. About five seconds later, the man's eyelids began to flutter again. *He's waking up.*

The man's lips moved inaudibly, forming words spoken to someone inside a nightmare. He turned his head left to right, right to left, with increasing speed.

"Uhhh!" He gasped, the air swiftly filling his lungs to capacity, inducing a coughing fit.

Sarah scrambled to pick up a bottle of water she discovered earlier in the mini-fridge on the other side of the room and put it to his lips. The man instinctively grabbed for the bottle and took a long drink, before putting it down and warily acknowledging Sarah's presence.

"Who are you?" He croaked. "You aren't... one of them."

"One of the hospital staff? No. I'm a patient, like you."

The man looked around the room before answering. Then, in a hoarse whisper he said, "We need to leave. Now."

"I know. That's what I was waking you up for. What do you—"

The man motioned for Sarah to come closer, then whispered in her ear, "There are cameras in here. They're watching us."

I knew it!

"That nurse's uniform will not fool them for long. Keep your head down at all times."

"But why do we need to leave so quickly?"

"They're keeping us here to silence us. This is not a game Sarah, something bad is coming and they don't want anyone to find out."

"What are you talking about? And how do you know my name?" *This guy really might be a lunatic.*

The man grabbed Sarah's forearm and looked deeply into her eyes. Sarah had the strangest sense that he was reading her thoughts.

"Look, I'm not as crazy as I sound. The fact of the matter is, the hospital is holding all of these people captive." He motioned at the rest of the sleeping subjects. "As far as knowing your name... I pay attention to new patients, who they are. We have to look out for each other in here. In case you haven't figured it out already, this is not your standard psychiatric hospital."

"Uh-huh."

"Listen, this is going to sound crazy, but they are hiding something, something about the very fabric of existence." He paused a minute before continuing, studying Sarah's face for signs of alarm. "There is an alternate world we live in that most people don't know about. Dr. Neely knows the truth and is trying to control the outcomes. She's keeping all of us that know the truth in here." He motioned with his head towards the glass rooms around him, "That's why we're all in here. Don't trust her. She's keeping all of us, in another hospital on the other side, tucked away, so no one can find out the truth. She's studying us, like damn guinea pigs. Is any of this making sense? But you must know, you woke me up..."

The man grabbed her arm and looked at her desperately, searching her eyes for any sign of understanding. Sarah could sense that she was his only chance out of here, in this strange turn of events. She thought she at least partially knew what he was talking about.

Gingerly, she peeled his hand off her arm and clasped it both of hers, like her mother would before diving into a serious discussion.

"Look, I don't completely understand what's going on here, or what you know, but my father and my intuition have guided me to the conclusion that this world is a lot more complex and much less predictable than I ever thought possible. This alternate reality you're referring to... I think I've been experiencing it in visions and dreams.

I don't know... it's hard to tell what's real and what's not. That's what landed me in here."

"That's what landed all of us in here," the man flashed her a half-smile. "That's why we need to run, before they put you in here too, and *believe me*, it's only a matter of time."

"Okay," said Sarah, "how do we do this?" She pulled up a chair to the man's bedside and hunched in close to him to keep from being overheard.

"First of all, we need to make a plan, and fast. I'm going to lay down and put my head to the side. You pretend that you're checking my vitals. This way we can talk for a bit. If no one's been down here, it means that we haven't been discovered... yet."

"Okay." Sarah scooched in close, pulling her chair near the bed.

After about five minutes, Sarah had learned that the heavily sedated man's name was Jeremy and that their best chance of breaking out of the hospital would be through the back exit. There was an extra set of scrubs in the adjacent room. They would try and walk out in uniform, undetected by cameras and hospital personnel as long as they could, and if they happened to be discovered, they would run.

Jeremy said he had a friend they could stay with, and Sarah had no intention of going back home. It was not an option at this point. It would only result in her landing back at the hospital.

Ten minutes later, after a rushed planning session, they were out the door. They waited a couple of minutes, to make sure no one was walking through that hallways and then quietly made their way to the back of the building, keeping their heads down.

Their attempt to remain undetected did not last long. Sarah's nurse pal spotted her and Jeremy about one hundred feet from the back exit. Sarah and the nurse looked at each other, standing there motionless, like statues in the wax museum game she would play in her drama class as a child, where you were only safe from elimination if you did not move an inch. For a split second, Sarah thought she might let them go. And then, the nurse picked up her walkie-talkie.

"I need assistance in hallway B. Please hurry, we have two residents trying to escape."

Sarah lingered for a moment and then with all the velocity of the Roadrunner escaping Wile E. Coyote, she and Jeremy broke through the back emergency exits, just as the security guards and nurses were closing in on them. A super-fast one broke past the rest and bolted after them.

Sarah ran faster, pushing herself until she could feel a burning sensation in her chest and throat. All she knew was she could not get caught. Jeremy suddenly began to disappear into an open sewer, a few feet ahead, with startling dexterity, *like a Parkour runner*, Sarah thought. He waved his hand out of the drain, motioning for Sarah to follow him. *Who is this guy?*

Without another thought, she plunged herself down the manhole, her feet missing the first few rungs of ladder. A surprisingly strong grip caught her around the waist and lowered her gently to the ground. He quickly replaced the lid, then gasped for air and coughed loudly. Grabbing her hand, he pulled her along at lightning speed. Sarah was grateful for the guidance but was barely keeping up. It was dark in those tunnels, and it was all she could do not to trip and fall.

Flashbacks of the cave filled her mind with images with owls, their intense, searing eyes and great, beating wings.

After about ten minutes of heart-stopping foot action, and halting twice to catch their breath, they came to another manhole.

Sarah bent down and coughed violently, gasping for air. This was the most intense run of her life.

Jeremy began breathing erratically and fell to the ground.

"Jeremy are you okay?! Are you asthmatic?" Sarah stood, hunched over him.

He closed his eyes and continued to gasp, turning pale under the light shining through the manhole.

"We need to get you to a hospital!"

"No!" He stammered, then gasped. Methodically, he slowed his breathing. "I'll be okay," he stammered. "Just give me a minute." After a few minutes, his breathing returned to normal and he picked himself up and made his way up the ladder to look outside.

"Are you sure you're okay?"

"Yes, I promise. Come on," he whispered. "We're here."

Where is here, and how does he seem to know the underground sewer system so well?

Sarah knew she didn't have many options at this point, so she decided to put her faith in him.

They peeped their heads out, a couple of nervous prairie dogs watching out for hawks. Sarah's eyes fell on a small red house, nestled into downtown Raleigh.

"That's my cousin Nikki's house, he said pointing. "No one's going to come looking for us here. We'll be safe, at least for a while."

24. DREAM LIFE: THE UGLY TRUTH

S am sat in a back booth of the diner, picking at a hangnail on her thumb, trying not to focus on her stomach, which was tying itself into a tight, sour pretzel in her gut. For the third time, the waitress came by to refill her coffee. Sam smiled up at her.

"Oh honey, let me get you a Band-Aid for that thumb, you've torn it to shreds."

Sam looked down at her now bleeding and throbbing thumb. She had torn the hangnail down too far and a ripe strip of pink flesh showed through.

"Thank you," she replied, dumping creamers into the mug and taking another slurp.

"You're welcome, and that's decaf now. I don't think more caffeine is going to help with those nerves."

The waitress's motherly concern, which would undoubtedly annoy some, comforted Sam. She wanted to pull her down into the booth and tell her everything: how the mother she never got to know just died, how her perception of reality was crumbling. But there was no time. Chip walked through the metallic diner doors, almost unrecognizable, in a brown fedora, sunglasses and leather jacket.

Not a very inconspicuous look. This was obviously some kind of ridiculous attempt at a disguise, or maybe he was just eccentric.

He looked sweaty, like he had been in a hurry to get there. Sam checked her phone. He was twenty-five minutes late.

"I'm sorry. I got held up. Thank you for meeting me again and for being discreet with your invitation."

Sam actually felt embarrassed about it. She had snuck over to the warehouse two nights ago and slipped the note under the door, containing only the most pertinent information, knowing he would remember the diner.

"Yeah... sure." It's all she could respond with. She knew that she needed to talk to him again, needed to make sense of things, but the words were like fish trying to escape a net, caught in her throat, or perhaps her mind.

She did not know where to begin and was thoroughly embarrassed, embarrassed for walking out on him before, embarrassed for the questions she wanted to ask him, for the conversation they would have, that she might be asking for any advice from a father who had been absent her entire life.

"Sam, what is it you wanted to talk to me about?" Chip leaned in intently, eyebrows raised, hands folded in front of him.

"I... well... it's what we were talking about before, I've had some experiences..." Sam began after a couple false starts.

"Tell me." A smile was beginning to creep across his face, which instantly triggered feelings of revulsion in Sam. This was not some colorful new puzzle she was eager to put together on Christmas morning. What was happening to her was scary and confusing, people had even stalked her. She ignored her father's growing enthusiasm and continued, gaining momentum as she chugged along.

It was a long conversation that continued without pause. After about two hours of turning down every alley on her winding road of questions and Chip giving his detailed, long-winded answers, she was beginning to get somewhere.

Sam had come to one surefire realization: the world was not her friend, but rather a stranger. It was rotating, spinning, in this reality and the next, in spite of her, and all the knowledge and experience she had amassed in her lifetime. In fact, she now felt that all she had learned, amounted to a pebble. She had spent her life scrutinizing it, turning it over and over in her palm, blinded to the mountain that existed beneath her feet.

The first of many startling discoveries was that that she had a body double, a second version of herself that existed on a different plane, in a different time zone. She learned that the waking world and dream world mirrored each other, with exactly a twelve-hour time difference. This other self was as real as Sam was in this present moment. The idea was unsettling.

Sam felt like the man in a television documentary she had seen once. In this film, he was living a double life with a second wife and set of children, all unbeknownst to his family, and now Sam was painfully aware of that poor woman's dilemma. But she could not be held responsible for anything her other self did, right?

However, the strangest, most mind-bogging discovery of all, was that her waking world self, actually believed that she was the dream world self and vice versa. It made her feel unreal.

Chip had recently figured out that Sam's other self was on a mission to find him. Chip also told her that he had developed a formula in this other world to escape the inevitable, in a sense. This pill created a bridge, a conduit, which essentially transferred the consciousness of a person to the body of their alter after death and was to be taken just before the moment of departure.

If the pill was taken and the person did not die, their consciousness would be connected to that of their alter on the other side. They would have access to their knowledge and memories. As his experiments demonstrated once a person was "connected" as he put it, the transfer of newly formed knowledge and memories was delivered to the alter after awakening from a sleep cycle. The opportunities this presented were beyond what Sam could comprehend at the moment. However, this pill was unstable and there was not yet enough evidence to know what it would physically do to a person that took it and did not die, as Chip did not complete the testing process.

Therefore, he said the pill should only be taken as a last resort, to transfer the consciousness of the dying individual into the body of the living alter, so they would not be erased.

This pill was the reason he was on the run, stating there were people after the formula, in pursuit of the power and knowledge it bestowed, especially if the formula was further tweaked. He had taken this pill himself, right before he was killed in the process of being apprehended by one of these people.

Chip had also known about Clara's death, and had miraculously managed to get the consciousness-transfer pill to her without anyone noticing. Clara's alter was named Addelyn Davis on the other side and was Sam's biological mother there as well. She was alive and well, though now unexpectedly flooded with new memories and abilities. Chip was clearly worried, as he stated this connection process would undoubtedly be startling to an individual who did not have an explanation of what was happening to them. They might think they were losing their minds.

Clara had taken the pill with her applesauce just moments before she passed. Chip stated that he was certain of this, because unbeknownst to anyone, he had instructions and surveillance set up in that very room to monitor Clara and to instruct her of what to do. He unfortunately, did not yet have a plan of how to debrief her on the other side yet.

Sam thought of her other self, escaping from a mental hospital, being pursued, searching for her father, and how terrible it would be to lose her mother as well. She thought of her mother, completely overwhelmed by these new memories, wondering if she should tell anyone about what was happening to her.

She remembered the Quantum physics class she had audited in college, out of sheer curiosity. She was taught that an atom could be in two places at once but could only be directly observed at one place at a time. It startled her how accurately that theory applied at this moment.

The final information that her father imparted was the part Sam was to play in all of this. She did not realize that by meeting her father, she would become a part of a mission, that the pretend spy act she assumed as a kid would become real. No, he didn't want her to work for the government. This was not some top-secret black-ops mission, where women in skin-tight, leather bodysuits and impractical high heels with eject-able knife blades scaled buildings. No, this was a much more cryptic and otherworldly surveillance project. Sam would have to be thoroughly prepared.

She would have to become connected to her other self so she could help her mother, and help Chip get ahead of his pursuers. He said he trusted Sam to do this more than anyone else, even more than her sister on the other side, Brianne, who he was afraid to involve in this.

Sam would have to become connected naturally. This was a process that the pill replicated, a process that occurred in someone after the dissolution of their ego, after they truly came to terms with who they were. Chip explained that this natural process would not be possible for the people in pursuit of this pill for the very reason that their egos, which drove their lust for power and greed, were driving them to steal the formula in the first place.

Sam wondered, if connection was possible naturally, then how many connected people were there, wandering around in emotional chaos? How many of them have figured it out? Chip suspected there were many who were connected, but also stated that the process was complicated, and essentially occurred when someone became enlightened. Additionally, if they were connected in both worlds, they were considered fully connected, something even more rare.

Later that night, Sam lay in bed, staring at the ceiling, chewing on the inside of her cheek, because she now had more than just a couple big secrets she was keeping from Elijah.

She felt herself changing. The person she used to be had been abducted and replaced by someone she hardly recognized. She wasn't fully ready, but tomorrow, her training would begin.

~~~

The next day, Sam was led into one of the larger warehouse rooms, filled with monitors, and rows upon rows video cameras of all shapes and sizes, drones, computers, headsets, bullet proof vests, some handguns, and bottles filled with all sorts of ominous looking chemical compounds. Phenobarbital and scopolamine were a couple Sam vaguely recognized. There was also an impressive looking chemistry lab.

Sam stared in disbelief at the towering metal shelves, filled with the plethora of equipment.

"It took years to amass all of this," said her father. "I've spent four years running. Your boss Larry Reeves gave me refuge here in this warehouse, and I began devising plans and gathering resources, which of course included some trustworthy allies," he winked at her.

Sam ignored the friendly jest. She was only beginning to warm up to this man, and she still did not feel completely comfortable around him. Maybe it was the strange start they had.

That day she got the full story. It was something they had to do in the privacy of the warehouse. Chip said there were too many names that were risky to mention in public. After a few hours they were both hungry and Chip went down the block to get lunch.

She plopped down into a swivel chair and put her feet up on a desk, clacking the toes of her newly purchased, black leather combat boots together. She thought if she was going to train like a spy, she might as well look like one. She reviewed what she learned so far.

Dr. Niles, the handsome stranger, known as Ignacio Benitez Mendoza, as well as a few others were working together, but for who, Chip did not know. Their objective: to steal his formula, that much he was certain about.

Over the years, people, some of whom Chip recognized, some he had never seen before, kept him on the move. He fled across the country from Florida to Vancouver to New Mexico. He even spent a couple months in Alaska.

Chip or Hurston, as he was called on the other side, explained that there was one man who took the super pill before him.

For Sam to fully understand, he started at the very beginning, and it was a long story.

Chip worked as a pharmaceutical scientist in both worlds before he got connected. He laughed when he told her this, stating that he must have been destined to be a scientist.

He worked for Blakely Pharmaceuticals for over a decade and had been working with his team to develop a new sleep medication for the majority of that time. On the other side, he was working on developing a new antipsychotic medication, when he began getting random visions of this formula from the other side. He had heard of inspiration hitting people out of nowhere and took it be something along those lines. He wrote down the formula from memory immediately, and his was particularly sharp, eidetic even, and went to work developing and releasing this sleep medication, which came to be called Somulex.

Working overtime had disrupted his sleep patterns and he began taking his own drug, this is when he noticed an increase in the visions he had already begun to experience. He wondered if these visions meant something. On the other side, he began taking Balixa for similar reasons.

Then, one fortuitous night, he sat down with his notes in front of him after a long day with his Blakely research subjects. He had begun seeing a pattern, and now he was sure there was something to it. His subjects were having shared experiences, shared visions. This is when he connected the dots with what was happening to him.

At that exact moment of discovery, Chip became connected. It wasn't long before he had the same realization on the other side and became fully connected. For him, he said, this discovery was a catalyst to his destiny, years of mind-numbing research had finally amounted to something, though he wasn't sure what he would do with this monumental information. He believed that it was the destiny of mankind to connect.

Chip knew he needed help with this next stage, so he told his superior, Larry Reeves, and shared his discoveries. This is when something truly miraculous happened. Mr. Reeves told him that he'd started taking Balixa himself, and that he, too, was experiencing visions. He thought he was losing his mind, however after thoroughly inspecting the research, he was convinced that this connection phenomenon was real.

Hurston had already begun his covert research to identify the link between Balixa and the connection process to the other world. He had tried to gain funding but was denied by the hospital and IRB. His friend Dr. Fowler however, agreed to help him procure the facility and equipment necessary to continue his research. Dr. Fowler was not connected, but he believed in Hurston's research, and more importantly in Hurston.

Reeves agreed to help Chip with his research on the other side, but he wanted to become connected as well. He suspected that for him, connection would have something to do with overcoming his addiction. He was known as Tommy in the other world and was a homeless, heroin addict. Hurston would have to find him, convince him of this dual world concept, and help him connect, a tall order.

However, Reeves and Chip were now beginning to understand the mechanism behind connecting. Chip essentially connected after he made the scientific discovery of his lifetime, which was preceded by some other deeply personal self-growth. Reeves was currently sobering up from his functional alcoholism, which he'd kept hidden from everyone until this point, and was working through a plague of childhood abuse that had been hanging over him his entire life. He wasn't connected yet, but he suspected it was helping. The common denominator seemed to be purpose and self-improvement. Reeves was sure that if Hurston helped his alter Tommy become sober, he would have similar results.

Hurston located Tommy after a careful piecing together of information from Reeves' visions, and they became fast friends. Hurston had a disarming quality about him that made him easy to talk to. Tommy and Hurston would sit in the back of the Walmart parking lot, about a block from where Tommy stayed in a tent off the bypass, eat a burger, and talk.

Tommy was deeply interested in Hurston's work. He himself had been a scientist in the day, a food scientist, before a series of tragedies unraveled his life. When Chip explained the connection concept to him, he was intrigued. He wanted to believe in something miraculous, the possibility of a better life on the other side. Tommy was terminally ill, in the late stages of kidney failure, discarded by family and friends after a series of selfish errors.

At this point in the research, Hurston was close to creating what he believed to be a Balixa/ Somulex super pill, something that brought the consciousness of a person on one side closer to the consciousness of their alter on the other side, a connection pill. The formula was finalized during a trip home to visit family, when he was working in his daughter Sarah's basement one night.

Reeves's advice proved to be futile, Tommy's health was in rapid decline and they both realized that he didn't have much time. Even so, he trusted Hurston and pleaded to be the first to try this super pill, stating that if there was even a chance that it would work, it was worth it to him, it would give his life meaning. Hurston knew he had to act quickly, so he rushed back to Texas from Raleigh.

However, when the medication was administered, something went terribly wrong. Tommy went into cardiac arrest. Hurston and Fowler tried to revive him, but his heart was too weak. Hurston was beside himself.

The miracle happened when Mr. Reeves woke up connected, with all of Tommy's memories and abilities intact. It had worked, just not in the way that Hurston had intended. He had no idea that even through death the connection process would persist.

At this point, Hurston had decided to discontinue the research. Someone had died. The pill was too unstable to administer, despite Reeves being happy with his personal results. Fowler urged him to continue the research, stating that this was too important to the world, to society. Hurston stood his ground and after a while Fowler relented.

What happened next propelled things into motion quickly. Hurston came home one night after a night at Fowler's, to find that his apartment had been ransacked. The odd thing was nothing of value was taken. He began to suspect that someone was after his research, information was somehow being leaked. It was too big of a coincidence. He knew he had to act quickly, so he took his little brown notebook where his formulas were written down, and burned it, as they were already committed to memory at this point, destroyed the super pills save a few that he popped into a pill canister to take with him, and gave Fowler a letter for Sarah in case she came looking for him.

That night he returned to his apartment to get his things. Moments after he entered the apartment, an unsettling feeling set in, a feeling of being watched. Not a minute later he felt a blow to his head, he fell over and turned around to catch a glimpse of his attacker, his face was obscured by a black ski mask.

He knew this could be it for him, so he unscrewed the capsule, threw back the last of his super pills and staggered away. His assailant jumped on him, and they tousled for a few minutes, when the man clumsily pressed a damp cloth over his nose and mouth, spilling a liquid that smelled of chloroform all over him.

The next thing he knew, he had woken up in this world. His clumsy assailant had accidentally killed him with a chloroform overdose.

So here he was, living out of the warehouse Reeves had supplied him and trying to gather as much intel on his pursuers as possible.

It was a lot to take in. Sam sat back in her chair and stared into the distance, lost in thought. She was out of questions for now.

25. Waking Life: Nikki

The beaded curtains rolled off Sarah's body as she entered Nikki's bohemian living room. The room had an immediate soothing effect on Sarah, her heart rate slowed as she felt her body relaxing.

There was nothing ordinary about this house, with its colorful wall tapestries and handmade decorations from around the world. Yet, the random constellation of objects and colors seemed to flow and fit together seamlessly. Sarah wondered if Nikki was some sort of retro Feng Shui master.

After a hurried explanation from Jeremy, an exhausted Sarah sunk down into one of the four knitted bean bags positioned in a circle around what looked like a hand-knotted, multicolored area rug. There was a low, Japanese tea table in the center of the room. Nikki brought over a steaming black tea pot from the kitchen and a few palm-sized cups and placed them on the table.

Nikki poured Sarah a cup a pushed it towards her. Sarah thought Nikki was as beautiful and eclectic in appearance as her house. She had a long thick ponytail of twists and dreadlocks in various shades of brown and platinum blonde, and beautiful multicolored beads and strands of gold filament woven into her hair. She had a smooth, medium brown complexion and dark almond shaped eyes. Sarah cradled it in her hands, savoring its warmth, the chills it sent down her back. A strong and spicy aroma rose up from the cup, piercing her nostrils with citrus.

"It's orange pekoe," Nikki said. "Citrus is a calming agent, it awakens the senses and centers the mind." She lit and blew out some incense sticks one by one, and set them in their intricately carved stone holders, embellished with lotus flowers and elephants. "That's sandalwood, it has a similar effect."

Sarah had some friends like Nikki in college and had a vague notion that she would have a cabinet of tinctures and tonics, a poster or two of Jimmy Hendrix or the Grateful Dead, hanging somewhere in the house, and definitely at least a few grams of marijuana.

She didn't even feel guilty concocting this stereotype in her head, because it soothed her, she secretly prayed that Nikki was exactly as she appeared to be, because no one was who they seemed to be these days. Sarah barely even recognized herself.

Nikki brought out a small box and some white rolling papers. Sarah sighed audibly, releasing the pressures of the day. She wasn't opposed to smoking, but having only done so a few times before, she was apprehensive. There was that time when she was thirteen and her neighbor decided to be generous with a few of the neighborhood kids. He was seventeen and repeating the ninth grade for the third time. Sarah didn't really know his story, but she was at that age where she didn't ask too many questions and went along with the crowd.

Sarah didn't remember feeling much, just a vague sense of wonder, as she wandered down the street that night, mesmerized by the glow of streetlamps, marveling at how beautifully and angelically they spread their pale-yellow wings against the night sky. Yes, she was stoned, and maybe a toke wouldn't hurt now either.

Nikki, ever perceptive and full of hospitality, crouched down beside her, handing her the joint and lighter. Sarah, in the guise of a professional, lit the end and took a long drag, inhaling deeply, like she had watched her college roommate do many times before.

Immediately her chest and throat were sent into rolling spasms. She coughed violently, gagging and choking as her chest ignited like a furnace. Nikki rubbed her back and smiled up at Jeremy knowingly, as if to say, you brought me a fledgling and I will teach her my ways. Finally, Sarah felt the head rush and smiled wearily. Jeremy and Nikki both smiled back at her.

After bringing Nikki up to speed with everything that had happened, the conversation began to grow increasingly personal. Nikki divulged that she was "connected" to her alternate self and how getting there was no easy task. She described the life-changing moment, when she left her parents' home for good. They were strict, rigid, ultra-conservative Catholics, "tools" as Nikki put it.

"I was their lapdog, every time they said jump, I would ask: how high? No pun intended. My father made me do track and field all throughout high school. It was miserable. But it wasn't until last year, when I turned twenty that I realized he couldn't *make* me do anything, and that I had *chosen* the life they so clearly laid out for me."

"So, how did you leave?" Sarah asked, soaking up every juicy word that fell out of Nikki's mouth.

"You can't make this stuff up." Nikki enthused before continuing, "I was at Le Maison Rousseau, you know, that upscale French restaurant on Yancey Street? Anyways, I was there with my parents one night. It was our usual Sunday dinner spot. I remember everything. I was wearing this Mary-Jane schoolgirl dress. Imagine me for a second, dressed like Audrey Hepburn from Breakfast at Tiffany's."

Sarah could not imagine Nikki, this ripped-jean-wearing, practitioner of relaxation, at an upscale French restaurant, dressed like a high-society doll.

"I can't," Sarah shook her head in bewilderment.

"Right?" Nikki laughed. "So, we were in the middle of dinner, and my frustration had been building since the night before. I was sitting with this big knot in my stomach. So, when my mother told me to eat the food I was staring at, I lost it."

"What did you do?" Sarah's eyes grew wider.

"I picked up the champagne on the table and began drinking it, right out of the bottle. You should have seen their faces," Nikki grinned, taking great pleasure from this memory.

"Tell her what you did next," Jeremy goaded her on. He clearly already knew the story.

"Well..." Nikki flashed them a mischievous grin and cocked her head sideways. "I poured the bottle all over the tablecloth, the entire bottle, until it was completely empty and then I walked out. No one even stopped me. There was just dead silence behind me. I didn't even turn around."

"So, I'm guessing that's how you ended up here?" Sarah squeezed the beanbag, relishing the texture of the small beans against her palms.

"My bags were outside on the porch the next morning when I came home. No note. Nothing. They were clearly mortified, and you know what? I don't feel bad about it. I mean, I did at first. But the more distance I had from them, the quicker I was able to dismantle that guilt. They haven't called me since, not even to check up on me. They were doing that through Jeremy for a while, until he got locked up in that hospital."

"So, when did you actually... connect?"

"Oh right, that happened almost immediately after I found this place. After the last trace of guilt had vanished, I was completely free, and I woke up one morning... remembering my other life."

"Just like that?"

"Just. Like. That."

"But you know, it really wasn't *just like that*," Jeremy taunted, throwing a Cheeto at her. "Nikki thought she had lost her mind, that is until I found her there, on the other side."

"So how did *you* get connected? What's your story?" Sarah wanted to know everything. Finally, she had found people who could relate to what she was going through.

Jeremy was about to reply when Nikki cut in.

"Now *that* is a story for after dinner. You guys hungry?"

"So hungry," Jeremy and Sarah replied simultaneously.

"Now there is something my upbringing was good for. I can cook."

"Yes. She. Can."

"And not only that, I make the best lasagna. It's your lucky night; I made some earlier that I can heat up."

"Sounds great," Sarah replied, turning her attention to her grumbling and aching stomach for the first time since they left the hospital four hours ago.

She turned to look out the window. The sun was beginning to rise already.

After a hearty plate of a wonderfully tasty and unapologetically meaty lasagna, Sarah was finding it hard to fight off sleep. She sat up straighter in her beanbag, determined to stay awake and not miss a moment of this.

Jeremy's story was considerably more somber, and it drained a lot of energy out of him.

"You see," he continued, taking a large bite of his third piece of garlic bread after finishing his second large helping of lasagna. "I had to change something about myself in order to become connected. We all do. And most of the time, we are so far from our true path in life, that the change is very painful. Nikki had one foot out the door, me on the other hand... I fought against it tooth and nail, until..." Jeremy paused, and sighed deeply, "until circumstances forced me to change."

Sarah learned that Jeremy had made a sacrifice that he never would have considered making at that time, because he had allowed himself to be pulled into the glitz and glamour of high school. He was the quarter back of the football team his sophomore year, and he was good, more than good, good enough to be drafted.

Before that, Jeremy had always felt a calling to politics, to fight against social injustice. He was the kid sticking up for the little guys in middle school, and working on a racial equality task force freshman year in high school.

But high school very swiftly began changing him for the worse. Jeremy described it as the fishbowl effect. He said he had become brainwashed into thinking that high school *was* life. He said he became selfish, egotistical. Sarah saw it as a pretty standard teenage experience: parties, drinking, chasing beautiful girls, and of course, soaking up the irresistible attention that came from being quarterback.

Sarah herself knew nothing of that life. She was the quiet kid with a few close friends that didn't seem to fit in with any clique. Still, she could imagine how incredible it would feel to be admired by so many.

But it had changed Jeremy, made him irresponsible. He described it as a pull away from his obligations, his moral commitments, and the breaking of his family's trust.

During his junior year, his father became ill, cancer began taking over his lung and he was too far down on the transplant list to have any hope of survival. Jeremy admitted that he was against donating one of his own lungs, at first. It would ruin his chances of playing football professionally, as he would need his full lung capacity for the NFL. His mother was ambivalent, torn apart with the idea that in order for her husband to live, her son would be robbed of his dream. She didn't want to push Jeremy into a decision, and she didn't. After a few months of watching his father deteriorate physically and his mother deteriorate emotionally, Jeremy made his own decision. It was the *only* decision as far as he was concerned.

Jeremy wiped the tears away with his shirt collar as he continued. He told them that it was only after he ran away from home to escape the pressure, and boarded a Greyhound for San Francisco, that it dawned on him.

He watched an old man in the seat in front of him, staring out the window vacantly, a lifeless expression on his face. It was then that it hit him across his "egotistical teenage brain," as Jeremy put it, that he would knowingly be putting his father in his grave. So, he turned around. He had decided then, that this would be his turning point, his salvation from the spiritual bondage he had voluntarily placed himself into.

After Jeremy had finished, Sarah couldn't help but feel that she had known the both of them longer than she knew most of her friends. Her own isolation suddenly became agonizingly apparent.

Jeremy also explained the research he began doing after he got connected. The mythology fascinated Sarah. There were apparently many references to this dual existence across cultures and religions. These references tied into creation myths, the passage between life and death, the spirit word, psychic phenomenon: it was everywhere.

It was a common thread in all cultures, Jeremy said, they called it by different names, but it was all alluding to the same concept of duality.

Sarah also figured out that her mission to find her father was now becoming twofold. She would have to become connected herself, and through some miracle, locate Jeremy in this other world and rescue him. He was being kept sedated somewhere, in another hospital.

Jeremy and Nikki both had unique contributions to this mission. Jeremy had a renewed sense of justice and Nikki was determined to release people from the chains of societal group think.

It was then that Sarah remembered Lucas Bremmer. He was still working her case from afar, and somehow, she knew that she should talk to him about this, that he would understand and keep her secret. *He must be wondering where I've been all this time.* She wasn't sure how Nikki and Jeremy would feel about her contacting

Lucas, but she had to, even if it meant breaking their trust. Lucas was the only one who had actively and whole-heartedly attempted to find her father.

Later that morning when everyone was fast asleep, Sarah sat wedged between the toilet and the tub, on the bathroom floor, cupping Jeremy's cell phone in her hands and staring out the opaque glass window facing the yard. She felt devious, but she promised herself that she would tell Nikki and Jeremy as soon as she could. Lucas was on her side. She quickly did a web search and pulled up his number, luckily his work number was linked to his cell.

"Lucas... hello?" She said in a muffled voice.

"Sarah? Is that you? Where have you—?"

"I was away Lucas, but no one knows where I am now, please, please don't contact anyone. I'm safe, I promise. Have you found out anything new about the case?"

"No, not really. Your father didn't leave any paper trail: no receipts, no credit card transactions, nada."

Sarah sighed before continuing.

"I'm going to come see you Lucas, actually no. I need you to come see me. I'll fill you in on everything. I'll text you the address."

"Okay, I'm out of town but I can be there in a few days. Is that okay?"

"Yes, that's fine. It will give me time to regroup and get everything together for you."

"Okay, but Sarah, are you sure you're okay?"

"Yes, I promise. I'll see you in a few days."

26. DREAM LIFE: KAWASAKI

The first mission would not be a simple one, because Sam did not yet know how to be in two places at once. There was, at this time, only a unidimensional focus to this plan. Sam would have to help her father with the surveillance of three key people he identified as significant in this super pill/dual world/corruption fiasco.

She turned the video camera on herself and opened up the side screen.

"Special agent Brennan reporting for duty. Operation Kool-Aid has commenced." Sam grinned into the camera and swiveled around in her chair. She brought the camera close to her face. "I have drunk, I repeat, I have drunk the Kool-Aid and am past the point of no return. I have gained access to classified information on subjects Dr. Neely AKA Dr. Niles AKA snake eyes, Ignacio Benitez Mendoza AKA Maurizio Pierro Accosi AKA ridiculously good looking, and Brady Ragland AKA Rocky Henson AKA shady looking character... Man! I am really good at this. I should have been a reporter in my past life."

"You are."

Sam jumped out of her seat like a startled cat and fumbled the camera in her hands, catching it just before it hit the floor. Chip was standing behind her and apparently watching her cheesy, impromptu, 70's crime show monologue. She felt the blood rush to her cheeks. *What is it with this guy and sneaking up on me?*

"We really do need to work on that startle response of yours." Chip chuckled and sat down across from her on a rolling chair with one jammed wheel.

"What do you mean by, *I am?*"

"I mean, in your other life, you're a reporter for the local newspaper, one of the best and brightest, I might add."

"Oh? She smiled and shook her head. "No wonder that personality test I took in high school said broadcast journalism was my best career choice. So, is my other self very similar to me?"

"Characteristically yes and spiritually yes. And by that, I mean, you both seem to have the same life path."

Here we go again.

Chip was long-winded. He had a detailed and drawn out explanation for everything, although at this point, Sam was grateful for any new information on this topic.

"First," Chip continued, "you are born into both worlds. In theory, you share one soul, so to speak, and although you are individually shaped by your respective environments, a lot of your biological characteristics and predispositions are the same."

"So, I guess I was meant to be a broadcaster journalist or reporter."

"Well, I don't think it's that simple. Your career is not the same thing as your purpose, what you were put on this Earth to do. I think there's a much grander, much more significant purpose for you.

Sam, from knowing you in both lives, you were born for leadership, but you haven't quite reached your full potential."

"Excuse me?"

"Well, do *you* feel like you've reached your full potential?"

"I guess not, but I think everyone is striving for something more."

"Ah, but that's exactly my point Sam!" Chip exclaimed, enthusiastically. "There's a difference between being diligent and working diligently to find your true purpose in life."

"I think I see. So, how do I know the difference? It doesn't seem like anything is missing in my life."

"Oh, doesn't it? Why do you think you sought out your birth parents? Began having these visions? Found all of this out? Just a coincidence?"

Sam stared at him for a moment before responding.

"None of this has felt like coincidence."

"And that, my dear, is called synchronicity, following your purpose. All I know is, the decisions you have made thus far have been a result of needing to fill some emptiness inside you, something that just didn't feel right. Am I wrong? In order to become fully connected, you have to let go of whatever barriers are keeping you from what you were put on this earth to be."

"That sounds very romantic and grandiose, Chip. Look, how can you be sure of any of this?"

"Because that's what it took for me, for all of them."

"All of them? So, who can I talk to about this besides you?"

"No one for now. Sam, believe me when I say, we cannot take the risk. It's too dangerous. For now, the main focus will be to get you connected. Surveillance will be too risky, never mind ineffective if you can't protect yourself in both worlds."

~~~

The connection process proved to be exceedingly more difficult than Sam imagined. After undergoing a series of mental tests and analyses administered by Chip, she still had no clue what she was put on earth to do, or what was holding her back.

She did, however, begin to have visions of herself on the other side with increasing intensity, about once every day. They came in a flash and did not last longer than a few seconds, but they were clearer and more vivid than ever. She began writing them down in excruciating detail whenever they occurred.

It dawned on Sam that she had been doing this her entire life. These visions were documented in her childhood dream journal amidst the doodles, drawings and poems. The idea of not being able to differentiate these visions from her childhood imaginings was simultaneously funny and terrifying, as if the dark shadows hiding in the crevices of her room really were monsters all along.

~~~

The next day Sam had decided she was done with the warehouse, at least for a while. She had wracked her brain enough trying to discover her so-called purpose, and it wasn't working. It was during the drive to dinner with Elijah that night that she saw it, the motorcycle dealership. Elijah told her she was insane, but she didn't care. She bought one the next morning and took a lesson that day.

~~~

Sam leaned her body left like they taught her to balance out her Kawasaki, around the sharp turn on the winding mountain road. She used to come to Long Mountain Parkway with her parents once in a while, always in the fall when the foliage turned brilliant red and orange as far as the eye could see. Never in her life did Sam see herself, a sensible businesswoman, on a motorcycle, but Chip encouraged her to try new things, to get out of her comfort zone. He said it might help with the connection process. Frankly, it was the most exhilarating experience of her young life, every sense was heightened and somehow accelerated by the velocity of the bike.

She could smell the river before she reached its mossy banks, hitting her nostrils as she zoomed ahead. The smells would change abruptly from honeysuckle to wet leaves to burning spruce, all in a manner of seconds. Time had slowed down, even though it flew faster than she had ever experienced before. It felt like running away. Sam relished every taste, smell and sudden change of temperature on her skin. She was living life in her own time zone.

Every time she stopped the bike after a long stretch of riding, she was overcome with disappointment. She was acutely aware of being back in the humdrum world. This motorcycle had brought on a new kind of realization. It was a turning point, a terrifying realization of her morbid unhappiness. Chip was right, she needed something more.

The next afternoon she walked away, cash in hand, after selling the bike to her neighbor, Mr. Clarke, who impulsively purchased it from her in the heat of a midlife crisis, much like hers. She enjoyed the bike as she was sure Mr. Clarke would, but it was not what she needed.

27. WAKING LIFE: DEAD AND ALIVE

I t was her second night at Nikki's house, and Sarah's insomnia was back. Since she was no longer running for her freedom and utterly physically exhausted, her mind picked up the slack. She lay across the paisley couch in Nikki's wooden-paneled living room and crossed her arms behind her head, sighing heavily. She looked behind her to the small digital alarm clock on the end table. It read 2:17 a.m.

How long has it been since I've taken my sleeping pills? Sarah realized she also had not taken her Lithium in two nights, and it had been over two weeks since she had taken the sleeping pills. There was no way she could go home for the Lithium, but she wasn't worried about it, she had gone without it before and could handle the hypomania and depression if it occurred. But sleep, she couldn't do without. Someone would have to go replenish Sarah's stash tomorrow. She still could not believe this stuff was sold over the counter.

The next vision came that night, just thirty minutes after Sarah took the pill. For the first time, Sarah could see herself. It appeared as though she was looking at herself through the lens of a digital camera. It was startling to see herself, so familiar and yet with distinct and subtle differences; her hair was longer, pulled into a neat, high ponytail and there was a small horizontal scar on the left side of her forehead, to the right of her eyebrow.

The visions came to her in brief snippets, a reality T.V. show, broken up by static and bad signal. In this vision she called herself special agent Brennan. *Brennan. That must be my surname... I wonder what my first name is...* She wondered if she really was a special agent. The video seemed more like a joke.

A few names her alter-self mentioned jumped out at her, including Dr. Neely and Rocky Henson who were apparently known as Dr. Niles and Brady Ragland in this other life.

This is insane! This means my other self knows what's really going on over there. But, why has this self not caught up? Get with the program Sarah!

Again, the images took over and Sarah saw herself through the camera lens, laughing and wondering out loud about her other self, when a familiar voice broke through. The voice ignited fireworks, blinding flashes of recognition that shot adrenaline straight into her heart. It was her father's voice.

Sarah sat up. There was no mistaking it. Outside somewhere an owl hooted, sending unsettling chills of memory through her. She had succeeded in her four-year-long mission. She had found him.

Impulsively, Sarah grabbed the pill canister from the end table and began pushing and twisting, her hands sweaty and fumbling to open the lid. She finally tore it open, removed two and tossed them back. *These pills are the key. They are my connection to Dad.*

She sat there, her sweaty tank top clinging to her stomach. She could not believe it. After four long years of searching, there he was, on the other side of the looking glass. She sat up gripping the edge of the couch, waiting for the effects to kick in, to fall down the rabbit hole after her father, as deep as it would go.

But as quickly as the happiness had come, came the all-to-familiar sense of defeat. She recalled the scene of Alice screaming at herself to wake up when Wonderland became a nightmare. The Queen of Hearts became an angry giant and her loyal deck of cards rolled over themselves in a furious wave to get to Alice. Sarah wanted out of this nightmare, so badly.

She just wanted to wake up and see her father, to really see her father. This was a new kind of torture. She squeezed her eyes shut and willed herself to see. Blackness. She rolled face-down onto her pillow and screamed until her throat ached. Still nothing... until... Sarah could feel it taking over this time, it was about thirty minutes later when her skin began to crawl, like it was covered with buzzing insects. *I know I didn't overdose... maybe this is a new side effect?*

Over the next few days, Sarah sent herself on a drug induced otherworldly binge. She could not just sit there and patiently wait for the whereabouts of her father to be slowly and disjointedly revealed to her. She had to speed things up.

To her dismay, the process only lasted three days. It did not take long for Jeremy and Nikki to put a stop to what they called her "dangerous drug abuse." It was true, Sarah had taken ten pills in the past three days, but she felt she had no other choice.

~~~

"Sarah, get up!"

A cold hand gripped her shoulder, shaking it back and forth. She felt like a disjointed marionette doll, lying limply on the floor.

"Is she waking up? She can't go on like this."

Sarah heard Jeremy's voice drift in and out. Slowly the beige and white square tiles of the kitchen floor came into focus.

"You have to stop this Sarah. I understand you think you're learning something, but this stuff is not helping you get connected.

You need to stop or you're going to overdose." Jeremy scooped Sarah up off the floor and carried her over to the sofa. "Sarah, how many pills did you take?"

Sarah looked at Jeremy through the slits of her eyes.

"Six," she mumbled.

"Six?!"

"Nikki, get in here!"

Nikki emerged from her bedroom and quickly came over, kneeling down over Sarah.

"Oh my god. She took a bunch of those pills again."

"Yep. SIX. We need to get her to a hospital, right?"

Nikki examined her eyes and breathing. She placed a cool palm against her forehead.

Sarah shivered, recoiling from the touch.

"Yes, she's overdosing, but she's just going to be sick. It's not that serious. Bring me a cold rag."

It was around 7:30 p.m. when four rapid knocks resounded at the front door. Sarah had gotten violently ill as Nikki predicted and was now sipping some orange juice. She pulled the fleece blanket around her shoulders. Clumsily, she slammed the glass down on the table, and willed herself off the couch, so she could get to the door first. Her body would not comply.

Until this moment, she had forgotten all about Lucas coming over. She hadn't checked her phone today either. She was so wrapped up in her own world, that it slipped her mind to inform Jeremy and Nikki.

"Wait," Sarah said weakly as Nikki suspiciously eyed the door. "Nikki, I know who's at the door."

"Why are you inviting people here? Are you insane? Do you want to get caught?!"

This was not a side of Nikki Sarah had seen yet. She was usually so mellow.

"No, he's safe, I promise. Just please trust me on this."

Nikki looked through the peephole. "Young Sherlock Holmes?"

"Yep." Sarah chuckled lightly, "That's him."

Nikki opened the door to a sliver and quickly motioned for Lucas
to come inside. He stood there, his thumbs in his corduroy pants
pockets, swaying back and forth on his brown, dress shoes.

"So, I'm here, what's going on Sarah? Everyone is looking for you.
There's even a missing persons alert."

"Wait, what?"

Watching television had been the furthest thing from Sarah's
mind. She was not sure if Nikki even owned one.

"Lucas, there's something, well so much we need to talk about.
I'll tell you everything, but you have to promise to keep it to yourself.
I have a new angle for the case."

"Actually, I've been doing some research as well. We have a lot to
talk about."

Apparently, several weeks of no contact did not deter Lucas from
doing his own digging. Sarah began to wonder if this quirky twenty-
something private eye even had a life outside of work.

Sarah dived into the details of her visions, the clues her father
had left her, how they brought her to Lucas's office, through
venturing into the cave of Lizard's Foot, to her stay at Forrester
Psychiatric, and finally to the present day, hiding out at Nikki's. The
entire time, Lucas remained quiet. So quiet, that Sarah could not
tell what he was feeling, except from the occasional parting of his
lips, raised eyebrows, or widening eyes. Otherwise, he sat there, legs
crossed, chin resting on his fist, pensively.

Sarah sat bundled up on the couch, croaking in the most
animated voice her drained and drugged body could muster. Jeremy
and Nikki watched tentatively on, from the outskirts of the living
room.

When she finished, Lucas remained in the same statuesque
position. Sarah fell back on the couch, utterly spent, turning her
head to observe Nikki and Jeremy's expressions, which were
predictably anxious.

"Sarah, I don't know how to tell you this." Lucas sighed and ran
his hand through his hair once. "I think I've been experiencing what
you're talking about, because I've... I've seen your father as well. You

see, ever since we met, I've been having these flashes of what I thought were daydreams fueled by sleep deprivation. I saw some of the things you described, and there is no way that my mind would concoct the very same details that you described, with such precision."

"What did you see Lucas?" Sarah could not wait a second longer.

"Sarah, maybe we should continue this conversation after you've had some rest. You look terrible."

"Like hell, Lucas. We are continuing this conversation right now." Sarah pointed her index finger at Lucas, only to see it shaking violently before her. Jeremy came out from the periphery of the room and crouched in front of her.

"He's right, Sarah, you're completely spent. You need to go back to sleep. Nikki, are you sure she doesn't need a hospital?"

"Trust me, I'm sure. She's thrown up most of it."

"No, no, no. I need to hear what Lucas has to say!"

"Sarah, I promise I'll tell you everything you want to know. I'll be right here when you wake up. I promise."

She narrowed her eyes at him.

"Fine." Sarah could not muster the energy to argue any further. She reluctantly pulled the covers over her and fell into a heavy, dreamless sleep.

Sometime later, a soft voice permeated Sarah's consciousness.

"I just don't know how to tell her. Because I really haven't solved the case. All I know is that he's alive. I've seen him."

The hushed whispers hit Sarah's ears clearly, as if she was tuned to pick them up, even through waves of sleep.

"Say it again," she called out, in her half-awake state.

"Sarah, you're up," Lucas said nervously, somewhere from the other side of the room.

"Take it easy," she heard Jeremy say.

Sarah peeled her eyes open and Lucas's face come into focus. He was crouching in front of her with one arm resting on the edge of the couch, eyebrows furrowing and lips slightly pursed. The words, reluctant to come forth.

She propped herself up on her elbow and looked into his eyes. "Tell me."

Lucas sighed and sat back on the carpet, hugging his knees and smoothing his curly, shoulder-length, brown hair behind his ears before continuing.

"Sarah, I found your father. Well, you know, I've been searching for him, using all possible avenues and leads ..."

"Out with it, Lucas! I know he's alive. I heard you say it."

"He is alive, Sarah. That much I know is true, but not in the way that you think.'

Oh, no. All the possibilities and impossibilities hit her at once, so that she could not separate her thoughts. Static.

"What do you mean?" She frowned.

"What I mean is, he's alive in that other realm, the one you spoke to me about. At least that's what I think is happening, based on what you've told me."

"But if you saw him, it means you were with him in the other realm, right?"

"Right, I think I was."

Sarah sighed loudly, shaking her head in disbelief.

"But there's something else... I just don't know if right now is a good time to tell you."

"Out with it, Lucas! I've come too far to get some half-baked answers."

"Okay... in these visions, your father told me that he's... gone... from this world. He only exists in the other realm now."

"Gone... like..."

Lucas dropped his head and looked down at the floor. "He's dead, Sarah, in this world, but he's still alive in the other one."

The static grew louder, surrounding Sarah with incomprehensibly loud buzzing. She could see everything, hear his words, but somehow it all felt unreal, like she was watching her life as a movie. She could see herself on the couch, vacantly staring at the corner of the room, Lucas sitting on the floor hugging his knees, Jeremy and Nikki standing by, looking at one another, conversing in a language of silent glances only a lifetime of friendship could decipher.

28. DREAM LIFE: A WAKING NIGHTMARE

"So, your anxiety is back?" Dr. Shandi crossed her legs as she clumsily spread cream cheese over her bagel. "I haven't seen you in a long time, Sam, and you haven't returned any of my calls. I've been worried about you."

"I know, I'm sorry. And yes, my anxiety is back. Actually, it's more like restlessness... and I think I'm a bit depressed too."

"I see. You think it's the same restlessness you experienced a few weeks ago, when you were having those visions and looking for your birth parents?"

"Yes."

"Have you found them?"

"I did, actually."

"Well, that's a big deal. How did it go?"

"Not well, actually." Sam fidgeted with her silver bracelet, thinking of what to say, and what not to. "My mother died shortly after we met."

"Oh no!" Dr. Shandi put down her bagel for a moment and waited for Sam to continue.

"Yes. She was sick, very sick. My grandfather is not doing great either. He's not handling her death well at all, he's an alcoholic, no offense to him, and my father... he's, well I don't know, I was never able to find him."

"I see. Well, no wonder you're anxious. You must be so distraught over this." Dr. Shandi put one free hand on Sam's knee and patted it gently. Shandi dusted the crumbs off her red and purple, African Batik skirt and leaned forward, looking into her eyes.

"I don't think this restlessness is part of one of my usual anxiety episodes," Sam responded.

"How so?"

"It's hard to explain. I know it seems like I have all the signs: agitation, trouble sleeping, racing thoughts. But somehow this is not my usual anxiety, no, it's much, much more significant."

"Well, I would certainly say so, given what you've just gone through."

Sam sat back against the sofa and sighed loudly.

"It's not just that..."

Dr. Shandi crossed her arms and sat back in her chair, giving Sam an inquisitive look.

"Sam, what is it that you're not telling me? You seem to know a lot more than you're letting on."

Damn. I knew this was a bad idea. She's going to pull it right out of me. Wait, maybe I can go about this in another way.

"Honestly, I don't know. But it feels like the answer is just below the surface. That's why I was thinking we could try the hypnosis again."

~~~

What felt like only a few minutes after beginning hypnosis, Sam's overzealous, visual cortex kicked in.

The place she was standing in was much colder this time. Sheathed by a heavy, midnight-blue darkness, so thick, Sam could hardly make out her own body. She was a faceless, body-less, spirit, floating around in an endless vacuum of space.

"Dr. Shandi?"

"I'm here Sam. What do you see?"

"It's dark, I can't see anything." Then like a command was given, things began to shift, almost like the environment was morphing to the sound of her voice. The midnight-blue began to lighten in the corners of her vision and slowly swirl around in front of her, in mesmerizing, Van-Gogh-like patterns. *This is exactly like my childhood dreams, the lights and geometric shapes.* The patterns became more defined and cloudlike, and pixels of light appeared in all directions. Sam was staring into the static of a TV screen universe. *What am I watching?* The light changed again, to accommodate her thoughts, the channel becoming clearer.

The same young girl stood before her. She appeared this time, without her scarf, and Sam recognized her instantly. She laughed to herself. The younger version of herself frowned at her in disappointment. *Note to self: Do not think.*

"It's really not that funny," her younger, telepathic self said. "Sure, you're finding yourself, but you've been lost for a long time. I'll show you where you need to go next." And without a moment to spare, she took off running.

Here we go again. Sam bounded after her with surprising speed, unlike in her dreams, where she felt like she was moving through liquid cement. The blackness passed by her on either side as she entered a lighter area, which slowly became more vivid with flowering cactuses and small shrubs blooming on either side of her as she zoomed by.

This is how it must feel to be the creator. The thought scared Sam, but there was a limitless feeling to this experience. That was until she came to a precipice, where her younger self stopped suddenly.

Sam waved her arms before her for balance, to keep herself from sending them both over the edge. *What is with this girl and heights? I don't remember liking heights as a kid.*

Again, her younger self turned to face her.

"That's not the point, now jump."

"Jump?" Sam asked in confusion.

"Just jump!" yelled the little girl, spinning around to face Sam, already mid-fall and smiling on her way down, her voice echoing off the canyon walls as she shouted from somewhere below. "It will only hurt a little, in the beginning!"

Hurt?! In the beginning? Sam looked up for Dr. Shandi's megaphone voice of approval, remembering that in this creepy universe, her thoughts were actually spoken out loud in Shandi's office.

"It's okay," she heard her say, somewhere far off. "Remember this is just a vision."

Okay... Sam inhaled deeply. *Here I go!*

"Ahhh!!" Sam screeched and squeezed her eyes shut as she leaped off the side of the canyon.

Then suddenly, everything changed, as if she had jumped into another dream. She remembered her dreams from when she was younger, always changing when a critical moment approached. There was a watery quality to the figures that appeared before her now, their pigments blending together, like the blurred lines of a watercolor painting. She remembered seeing these colors before, in the watercolor kit her grandfather bought her one year for her birthday. She walked around the room she was in, or maybe she was outside. There wasn't a ceiling and the walls were rounded.

Sam screamed as an overwhelmingly loud vibration resounded all around her, her eardrums on the brink of bursting.

"Sam, calm down, nothing here can hurt you."

Dr. Shandi's voice only exacerbated her fear.

The noise came in again, like a burst of gunfire, hammering her ears. Sam covered her ears and squeezed her eyes shut. After a moment, she looked around her again. This time she could see the source of the horrendous noise, a pointy needle-sharp beak, was breaking though the wall above her. *I'm inside of a tree? Oh, god. Someone get me out of here!* This time her words were not effective. The floating, amorphous shapes around her began to take form. The first of the figures was highly disturbing.

Mr. Reeves' face leered at her from above, grinning, his teeth, replaced by his two scantily clad assistants.

Great, I'm stuck inside a nightmare. Dr. Shandi, get me out of here!

"Focus Sam, you can get out of this yourself."

Thanks a lot... Sam squinted with exhaustion and began climbing, out of instinct, towards the ever-widening hole above her, the tree reverberating with that deafening, drilling sound.

The next face that appeared was more welcoming. Elijah smiled at her from above and reached a hand down to her. She reached up and grabbed right through it, as if he were a ghost. A look of confusion came across his face. He looked... hurt, and it cut right through her.

She climbed faster to reach him and lost her balance. This time there was nothing to hold on to. The tree hollow grew deeper, darker, and louder. She was falling into a bottomless pit.

Sam opened her eyes and was back in the office.

"Where were you, Sam?"

29. WAKING LIFE: HOSTAGE

S team floated from the mug of piping hot chai into Sarah's nostrils. The sweet scent of fresh baked bread and danishes brought on a nostalgia she could almost do without. Almost. It did not take long before the claustrophobia began to set in. After one week, she had to leave the house, just for a little bit. She managed to escape unseen one morning to a local bakery, dressed in a black hoodie and a pair of Nikki's navy slacks. She knew it was risky, but she just couldn't think in there, with Jeremy constantly talking about finding his comatose body in the dream world, and inhaling Nikki's endless clouds of marijuana smoke. It was becoming stifling. Sarah just needed a change of scenery, some time away from the people she had grown to care so deeply for in a very short amount of time.

For a while, Sarah just sat there listening, like she used to on her breaks at NC Roasters, taking in the sounds of the tables around her. A therapist was having a session in public with her client. They were discussing her arachnophobia. The woman's greatest fear was being bitten on the butt by a spider. Sarah suppressed a laugh and focused on another table. A couple was talking in a foreign language. *Probably Russian,* Sarah thought.

She turned her attention inwards. This was her time to formulate, to do some clear thinking, without the drug-fueled dreams she had been inducing for the past week. She needed a plan to connect, to find her father, to find Jeremy in the other world.

So, as she did many times before in the basement of her house, she began her internal monologue: I can't stay here. There has to be a better way to get connected than to sit in a house all day thinking about it. Maybe Lucas can help. If he was connected, he would be much more useful at finding Jeremy and my father. Either way, he might know how to help me get around undetected.

Sarah's silent brainstorming session was suddenly interrupted by a strange feeling. It felt like she was being watched. Instinctively, she looked over her shoulder towards the back of the coffee shop. There was no one there that she recognized. Still, the feeling remained. She got up quickly, then immediately sat back down to regain her composure and check for any sideways looks in her direction. Sarah listened again, focusing on the voices at the surrounding tables.

"Sarah said..."

Sarah turned her head in the direction of her name. A woman she did not recognize was sitting at a table diagonally from her, talking to a few people.

"Sarah said..." she heard her say again, over the other voices.

Okay, clearly she's taking about another Sarah. So, who's looking at me?

After another minute or so, Sarah got up, threw her trash away and quietly exited the coffee shop. She wrapped her arms around herself, dropped her head low, and headed down the sidewalk in the direction of Nikki's house.

She had not made it fifty feet before that same paranoia set in. She turned to look behind her. No one was there. Quickening her pace, she turned a corner to take a shortcut through an apartment complex.

There is definitely something wrong. Run!

Sarah broke into a full-speed run. After a few minutes she stopped to catch her breath, slumping down against a tree on the other side of the complex. She was almost home free.

A swing set swayed in the grassy field to her right. *Funny, there's no wind. Maybe the kid just went inside before I got here.*

The sun was beating down hard. Sarah pulled at her sweater, wafting some air against her overheated body. She stared ahead at the road, swaying under the unusual October heat wave. The powerful lull of the sun was making her sleepy. She closed her eyes for a moment and thought to herself, *maybe this time I am just being paranoid.* That was when she heard the footsteps. This time she knew there was someone there. Her breath caught in her throat and she prayed that the figure she now felt standing directly behind her, was just a concerned member of the neighborhood watch. Slowly, as if she could slow down time, she turned around, and found herself face to face with Rocky Henson.

~~~

Water dripped from a faucet of the dank smelling room. She could hear and smell from the muskiness that she was in a basement.

Sarah had been bound to a chair, her wrists sore from the tight plastic restraints constricting her blood flow. She had been sitting in that room, blindfolded, for what felt like an hour before she heard footsteps approaching. Her heartbeat quickened.

Rocky took off her blindfold and flashed her a sleazy, crooked smile.

He had changed clothes and was now wearing a white sleeveless shirt and dirty jeans. Sarah did not like the implications of the wardrobe change.

Rocky came close and reached a hand out to her eye, which he previously injured, as if in remorse.

Sarah recoiled.

"Do you know who I am?" The man suddenly spoke, crossing his arms across his chest.

"Am I supposed to? What are you doing? Let me go!"

"Uh, uh, uh," Rocky shook a chastising finger at her, "not until you tell me what I need to know. You're a scrappy one, but this time it was just too easy to catch you."

"Let me go! I didn't do anything! You've got the wrong person." Sarah struggled to break loose, wincing in pain from the cuffs digging into her wrists.

"Oh, you're the right person, Sarah Davis. Believe me, you're exactly who I want to talk to." Rocky walked around the dark room for a minute.

There was a single overhead bulb shining uncomfortably bright over Sarah's head, like some sort of interrogation room light. Again, she shuddered at the implications.

"You must know why you're here."

My dad. He wants information on him. I just know it.

"I have no idea. Now, let me go!" Sarah yelled again, this time, with a hint of fear in her voice.

"Now I can't do that, not until you give me what I need."

"And what's that? What do you need?"

"Your father."

Sarah swallowed. "My father? What do you want with my father?"

"You're not here to ask the questions."

"I don't know anything about where my father is. I haven't seen or heard from him in years."

"Now we both know that's not true. You've seen and you've heard things."

"I don't know what you're talking about."

"Okay, be difficult, but know this, I can be difficult too." Rocky walked to the back of the room and out of sight.

Oh my god, he's going to torture me!

Rocky came back wringing a wet towel between his hands. "Okay, let's start over. Tell me where your father is."

"I said I don't know," Sarah glared at him.

"Wrong answer."

In one swift motion, Rocky twisted the towel into a rope and snapped it sharply, against Sarah's shoulder.

"Argh! You asshole! I said I don't know anything!" Sarah looked down at her shoulder. A red welt was beginning to form.

"Wrong again." Rocky snapped the towel at her twice more, bringing out two more welts on her neck and chest.

"What is this? High school locker room torture? You're pathetic! What do you want with my father anyways?" Sarah continued struggling against her restraints, pain shooting through her wrists. At this point, she was pretty sure her wrists were bleeding.

For a moment she believed the violence was over, that she had jabbed the knife where it hurt.

Rocky smiled at her and sighed. Shrugging his shoulders, he walked out of the room again.

No. He can't be done with me. He's going to bring out something much worse than a towel. What does he want me to tell him anyway? That my father's dead? I still don't know where he is. I should have never left the house! Oh my god, what if no one finds me?

After about ten minutes, Rocky returned.

Sarah tried to make out what was in his hand and then she recognized the familiar shape she had seen in all those episodes of Cops. *Shit, it's a Taser! No no no no no no no! I am NOT cut out for this. How am I supposed to endure this? But I can't... I can't betray my father. I won't. I won't. I won't.*

"Sarah..." the whiny-voiced man taunted, interrupting her petrified chant.

It was hard to imagine this man interrogating people for a living, he was so unassuming. Still, he seemed to have all of this planned out.

"Sarah," he said again.

"What?! What do you want me to tell you? I don't know anything. I haven't seen my father!"

"Sarah, I don't want to do this the hard way. But I'll hurt you if I have to."

"Then don't! Who is putting you up to this?"

"Shut up!" Rocky snapped back, switching on the Taser.

Sarah flinched from the loud electric buzz.

Rocky slowly inched the jumping, blue light closer to Sarah's chest.

"Stop! I told you I don't know where he is. I swear!"

Rocky smiled again.

Ugh, he's enjoying this. Don't scream. Don't say anything. Don't give him the satisfaction.

The electricity coursed through her violently. She felt every muscle seize up and convulse uncontrollably. It was the worst pain she had ever felt. When he was done, her body collapsed. Silent tears flowed down her cheeks. She didn't want him to see her pain. Too late.

With a forceful finger, Rocky flipped Sarah's chin up, so that their eyes met.

Yep, he's a fucking psychopath.

"Now, what is it that you wanted to tell me, Sarah?" Rocky spoke in a calm voice, like he knew he had won.

No, he hasn't won. I won't tell him anything... but, maybe... if I tell him the truth, that he's dead, then he'll stop asking?

"He's dead," Sarah said after a few moments of deliberation.

The man looked like he had just been tased himself. He backed up slowly, shaking his head in disbelief.

"Impossible. How is that possible? My people saw him... they just saw him!"

"Saw him where?"

"On the other side. He is alive. Are you sure he's dead?"

"I swear. He's dead. I just found out myself."

"How long?"

"It's been a while."

"But... if he's dead here... and they still see him there... then... then..."

2

SONYA DEULINA WILLIAMS

30. DREAM LIFE: SURPRISE PARTY

S am was shaken by her last hypnosis session. After processing it with Dr. Shandi, she determined that she was no longer feeling satisfied with her life at present, not with her job, and not with her marriage. She was reaching for the wrong things and getting nowhere with her connection process right now, so she focused her attention on Elijah's upcoming thirtieth birthday party.

That weekend, Sam ambled through the refrigerated beer section at Hops and Vino, a beer and wine shop downtown, looking for a microbrew to please the birthday boy's picky palate. But that night, beer and birthday parties were the furthest thing from her mind. She couldn't shake the feeling that things no longer felt right.

She grabbed a funky looking pack, displaying a picture of an evil, grinning clown, holding out a mug of overflowing beer. She shuddered. It reminded her too much of the nightmarish experience she'd just had at Dr. Shandi's office. She put it back and picked up a local IPA sitting right next to it.

Sam realized that Elijah deserved some unadulterated happiness on his birthday, without her morose cloud of confusion dampening it. That night, Sam would throw Elijah a small surprise party in their studio apartment, with their closest friends.

She had decorated the apartment with colorful streamers, banners, and balloons. She had purchased a chocolate ganache cake and an expensive watch Elijah had been eyeing for several months. On one hand, she was pretty impressed with herself for pulling this off, diligently assembling the friends with only a week's notice and taking off work early to make it all come together. On the other hand, she could not be in the moment. She felt guilty for not telling Elijah all that had happened, knowing that if he really knew what was going on, he wouldn't want this party to be happening in the first place.

Sam stood in the middle of the living room. Everything was ready, and the guests would be arriving soon. She was trying her best to ignore the sinking feeling. Normally, she would have been overjoyed at her scheming and crafty handiwork. But not today.

Oh crap, I forgot to wrap the watch!

Sam walked into the bedroom and pulled out the black leather, Larso and Jennings watch. She held it in her hand for a moment, examining the sleek and intricate layers of numbers and glass. There was so much glitz and glamour in this small accessory, that its main function seemed to become contrived. Sam could not see what Elijah saw in this watch.

Suddenly, a thought occurred to her: *There was no time like the present.* It dawned on Sam that the life she had built for herself had been a huge waste of time. What goals did she even set for herself, and did they really mean anything to her anymore?

Thinking back to her basket weaving days, Sam remembered the excitement she felt peddling those baskets around town. She targeted the ladies, and in that town it was the older ladies, specifically ones living more stereotypically gender-normed lifestyles. She found that they loved their baskets. She would say, "You can use it for so many things. You can put fruit in it or pack a picnic or use it as a knitting basket!" She knew her audience.

But that joy, where did it really come from? The sale? The look on the customer's face when they received their basket? No, it was none of those things. She closed her eyes for a moment and frowned. She shook her head, thinking of her therapy sessions with Dr. Shandi, specifically the ones where they discussed going back to the source of her true emotions. Sam smiled. She realized that it was the creation process. She remembered when she made her first basket, how proud she was, even though it was clumsily woven and lopsided. Of course she'd never sold this one. She thought about it now, stored in her parents' basement with a plethora of other nostalgic remnants of her youth.

Eventually her baskets got better. She even began giving them her own twist: a wooden bow here, a brightly painted star, there. She remembered that the selling part was her father's idea from the start. It was then that she discovered, she had a knack for it.

The truth was really a lot further below the surface, below the actions of everyday life, below her job responsibilities and achievements, even below her marriage. *What was I put on this earth to do?*

Sam was pulled sharply from her introspection by three quick rings of the doorbell. It was her friend Cary's signature. Before Sam could get to the door, Cary was inside, sighing dramatically as she unloaded her bags on the kitchen counter.

"Hey, girl! So, I brought the cake and the streamers."

She took them out of the bag and waved them around.

Sam had already purchased a cake, but Cary was the type of friend that marched to the beat of her own drum and didn't pay too close attention to other people's instructions.

"Thanks," Sam responded flatly.

Sam was used to Cary's antics, and this deflated emotion was not because of her.

"Are you okay? You seem upset."

"I'm fine, just feeling kind of drained."

"Oh no, that stinks! Are you sick? Here, help me with this bean dip party platter," Cary continued without waiting for Sam to respond.

It wasn't long before the house was decorated and everything and everyone was in place. Looking around, Sam felt a little better. Black, gold, and Cary's bright blue streamers filled the living room. The large blue Happy Birthday banner hung above the kitchen island. The chocolate cake sat frosted in all its glory next to the coconut cake Cary had brought, and of course, all of Elijah and Sam's closest friends, crouched like hide-and-seekers behind the furniture.

After about fifteen minutes of crouching, and shushing each other in false alarms, the doorknob to the front door began turning. The sound of keys clanked against the doorknob. A hush fell over the crowd.

With a slow creek, the door opened.

Sam looked at Elijah and lost any words she may have prepared.

Elijah took a few steps into the house, holding a bag of frozen peas and carrots against his temple. Confused and tired, he stumbled across the room towards the couch.

"Surprise!" Everyone yelled in unison, popping out from behind the furniture.

Elijah groaned in pain and an abrupt hush fell over the crowd, their joy quickly replaced by a painfully awkward silence.

"What happened?!" Sam rushed over to Elijah, guiding him to the couch to sit. The crowd of friends stood tenuously around the room, creating a bubble of space around Sam and Elijah.

"You'll never believe it… some asshole attacked me. He was this short guy, with a scar on his head. He approached me like he knew me and then he said the strangest thing to me: "Tell your wife if she doesn't give up the information, you're a dead man. He must have been insane, and then out of the blue he just pulled out a gun and hit me over the head, knocked me out cold."

"Oh my god!"

"Did you call the police?" Elijah's best friend Kenneth said, breaking the stunned silence none of the other friends had yet dared to penetrate.

"Not yet."

"Well, you probably should. Do you have a good description of him? If you describe him to me, I could probably draw him. We covered composite sketches in my forensics class."

"Yeah maybe," Elijah said. "I just need a minute to think."

Sam looked at their friends.

"Guys, I think it's safe to say the party's over tonight. Thank you so much for coming. It means a lot, but Elijah and I need some time to handle this."

"Ok," Cary said, "are you sure you don't want some of us to stay and help?"

"Thanks, Cary, but we'll be fine."

"Hey man, you want me to hang around to do that sketch?" Kenneth asked.

"I don't know, no, I'll just call you later once Sam and I figure things out. Thanks for coming out everyone. I'm so sorry. I promise we'll reschedule, and hey, please take some food with you."

Their friends began picking up their things and saying their worried goodbyes, hesitant to leave, but not wanting to intrude.

Sam thanked everyone and smiled apologetically. Cary sighed and gave Sam's shoulder a tight squeeze before heading out.

Sam knew something significant was happening. Her father had been warning her about the people looking for him and this guy sounded familiar. Sam quickly thought through the list of people her father had told her about. A particular name came to mind: Brady Ragland. He was known as Rocky something on the other side. She never foresaw Elijah getting involved in all of this. Chip never mentioned what she should do if this sort of situation arose.

"What do you think he was talking about, Sam?"

She froze.

"I don't know... he must have been insane."

"Maybe... but why would he say *your wife?* Are you sure you don't know what this is about?"

After a few seconds she responded.

"Absolutely not."

Elijah frowned, and looked at her incredulously.

"Elijah, of course I don't know what he's talking about! What information could I possibly know that someone would hurt you for?"

"I don't know... maybe trade secrets, or something from Blakeley Pharmaceuticals?"

Oh, he is clever.

"I don't know any trade secrets, besides, everything I know is already public knowledge, well... except Balixa, and that will be public knowledge very soon."

"Is there something about Balixa?"

Too clever.

"Elijah, you better lie down. You're talking like a crazy person." Sam grabbed a couple pillows from the other side of the couch and propped them under his head. "What could someone want with information about a sleeping pill? I mean, it's good, but it's not that good. Not good enough to kill someone over."

"God, you're right. I'm sorry. I'm just not thinking straight. Besides, it's not like he mentioned your name or anything. He was probably psychotic, and I just happened to be in the wrong place, at the wrong time. I'm sorry, babe, it's just... it's not every day your life is threatened."

"I can't imagine... well, we should probably call the cops. It's too dangerous to have someone like that walking the streets."

"You're right." Elijah began reaching into his jean pocket. "Ughh! He groaned. Maybe I better wait until my headache calms down a bit."

"Okay. I'll be right back – I'm going to get you some ibuprofen."

Sam walked into the kitchen and stopped in front of the medicine cabinet. She put her hands on her hips and exhaled loudly, shaking her head. *What the hell do I do now? I need to talk to Chip, but I can't leave Elijah like this.*

She opened the medicine cabinet and looked over the assortment of medicine bottles. *Let's see…vitamins, Benadryl, no, no…*

"Honey! We don't have any ibuprofen. I'm gonna jet to the pharmacy and pick some up for you," Sam yelled from the kitchen. She grabbed her purse, softly kissing Elijah's forehead. "Just whatever you do, don't go to sleep in case you have a concussion. Call me if you feel the least bit sleepy. I'll be right back." She began making her way towards the front door, then stopped. "Hey," she said turning around, "maybe we better just go straight to the hospital."

"No, I'll be fine."

"No, no, you're definitely going to the hospital."

Her answers would have to wait.

~~~

It was well after midnight when Sam stepped foot into the warehouse. Luckily, the neurological testing and X-rays were negative for concussion and internal bleeding. Elijah was cleared to go home that night and was fast asleep when Sam snuck out.

Chip was already there when she arrived, pacing the floor nervously. Sam wondered why he was so frantic. He stopped his pacing and looked at her.

"What's wrong? What happened?"

"It's Brady Ragland. I think he figured out that I'm involved. He came at Elijah today and pistol-whipped him."

"What? Is he okay? What did he say to him?"

"He's fine. We were at the hospital earlier… He said something like, tell your wife to give up the information or you're dead."

Chip sat down in a swivel chair and looked down at the floor.

"That's not good at all." Chip looked up at Sam. "But we will not be manipulated by scare tactics." Chip's voice grew high with anger.

Sam stared at him. Either he's terrible at showing concern or he really just cares about his own agenda.

"Well, what are we supposed to do?" Sam stammered and tapped her foot rapidly.

"We will need to keep moving."

"Keep moving? *We?*"

"Yes, Sam, *we*. They know you've found me. This is bad. You can't stay here anymore. If they know you found me, they will dig into your life and use you to get to me, to my formula. I've kept tabs on them, stayed two steps ahead, even started to piece together a few things, but the tables are turning now. We have to move."

"That's ridiculous. We have to go to the police. I mean they got Elijah involved now. I have to stay. I have to tell him what's going on."

"No," Chip said sharply. "There is no going to the police with this. Remember, there are government officials involved in this, and believe me, they have the police wrapped around their fingers."

"Unbelievable!" Sam threw her hand up. "You expect me to just leave my husband, to just run off without telling him anything? And after he was attacked? You can't be serious."

"I'm very serious. It's imperative, Sam."

"What about the FBI? Can't we go into witness protection or something?"

"Sam, sit down." He motioned for Sam to sit in a chair next to him.

"No, I'll stand, thank you. Make it fast; I have to get back to Elijah."

"Sam, the fact of the matter is, they now have information on you, your adoptive parents, probably the location of all your family members, not just Elijah."

"Oh my god... but that's all the more reason to stay."

"Yes... that's why I've been staying away. We were not supposed to be... spotted together. Now I'm afraid we have no choice but to move elsewhere, set up a new base. They will find us very quickly and believe me, they'll do whatever is necessary to get my formula."

"This is ridiculous! How dare you drag me into this? My entire family."

"Sam, this has been going on for a while now, it's much bigger than you and me, and I have reason to believe that you can help."

"No. If I leave, they may hurt my family to get me to come back. I have to stay here and warn them. We need to tell the police, the FBI, somebody!"

"And tell them what? That people are after your father's top-secret formula that prolongs life after death? They'll lock you up in the hospital, Sam, just like they did on the other side."

Sam felt anger rising from the pit of her stomach.

"Look," she said, her voice quaking, attempting to suppress the volcanic eruption rising to the surface. "I will figure this out, I have to. Now are you going to stay here and help me or are you going to run like a coward?"

The words hit Chip hard. He stared at Sam blankly, his pain tangible.

She didn't care. She could not believe the selfish man before her was her biological father. It was not possible.

"Sam... if I stay, they will catch me."

"And if you go, they will catch *me*! Or my family! Is that what you want?"

"Of course, not..."

"Then stay. Stay and we will fight them together, whatever it takes. Or you can leave us, and we will figure it out on our own. Those are your options." Sam stared at him.

After a short pause and a deep exhale, Chip replied.

"Okay. I'll stay. But we'll need reinforcements."

31. Waking Life: Lucas

Fortunately, Sarah did not have to endure the Taser for long. Her captor was so flabbergasted by the new information she had unloaded on him that he stopped mid-torture. He must have finally figured out that Sarah knew about as much as he did about her father's whereabouts. Still, Sarah wondered if she had said too much.

Rocky had gone back upstairs, Sarah assumed to call his superiors and come up with a new plan. It wasn't more than an hour later when she heard a loud thump and someone coming down the basement stairs. To her great relief and surprise, it was Lucas. He had come down the stairs, breathless and sweaty, with a P22

Walther holstered to his jeans. Sarah looked up at him in amazement. *Who is this guy?*

For a moment, she forgot where she was. Lucas had transformed from a wiry and nervous bookworm, to a slightly more dapper FBI agent. It was true, he was only a modified version of himself. Even so, Sarah wondered where this transformation came from. And how did he find her? *Of course, he's had police training. That would explain it. But still, something about him is different.*

"Lucas, thank god! How did you find me? And how did you get past Rocky?"

"I shot him."

"Seriously?!"

Lucas smiled.

"I'm kidding. He's just knocked unconscious in the other room. We have to hurry and get you out of here before he wakes up."

Sarah stared at him, wondering if this last statement was a joke too.

"We went looking for you. When we couldn't find you, I checked my sources. Naturally, we thought of Rocky. I was actually able to find his address. Clearly he wasn't very clever in bringing you here."

"Yeah... that's amazing, Lucas. You found me so fast."

Lucas flashed her a genuine smile and brushed a strand of hair from his face.

With a pocket knife, he carefully removed the restraints and they were off.

She carefully stepped over the unconscious body of Rocky Henson, who lay sprawled out on the living room carpet, the back of his head matted with blood. The weapon of choice: a broken vase, laying in shards around him.

Sarah shuddered and covered her mouth in horror, this was not a sight she was used to seeing. She looked away and kept walking. At the same time, she could not help but laugh as she pictured Lucas sneaking up behind this man and smashing a vase over his head, like some kind of maniacal cartoon character.

By the time they made it across the parking lot, Sarah could see a crowd gathered across the street, near a large fountain in the park.

"Come on, it could be a good cover in case he gets up quickly. We'll cut through the crowd to the opposite street," Lucas pointed.

"Okay."

People cheered and clapped loudly as Sarah and Lucas jogged up and wedged their way into the center of the crowd. As they walked through, Sarah turned her head to get a glance at whoever was in the center.

A flash of blue light shot up into the sky from the center of the crowd, it exploded and was promptly followed by a bright red and green light.

A kind of light show danced across the sky making vaguely familiar patterns: a star, a sun, a lightning bolt. The man in the center juggled his explosive glow wands with lightning-fast speed.

A type of fireworks, maybe?

For a moment the performer locked eyes with Sarah. There was a yank on her arm. Sarah jumped.

"Come on, don't linger." Lucas pulled her along.

She glanced back one more time. This time she noticed three different pairs of eyes staring at her, from various sections of the crowd.

"Lucas, I think we're being followed."

"I know. Rocky's apparently not here alone. Come on!"

They took a sharp turn to the left, past the large oak tree and ducked into a nearby alley, binging a taxi to a screeching halt as they ran across the road. The three pairs of eyes extracted themselves from the crowd and became three men, approaching rapidly from behind. Lucas and Sarah had broken into a full-out sprint.

"This way!"

Sarah's heart pounded as images of escaping the hospital flashed through her mind in rapid bursts.

Finally, after what seemed like an eternity of running, Sarah and Lucas made it back to the house. Lucas slammed the door shut and stared out the peephole as Sarah bent over, hands-on-knees, breathing heavily, until the taste of iron left the back of her throat.

"I knew it couldn't have been that easy to get out of there," Lucas said after a brief pause. "Rocky, he has more people working for him. Listen, I think they're planning something. They're after you and your father, probably his research. We need to leave here right away."

"But, where do we go?" Sarah could not believe how fast things were moving. *What is happening here?!*

"I don't know, but we can't stay here. Something has happened to me Sarah, in these past few days..."

"What do you mean?"

"There's not a lot of time for me to explain... but since we met, I knew that your case was different, something I just had to take on."

"Okay..."

"I just felt this immediate connection to it, I don't know how to explain it, but I knew I had to help you."

Sarah smiled, remembering the nervous spiel Lucas delivered at their first face-to-face meeting.

"So, two days ago," Lucas started back up, looking down at his hands as he opened and closed them, "two days ago I came across this relic from my childhood, an old pocket watch my grandfather had given me."

A chill ran through Sarah as she remembered her father's pocket watch, Bri had given her.

"And then I noticed something unusual, something I hadn't noticed before."

Sarah blinked at Lucas, realizing that she had momentarily zoned out. She nodded.

"The watch had an engraving, an inscription. How it got there, I don't know, and then I realized... this was not the same watch, someone had switched it out."

"What? Why?"

"Sarah, I think there's a greater reason for you seeking out my services."

By this point, Sarah was filling in the blanks with a number of bizarre scenarios.

"What do you mean? Why would someone switch out your pocket watch?"

"I believe, and I don't know how he would do this, but I believe it was your father, or rather someone that works for him."

"What?! That makes no sense. He's dead!"

"Because..." Lucas looked Sarah squarely in the eye with a grave expression, "the message he left was quite distinct. It read: Seeds of faith are always within us; sometimes it takes a crisis to nourish and encourage their growth."

"Does that mean anything to you?"

Sarah shuddered.

"Susan L. Taylor. She's an American writer and journalist. She's considered the most influential black woman in journalism today. She was one of my idols growing up. But how did you..."

"Right, I figured as much, after what you told me about your journalism career."

Sarah flashed Lucas an irritated look. *Is he always this much of a know it all? How in the world did he connect those dots? They were a galaxy apart.*

Lucas appeared genuinely unfazed by Sarah's annoyance.

"Well, this message hit me hard. It was something my grandfather used to say. It was actually one of his favorite quotes when things were getting hard, when his cancer..." Lucas paused. "He was the one who encouraged me to go into detective work. It was my way of honoring him after he passed."

Sarah opened her mouth to respond, but Lucas kept going.

"A few days ago, I realized that I was helping you for the wrong reasons. It's funny, even though I only started this detective work a few years ago, it was losing meaning for me. You know, I originally wanted to study physics. I just wound up in this career by sheer circumstance. Anyways, when I read this inscription, it all made sense, why I met you, why I was supposed to help you, why I got into all of this in the first place, and then..."

"And then?"

"It hit me Sarah, my entire life in this other world. I suddenly had all this know—"

Sarah stopped listening and retreated into herself again. She suddenly felt like she was in sixth grade again, playing checkers with her sister on the living room couch, while Maggie Pinkerton and the rest of her classmates rode ponies at her ultra-exclusive, birthday party. Conveniently the next day, Maggie informed Sarah that her invitation must have gotten lost in the mail and that she was "so sorry." This was of course, a load of bull.

Sarah stood there, blinking, not knowing what to say, feeling like the only kid not invited to the party.

Jeremy who had been in his bedroom, suddenly emerged. "So, you're connected too now, Lucas?"

"Yes, I guess I am."

"I heard you've got some FBI experience on the other side, if you're connected there too, I could use your help finding my alter."

"I am fully connected, it's an amazing feeling."

"Were you spying on us?" Sarah cut in, thankful for the spontaneous intrusion.

"Listen," Jeremy continued, ignoring her jest, "Lucas, you're a detective and now that you're connected, maybe you can help me find where they're keeping me on the other side. I'm sure I'm still locked away somewhere in that hospital."

Lucas smiled softly, raising his eyebrows.

"Okay, but it's gonna cost you."

32. Dream Life: Incognito

Sam was tired of waiting around for Chip's orders. He was a man who worked under extreme caution, with a not-so-subtle air of paranoia looming about him. It made sense to Sam. After all, he had been on the run for four years now.

Still, being a sitting duck was a good way to get caught. She needed to take action now, and Chip's call for "reinforcements" was nothing more than increased surveillance and security measures for the warehouse.

Sam was unsure if and how she would tell her adoptive parents about this mess. Her mother was so anxious. Maybe she could tell her father first. An attorney's skills could be an asset to them. But would he even believe her?

Sam had been toying with the idea of using social media to discreetly contact the people Chip had warned her about, not to provoke them, but to send a message. She quickly realized that this would be dangerous and stupid.

But it wasn't long before a new plan of action presented itself, in the form of a new team member, named Lucas.

Apparently for the past couple of months she had been working with this man in the waking world and when he got connected in this world, he came to find her. Lucas introduced himself to Sam one evening outside her job. At first glance, he appeared to be a bit nutty, making Sarah a bit nervous when he approached her. But, as he got further into his story, things began to make more sense. He was one of the good guys.

She invited him back to the warehouse that night to meet Chip, who after putting him through an intense interrogation, also realized he was one of the good guys and explained everything to him. After a long night of breaking through the eggshells of countless rotten ideas, they finally hatched a detailed, credible plan.

Jeremy, who was known as Tyshawn Wheeler in this world, was being held in Northern Weaver Psychiatric Hospital in Raleigh, about a three-hour flight away. They would need to leave very early the night before to get there for opening hours.

Lucas, whose name was Eugene in this world, liked to go by Lucas, his other worldly name.

Lucas had uncovered information about a current patient at Northern Weaver, named Margaret Keener. Remarkably, this woman had an uncanny resemblance to Sam. They would need to enter the hospital incognito to avoid detection.

Lucas smiled, tapping at a picture of an affable looking, mustachioed man, in his mid-thirties.

"We'll go as Aunt Janie and Uncle Stephen. They are on the visitor list."

The guy really knows how to find personal information. I wonder what he's got on me.

"We can't go as them, you look nothing like him! Admit it, you just want an excuse to wear that ridiculous mustache." Sam smirked, crossing her arms across her chest.

"Ha!" Lucas let out a short burst of laughter. "Maybe, but hey, have you seen Chip's collection of makeup and wigs?"

"Yes. It's ridiculous and kind of awesome... Listen..." Sam started back up, as they made their way to the back of the warehouse, "how do you know so much about this stuff? You know, hacking into databases, obtaining confidential files?"

"FBI training."

"Wow! That makes sense. So, you're an agent then?"

"Yes I am."

Sam wondered how Lucas had gained her father's trust so quickly. They had barely known each other two days and Chip was already showing him his wig collection.

After brushing her blonde wig out, Sam pulled the long hair into a neat ponytail. She looked at Lucas coquettishly, batting her eyes and pursing her lips.

Lucas smiled.

"Perfect, just like the picture. Now this stuff is really going to do the trick." Lucas pulled out two small tubs from the closet and plopped them down on the table in front of Sam.

"Oh yes, I've seen this before: casting plaster and liquid latex."

Lucas raised his eyebrows in astonishment.

"I was in theatre for a while in college."

"We can make molds into the exact shape of their noses, chins and whatever other features we need to augment."

"Won't they be able to tell they're fake? Especially if they're standing close to us? This is insane, Lucas!"

"Not if we work meticulously."

Sam began to wonder if this plan was more than half a bubble off plumb.

After four hours of perusing files, quizzing each other on family facts, and completing hair, makeup and wardrobe, Lucas and Sam stood before the mirror, inspecting their work. Sam smoothed her seafoam-green blouse and blotted some more red lipstick around her mouth, to accentuate her now surprisingly plump lips.

Lucas looked like a masterpiece himself. She inspected him, then looked back down at the picture of Uncle Stephen.

"You *are* him! Even I can't tell the difference between you and the photo!" Sam laughed. "Oh, this is so weird."

"I know," Lucas stared at himself in the mirror, turning this way and that.

"Okay, don't get too conceited with your new, pretty face," Sam smiled at him. "Do you think we're ready? What if Margaret doesn't recognize you? What if you screw up and say the wrong thing?"

"I shouldn't have to be with her for long. I'm counting on you to pull this off, Sam. Oh, and one more thing, take this."

Lucas handed Sam a small oval pill.

"What's this?" Instantly, Sam thought of the James Bond villain who took the cyanide pills.

"Don't worry, it's not cyanide." Lucas smiled, reading her mind. "It is however, one of *those* pills."

"Those? Oh."

Sam knew what this meant. She would have to take one if they got captured, in case they got killed, so her consciousness could cross over and continue to exist in the other world.

"Do you understand?"

"Yes, we take them if we get captured. It's my father's super pill."

"Exactly, and not a moment too soon."

Sam sighed. Her life really had become an action movie. The problem was, she didn't ask for any of it. Or did she?

This magic drug her father invented was unnamed for its own protection, but she was getting tired of the vague references. So, just for herself, she decided to refer to it as "super pill." It was a cheesy name, something you would hear in a science fiction movie. The irony was too real.

~~~

"Janie and Stephen Miller," said Lucas confidently, as they approached the receptionist desk. "We're here to see Margaret Keener, my niece. We should be on the visitor list."

"One minute, let me check." The receptionist adjusted her large leopard-speckled glasses. After a couple minutes of clicking, she replied, "Yep, there you are. May I see some identification, please?"

"Sure," Lucas said.

Both Sam and Lucas simultaneously reached into their wallets and laid their counterfeit driver's licenses before the receptionist.

"Thank you," she said, after a cursory inspection. "Let me check the schedule and see where she is right now."

"Excuse me, ma'am," Sam started in, "where are your restrooms?"

"Right down that hallway and to the right," the receptionist pointed. Sam, of course, already knew the route she would be taking, drawing the blueprint in her head. She quickly made her way down the hallway, taking a sharp right into the bathroom and pulling the tightly folded scrubs out of her purse. After a quick change, Sam left her empty purse atop the toilet lid. She adjusted her name tag, which read: Cindy Bailey.

This would be no easy task. Sam had already thought through all the possible scenarios: she could be detected as an imposter, or worse, as herself, or maybe someone would ask her a question she could not answer and it would give her away. There was no more time to second guess. Sam stepped back out into the hallway with doubt clouding her head. Her gut churned.

Weaving through the hallway with an air of false confidence, she continued to follow the roadmap in her mind's eye, the one she went over several times, in her intense planning session with Lucas.

Finally, Sam reached the coded-lock door at the end of the hallway. She looked into her palm, where she had written down the seven-digit combination: 2953724. Lucas recovered this combination from an ex-employee he'd scoped out, with a vendetta against Dr. Niles. It didn't take much convincing to get it. Apparently, they never change it.   The doors made a slight whooshing sound as they slid open automatically. Sam stepped through.

The place was much more high-tech than the small sleep lab at Blakeley Pharmaceuticals. Bright, florescent, overhead lights filled the room with a larger-than-life glow. A few people moved about the area, nurses going in and out of patient rooms, doctors checking computer monitors and conversing with hospital personnel.

A sharp-featured brunette in a white lab coat approached Sam. "Can I help you?"

Sam could sense that her presence here was unwelcome, so she needed to drum up one of her valid reasons. She perused her memory for one of the many rehearsed responses she developed for this exact situation.

After a short and hopefully undetectable hesitation, she responded.

"I'm here to administer meds to Ruth Shelly. I'm new. Can you please tell me in which room I can find her?"

The woman gave Sam an incredulous look.

"I haven't seen you here before."

"Oh, that's because I just started this week. I've been in training. This is my first day inside this wing of the hospital."

"I see, well let me check her file."

Okay Sam, you can do this.

After a quick search, the woman simply said, "room 447" and went back to her work.

Sam exhaled an invisible cloud of relief. Again, she was astounded by Lucas's detective work. Feeling only somewhat relieved, she made her way, as calmly as possibly, down the hallway. Based on the floorplan and Lucas's calculations, Tyshawn would most likely be held somewhere in that sleep lab, possibly in an area labeled *restricted access*, somewhere not annotated in the blueprints. Unfortunately, this time, Lucas was unable to find any concrete information.

As Sam approached room 447, she knew time was running out. Finally, after several minutes, she saw it. The unassuming door on the left, at the end of the hall, could have easily been mistaken for a linen closet, except for the black pin pad to the left of the door handle.

This must be it. Damn it, Lucas! I don't have this combination.

33. WAKING LIFE: RUNNING WITH A STORY

"**I** used to just *do* things as a kid, you know, just because I felt like it." Sarah hopped up on a raised, cement sewer drain. "Now I say to myself, 'No Sarah, you are too adult for that. Act your age.' You know what I mean?"

"I think I do," Lucas responded amusedly. He smiled down at the ground, recalling a memory. After a moment he spoke again. "I used to climb trees, every chance I got. Especially large, oak trees. They were my favorite. Oaks are the best for climbing, you know. They have these low, sturdy branches, so you can get a good start up the trunk. I would run at them at full speed, then jump up into them as high as possible. You should have seen my mom's face." Lucas chuckled, shaking his head.

Sarah hopped down from the drain and they continued their intensive planning session/stroll down the Greenway, lowering their voices whenever somebody passed them.

"So, what do we do now?" Sarah said, "I don't understand how you expected me to get Jeremy, I mean Tyshawn, out of the hospital, with me not connected. Do you really think it was wise sending me in there?"

"Yes, it was our only option. But honestly, something went wrong. I woke up today in the middle of the night and I..."

"You what?" Sarah probed.

"Well, I... I remember everything. Two guards captured me and took me to a back room, one of them pulled out a knife, and then everything went black."

"What? What do you mean, everything went black?"

She could see in his eyes that something was very wrong.

"Sarah... I think I died."

"You what?!"

"I think they killed me, at the hospital yesterday."

"But maybe you *are* alive? How else could you know all this right now? Unless..."

"I took one of your father's super pills. I shoved it in my mouth seconds before they apprehended me."

"But, are you sure you're dead on the other side?"

"I don't quite know how to explain it. I just feel like a part of me is gone. I still have that deeper awareness, that fuller perception of myself. I know that my alter and I are integrated fully, that he's not there anymore, he's here, if that makes any sense."

"That's kind of creepy."

"Not really, it's not like I'm living with another person it's still me, just a better, more complete version."

"What are we supposed to do now?" Sarah cried out. "Lucas, this is terrible! Please tell me that we at least got Jeremy out."

"I don't know... You were the one in charge of finding him and they got me before you got back to me. God, I hope they don't have you too, Sarah."

"What if they do? What am I supposed to do? They'll kill me too and I'll never see my father again! What if I'm already dead?!" Sarah could feel her chest tightening like a snake around her heart. She breathed deeply, trying to unravel it. She was having a panic attack and there was no stopping it.

"Slow down, Sarah, just breathe," Lucas said reassuringly, rubbing her back. "I think you would know if you were dead."

"And how would I know?" She snapped back, barely able to get the words out between gasping for air. "I'm not connected... and I've stopped taking Balixa... so I'm not seeing visions... anymore."

"Shhh... that's it, slow deep breaths. We'll figure this out, I promise."

No, there is no stopping this one, Sarah thought as her legs turned to limp noodles underneath her and her vision tunneled to black.

~~~

Sarah slowly opened her eyes and looked around. She was in someone's basement. No, not the familiar basement of her father's house, but an equally messy one, covered, in stacks of notebooks and papers.

"Lucas, did you bring me to your house? Because that can't be a good idea right now."

"Take it easy," said Lucas, coming to her side and supporting her back with his hand. "No, this is not my—"

"Listen," Sarah interrupted, "I think I have an idea. When I was out, I had a dream. In this dream, I made a plan... If those guys can get people on their side using their power and influence, then so can we."

"What do you mean?"

"I mean using the media."

"I'm listening." Lucas picked up Sarah's legs off the couch and draped them over his lap as he sat down next to her. It made her think about Joey.

Sarah decided that Joey must hate her by now. Their relationship must inevitably be over. She had no idea if he had called her, since she no longer had her old phone.

"Sarah?"

"Yes," she continued. "We can fight these guys. I have contacts at *Resonance Weekly* and I think I can figure out an angle that will expose these people for who they really are: scam artists, manipulators... murderers."

"But how are we going to prove any of this stuff?"

"That's where the tricky part comes in. You see, we can't use the dual world angle, not just yet. The public's not going to believe a word of it, not unless we have solid, tangible proof."

"So, what are we gonna write about then?"

"We will expose the dirty stunts they pulled with Jeremy and I at the hospital and hopefully at some point tie it back to Senator Remmer."

"Sarah, what makes you so certain the senator is involved in any of this?"

"I don't know, didn't my father tell you that he was approached by one of the senator's lackeys? That he offered him big money for his formula, but he declined?"

"Yes, that's true. But, how in the world are you going to tie any of this back to the senator? He covers is tracks too carefully. And who would let you write this story?"

"You're right, I'm sure he does. But I know someone who'll let me write the story."

~~~

Sarah sat tightly bundled in a fleece blanket, her pen frantically hovering over a legal pad, in Lucas's longtime college friend's basement.

"Let's see, I will need at least two independent sources," Sarah sat there chewing the end of her pen, "Well, I've got that," she continued her monologue, jotting down a few names. *I could tell Mr. Chesterfield I was going undercover for the paper. Of course, I've been fired, but if I don't have a good enough angle... why did I do the interviews without a tape recorder? Damn it! Not that it would have helped me.* Sarah scribbled down a few more things.

"Lucas, tell me what you think of this." She held the paper out to him from the couch.

Lucas looked up from the laptop he was hunched over.

"I have a few reputable people I can interview for this story, you and Jeremy being two of them. You'll be speaking from a law enforcement angle, and Jeremy, well, from what I've figured out about him, his hospital story might pull some weight."

"You know," Lucas said, "if you can get your old boss to run the story, maybe I can get it out to some of my sources as well. We can at least put a stop to this hospital rouse and maybe get the authorities involved."

"Exactly. If we can't tie this back to the senator, we can at least stop his foot soldiers. Hopefully, all those comatose patients will be set free."

"Do you think it'll be enough for Mr. uh... what's his name?"

"Mr. Chesterfield... maybe, I'm going to try my hardest."

"So, what do we do after the story's released? Let's say we go to all the major news outlets and we're successful, what then? They'll come after us. We'll be in danger again."

"Maybe... but we still have to do this, Lucas. All those patients are being held against their will, being experimented on. There are people after my father's formula to do god-knows-what with it. We can't just sit here and let it happen."

~~~

"Absolutely not!" Mr. Chesterfield slammed his fist on the table, rattling the tall glass of ice water on the edge of his desk.

Sarah had hoped to pique his interest with the story in the first fifteen minutes, when his shock at her return was still potent. But his amused, bewildered state quickly passed. He had been informed of Sarah's hospitalization by her mother and to her dismay, had her position filled immediately thereafter. But Sarah had bigger concerns than getting her job back. Besides, knowing Mr. Chesterfield, all she needed was a fantastic idea to get her foot back in the door.

"Listen," Mr. Chesterfield began his half-hearted explanation, "when you said you were getting a lead on the hospital story, I didn't think you meant getting locked up in one, no offense. I had to fill your position, Sarah. How could I have known how long you would be in there?"

Oh, how sincere.

Maybe she could build on this wobbly sense of guilt she was sensing. She knew she had to pull out all the stops. She had to convince him to let her run the story.

"I understand, but I'm not asking you for much. All I'm asking is that you read the story. I promise I'm not trying to take a job away from someone else. It's just that this story is too important. It's partially the reason why I got locked up. You see, I did get that lead and I followed it. Some of it is based on my experiences from inside the hospital. Now when have we ever run a story like that, huh? You won't believe what I found in there! It's just too good to pass up. Trust me."

"Slow down there, kid! Okay, leave it on my desk and I'll give you a call this afternoon and tell you what I think. And remember, this doesn't mean you get your job back."

"Thank you so much! I completely understand. You won't be disappointed. This is the one, Mr. Chesterfield."

"The one?"

"You know, *the one*. The story that makes a career, which propels you into journalistic stardom. But you know what? I don't even care about any of that. The story just needs to run. It's too important not to run."

"Sarah..."

"Okay, okay. I'm gone. Thanks again!"

34. DREAM LIFE: CODE BREAKING

S am could feel her time running out as she stared at the coded lock with growing fear. *We didn't plan for this! Why didn't Lucas plan for this?* She knew that Lucas couldn't have planned for everything. He was only human. Still, that didn't change the fact that she was now in an impossible position.

Sam decided that the only thing she could do was wait for someone to come out of the room and then to catch the door before it shut. Trying to not appear out of place, Sam walked a little further down the hallway, stopped beside a patient room and looked down at her clipboard, pretending to review the patient chart. She didn't know what else to do.

After a few minutes, she decided this act was futile and that she better make her way back to Lucas and regroup. This whole thing was a mistake. *Why in the world did I take instructions from someone I barely know? Put myself in danger like this.*

The prickle of paranoia began to set in. Sam felt as though the people walking around the hallways were eyeing her suspiciously, like they could see right through to her real intentions.

Sam walked passed the sharp-featured woman again, smiling at her. The woman stared back at her and frowned, then looked away.

Her worst fears were coming true. They had spotted her, a rotten oyster. *I need to get to Lucas!* She quickened her pace and kept her head down, walking directly into someone.

"I'm so sorry." She looked up and shivered. It was him, the handsome stranger, Ignacio Mendoza, the one whom had followed her. He definitely recognized her. His green eyes said it all. He knew her secret.

He squeezed her arm and continued to stare into her eyes, not changing his expression. Then, without a word, he swiveled her around towards the doorway, like a doll, and led her out of the sleep lab, nodding to Dr. N as he took Sam out of the hospital through a back exit.

Where is he taking me? Oh god, he's going to kill me!

Sam began to wiggle this way and that, attempting to break free of his grasp. Ignacio held her tighter.

"Let go of me!"

He pushed her further down the hospital parking lot towards a black Lexus.

"I said, let go!" Sam tried to run away, using what felt like every muscle in her body. She could not budge from his grip.

"Get in," her captor said flatly as he pushed her head down, like a cop, seating her in the driver's seat. She scrambled to get out, kicking him.

Ignacio sighed and pulled a gun out from his jacket, pointing it at her face.

"I said, get in." His voice was no more menacing than before, but Sam could take the hint.

She huffed angrily when she realized resisting would be futile.

"Now go to the back seat."

She sat there, staring blankly.

"I said go!" His voice grew a bit louder and more irritated.

Sam crawled into the back seat, as Ignacio got into the driver's seat and locked the doors behind them. He looked back towards the hospital, keeping his gun aimed at Sam. Sure enough, Dr. N stood there, leaning against the back door with her arms crossed. Ignacio quickly pulled out of the parking lot.

I'm dead. Should I try jumping out of the car? Maybe I could barrel roll, like they do in the movies.

Predicting her next move, Ignacio sped up and quickly got onto the highway.

Sam could not take her eyes off him. There was something about him she couldn't read. Sure enough, about a mile down the road, after extensively checking his side and rearview mirrors, Ignacio exhaled deeply. His entire body went from rigid to slack in a heap of relief. He turned to Sam. His eyes now looked sincere, apologetic.

She wondered how someone could say so much without talking.

"I'm sorry Sam, I didn't mean to frighten you. I just had to put on a show, you know, for the witch."

"The witch? You mean, Dr. N? And like hell! You had a gun pointed at my face! Let me out of this car, immediately!"

"Yes, if you want. But please, just give me one minute to explain. I mean you no harm. The gun was just an act. I didn't want to do that to you, but she was watching, and you were not cooperating."

"Well, of course I wasn't cooperating. You put a damn gun in my face and dragged me into your car!"

"I'm so sorry I scared you, but I promise, I'm not working for her anymore. She only thinks I am. Sam, you're in real danger and we need to get you out of here quickly."

This is not my life. This cannot be my life!

"But... where is Lucas?"

"I don't know. I saw some orderlies grab him and take him into a room. I don't know what happened after that. But I couldn't help you both Sam, I'm so sorry. I had to get you out."

"No! We have to go back for Lucas! What if they hurt him?"

"No, we can't. I'm sorry. It's not safe. Sam, whatever could happen to him, probably already has."

"What are you saying?"

"I'm saying... Lucas is probably dead."

"What?!" She blurted out. "What do you mean? Why would they kill him?" A wave of nausea hit her.

"These are very bad people Sam, dangerous people, and they are puppets for the witch, the worst one of all. That is how they operate – they get rid of people they have no use for."

Sam remembered the cyanide capsule.

"Lucas wouldn't say anything. He would keep quiet to protect me. But they can't get away with this. We have to do something! My god, Lucas was just here. But if he's gone then he's taken the capsule. I can still contact him... but I'm not connected. Damn it!"

Ignacio looked at her quizzingly.

Sam held her head in her hands and moaned loudly. She looked up at Ignacio.

"Are you sure we can't go back for him?"

"I'm positive. It will be impossible. Her people are everywhere. Besides, these people work swiftly; whatever was going to happen, has already happened."

"Stop saying that! You don't know that!"

Ignacio sighed and shook his head.

Sam did not like this, not one bit. She felt like a traitor and completely helpless. She was not even sure she could trust this man, as sincere as he sounded. How could she know that he wasn't a mole for Dr. N or that he didn't have his own devious plans?

If panic was in effect before, full on terror had set in, to erase any doubt, the minute Ignacio turned the street corner a few blocks from the warehouse.

He knows. Which means... they know... which means...

~~~

Her father's warehouse had been turned upside down. Chip was gone. Sam walked around the turned over tables and emptied boxes, paralyzed with terror.

"They were looking for his formula," said Ignacio.

The nausea suddenly turned into a bubbling suspicion, rising through her with the force of the elements. *How did he know all this information? Have they all been spying on them? How did they find the location of the warehouse?*

"And how do you know about this?" Sam turned towards Ignacio. "Who are you, huh? And how can I know that you're not just luring them here, right now, so they can torture whatever they're looking for out of me?" Sam pushed Ignacio several times, attempting to incite his anger, to jostle his true colors to the surface.

"Sam, stop, please stop." He backed up, shielding himself from her blows. "I'm not with them, I swear! The witch threatened to take everything from me when I found out what her true plans were. She has them all fooled, everybody!"

"So, tell me!" Sam pushed him again, losing her footing and a bit of her dignity, tripping over a pile of books.

Ignacio suppressed a laugh. She glared at him, trying to recover her pride, and then plopped down in a chair.

"And will you stop calling her, *the witch*? It makes her sound like a Disney villain."

Ignacio sat down too.

"Fine. But that is what she is to me, a witch."

Ignacio explained how he first become involved with the hospital, how he began as an orderly, and when promised a tremendous pay raise, agreed to follow Dr. N's "special instructions." It was hard to resist that kind of money. His sister was battling her second round of stomach cancer and was not making enough to pay the hospital bills. His parents were long gone, and he could not pass up the opportunity.

Ignacio filled Sam in on everything he knew. Dr. N was working directly with the California senator, Nathaniel Wood, known as

Thomas Remmer, the North Carolina senator, in the other world. He was her brother and Dr. N was his main foot soldier in both worlds, and although she wasn't connected herself, they had created a system using people both connected and not, to provide them with a constant stream of information. This was partially how she used the sedated people in the hospital. They were all connected, and she would send them out to gather intel in both worlds and have them report back to her. None of them ever went for help, because she had them trapped, in more ways than one. Dr. N was the senator's partner in crime and the face of all the evil committed, while he hid behind the scenes, until his grand debut in the November elections.

Dr. N and her people knew all about her father's super pill. How? Ignacio wasn't sure about this part. But they were well versed in the dual-world phenomenon. Apparently, the senator was going to use the super pill, and although Ignacio didn't know for sure how, he suspected it had to do with getting connected, becoming a more powerful man, and ultimately gaining full control over the formula. From everything he had heard, the senator was as sleazy as Dr. N, and although they were working together for now, there was no honor among these thieves. This highly disturbing truth was all he claimed to know. Most of the information was gathered from eavesdropping on clandestine phone conversations between Dr. N and the senator.

Then, Ignacio began questioning the assignments he was given. One day, after being asked to spy on Sam at work, Ignacio learned about the senator's plans to get his hands on the super pill. Before, he always did what he was told, but after overhearing Dr. N's conversation with the senator, he decided to confront her. He told her that he no longer felt comfortable doing her dirty work, and was promptly instructed to proceed anyway, with the vague added threat that she couldn't guarantee his sister's safety if he stopped.

Sam was highly disturbed. Now she understood why Ignacio had followed her. She hoped that he was on the right side of the fight now.

After a few rounds of questions and answers, Sam was becoming convinced. If this man was not on her side, then he was a great liar. Either way, he offered her inside information that she could not pass up. Her mission was becoming clearer. She would need to rescue her father and stop the senator via stopping Dr. N and her minions.

"I think I know where they took your father," Ignacio said.

~~~

Acrid smelling fumes rose up through the floor vents. Sam put her hand over her mouth and held back the violent cough that threatened to erupt from her throat, terrified that she would give herself away. Her eyes watered as she looked at Ignacio. He put a finger to his lips to quiet her, craning his head to look around the corner of the hallway, gun stretched out before him.

Ignacio and Sam stood inside a remote underground, chemical research facility, just outside of Raleigh. Although Ignacio had security clearance, he had to sneak Sam in unnoticed.

Sam took some long deep breaths through her shirt to steady her heartrate. A drop of sweat ran into her eye. She wiped it away tentatively, hyperaware of every sound her body made. It dawned on her that she would have to become accustomed to this new lifestyle: sneaking into dangerous places, with even more dangerous people.

She had never heard of this place before. In fact, as Ignacio had explained to her, there was a box factory above it and all the road signs leading up to it said so. The box factory, of course, was run by the Senator's people. It unnerved Sam to think how many people were working for the senator. It was like he had amassed an army, his soldiers hiding in plain sight.

"Ready?" Ignacio whispered.

"Ready as I'll ever be, I guess."

They inched their way down the hallway, Ignacio with his military grade handgun and Sam with the P22 Walther he had given her. She had never carried a gun on her before, and until she met her father, she had never fired one. She just never had any need or interest in doing so.

But now she was feeling all of its malicious draw, the power the weapon carried, the potential damage it could inflict. She prayed there would be no need to use it, but the way things were going, those chances were slim. She tightened her white knuckles harder around the grip, clenched her jaw, and inched her way further down the hallway.

As they walked past door after closed door, she wondered how deep they would get before they reached them. How many bad guys would there be? They were armed, undoubtedly.

She imagined a big gunfight, her father being taken hostage by the ringleader, who would put a gun against his head and make his demands. They would make their escape, probably in a Bond-style car chase, running over fruit stands and mailboxes along the way. She tried to shake these ridiculous thoughts from her mind, but what else was she supposed to think? Ignacio turned out to be a man of few words in this situation, which was not helping her.

Sam's heart beat in her temples as she realized she could die, that this could be one of her last moments on earth. She thought back to her last conversation with Elijah, how he told her he loved her after she tucked him in to sleep after he came back from the hospital. She remembered her last conversation with her parents: some mundane exchange of words with her mother about buying eggs, about how her father would be cutting the grass that weekend. No, Sam decided that this was not a suitable time to meet her maker. She was determined to stay alive.

Just as another one of her hypothetical, action movie reels began to roll, she felt Ignacio's strong arm push her backwards. He looked back at her and pointed forward with his head. Sam looked around the corner and saw them: a group of men in white lab coats stood around some very large, high-tech machinery. What looked like the gigantic MRI machine from the hospital sat inside a small, glass room. The machine was on and humming. Seemingly, someone was inside. Her father? Two men were looking at the computer monitor from behind the glass. She could hear them talking.

"Do you see anything yet?

"No, he's closing his mind to us. You need to increase the Scopolamine."

Scopolamine?

Sam remembered seeing that drug in her father's lab, Devil's Breath, how he referred to it. It was used for rendering a person incapable of making sound decisions: essentially, the worst kind of roofie imaginable.

Two stern looking men, with the physique of WWE wrestlers, stood in each corner of the room. Bodyguards, no doubt.

Sam quickly did the math. The bodyguards in the back were definitely armed. The men in the lab coats did not look like the sort of people that would be, but who knew? They were outnumbered and it was now or never. They had to take them out. Sam looked over at Ignacio. He nodded to her in affirmation.

35. WAKING LIFE: DR. FOWLER

S arah couldn't help getting a bit sidetracked, to get a piece of normalcy out of this whole experience. Dr. Fowler's house was on the other side of a scenic park, so Lucas and Sarah decided to cut through it, before continuing headlong into their mission.

The blooming red and purple pansies and poppies reminded Sarah of home. Lucas and Sarah took the gravel path towards the fountain. Out of the corner of her eye she noticed two older men sitting on a park bench across the way.

"Young lady," she heard one of the men say.

She turned in the direction of the voice.

"Young lady, come here," the old man beckoned.

The one beckoning Sarah over, looked about ten years older than the one beside him.

Maybe they're brothers. As she began to approach them, she noticed the other man began shaking his head at her.

"Don't come over here."

"Don't listen to him. Come over here," the other man implored again.

Sarah froze in her tracks, unsure of how to proceed.

"You two are confusing me."

"Come here," the man beseeched.

"If you would like to ask the young lady a question, you can ask her from here."

"Do you want to ask me something?" Sarah asked.

"Yes, I want to talk to you, come here."

Again, Sarah made her way towards the bench.

"Don't come over here," the other man retorted again. "He's not right in the head, if you know what I mean."

Oh.

At this comment the other man grimaced at his companion and shooed him away with his hand.

"Come here," he continued, smiling at Sarah.

Sarah didn't know what possessed her to approach this Tweedledee and Tweedledum duo, but she found her feet moving forward, despite the other man's insistent reservations.

Lucas stayed behind and watched on, tentatively.

When Sarah got close, the goading man looked up at her and smiled. Then, with the swiftness of a storm cloud moving over the sun, his expression changed. He grabbed her wrist and pulled her to his side.

Startled, Sarah tried to pull away.

"I told you not to come over here. Let go of her Mort!"

"Watch out Kathleen!" The man said, looking right through her as if she were a ghost. "Don't go in there Kathleen, it's not a safe place for a young woman."

Sarah sharply withdrew her wrist and backed away.

Still a bit shaken, Sarah and Lucas arrived at Dr. Fowler's later
that afternoon, and over a lunch of turkey sandwiches and
lemonade, Sarah explained the happenings of the past month. Lucas
trusted Sarah and so he too disclosed what he had learned about
the key players and about Sarah's father.

"Yes," Dr. Fowler said after a time, stroking his long beard, "I've
been doing some of my own research after your departure. Sarah,
I'm so glad to see that you're alright."

"I'm fine. They kept me locked up for their own agenda, but I got
out before they could hurt me."

"Yes, that's what I thought as well. You seemed like a sensible
girl, just frightened, that's all. Anyone would have the wits scared
right out of them, seeing what we saw in that cave. It's true that your
father was doing research that would be considered otherworldly,
parapsychology, if you will. It makes perfect sense why he needed to
keep it hidden from the scientific community, even from me. I
returned to that cave for his journals. Here, follow me, I want to
show them to you."

Sarah and Lucas stood up and followed Dr. Fowler through the
living room, into the kitchen, then down a steep set of stairs that
lead into the basement, probably his working area. Sarah noticed
the basement door looked differently from the rest of the doors in
the house, it was made of metal rather than wood. The surrounding
walls had a metallic look as well.

Sarah got the strange feeling that she was inside of a large,
industrial cage. An uneasy feeling began to set in. Lucas was
apparently on the same wavelength.

"Listen Dr. Fowler," he began, "We can bring the journals
upstairs, the lighting is much better up there."

"Nonsense!" Dr. Fowler retorted. "There's plenty of light down
here. Here let me switch on these overhead lights." Dr. Fowler made
his way around the room, flipping switches. "And if you're wondering
why this room looks so different than the rest of the house, it's

because this is my work area, where I go to do all my most crucial, confidential work."

Confidential work. Hmm... I wonder if this guy works for the government, the feds maybe... or the CIA. He would probably never tell us that.

"What kind of confidential work?" Lucas asked, scrutinizing the table covered in journals and folders, but trying to be tactful and not touch anything.

"Ah, now that is not something I cannot disclose to you. It's classified after all."

"I see," Lucas said.

"Now my dears, I'll be back in a moment. I'm going to bring down the letter I received from your father again, Sarah. There's a clue in it I was able to decipher from his journals. Would you like anything to drink while you're down here, a lemonade perhaps?"

"Maybe some coff—"

The door slammed behind Dr. Fowler before Lucas could get his words out. Sarah was already up the stairs, trying the door. It was locked.

Banging and screaming proved to be fruitless. It was painfully clear that Dr. Fowler got the best of them.

"Oh god! And I told him everything! He knows everything, Lucas!"

"I know."

"And I thought I could trust him, I mean my father gave him the letter, didn't he? Oh no, he probably stole that too! Or maybe he framed him."

Sarah sat on the floor, clutching her head in her hands. She began to rock herself back and forth. Lucas was silent. He kept the same confused expression on his face since Fowler closed the door. He seemed to be turning something over in his mind.

"What are you doing just standing there?! Help me find a way out!"

Sarah sprung up off the floor and began frantically running around the room, trying to find an opening, a door, a window, a latch, anything that could possibly help them escape.

She quickly realized, it was of no use. She might as well be trying to claw her way out of a cinderblock.

"It makes perfect sense."

"What does?" Sarah whined and plopped herself back down on the floor, wrapping her arms around her knees.

"Dr. Fowler was your father's closest confidant, right?"

"So he says."

"Well, what I imagine happened is that he did let him in on some of the research he was working on, but things went south. Dr. Fowler probably wanted to use the research for his own purposes. When Fowler saw you that day you first came to Lizard's Foot, he knew that he could use you somehow, maybe to get to your father's research, and now that he has us..."

"What?"

"It's only a matter of time before..."

"Before what? Spit it out Lucas! What are you thinking?"

"I'm thinking that there's a reason he locked us in here. We're sitting ducks. I think he might be bringing them here."

"What do you mean bring— oh... oh no! He's probably working with Dr. N. You know, I remember the director of West Forrester Care... he became so scared when I asked him about speaking to someone about my father... he gave me Dr. Fowler's name and address."

"Do you think he's in on it, too?"

"No, I don't. I don't think he knew what Dr. Fowler was doing. I honestly think he was trying to help me. They've got Dr. Blanch scared. I don't think he's on Dr. N's side. You should have seen the way he looked at me... he was definitely scared."

"Well one thing's for sure: we need to find a way out of here before whoever's coming, gets to us."

Sarah looked at Lucas with annoyance and thought that for someone as intelligent as he was, he had a knack for not contributing anything useful to a conversation. Captain Obvious Syndrome, she called it.

She began pacing around the room again, a bit more aimlessly, pulling open drawers, looking through documents, searching behind corners. Lucas followed suit.

"Look, here's a flower vase with daisies." Sarah picked up the vase off the desk in the back of the room and waved it around.

"How thoughtful of him to give us something pretty to look at... You know, it's kind of heavy for a vase... actually... how often do you see a metal vase?"

"Sarah..."

An expression of horror came over Lucas's face.

"What Lucas?" She snapped back. "You know, it almost feels like there's something inside it..."

"Sarah, don't! That's not a vase, it's an—"

Lucas rushed over to her, in an attempt to grab it from her hands. But it was too late. Sarah dumped the contents on the table. A cloud of powdery smoke rose up around them, sending them both into coughing fits. She looked down and frowned in a moment of confusion. Then it hit her. Her eyes grew large and watery. Lucas grabbed Sarah up in his arms and held her tightly. She trembled violently.

"Lucas, I think these are ashes. Oh god, I think... these are my father's ashes!"

36. Dream Life: Taking a Bullet

The first shot resonated around the room with a loud reverberating clang. Then there was silence. It dragged on painfully, the way it did during a car accident, right before the moment of impact. Every sense was heightened.

She looked down at her hand, it was trembling. To her astonishment, she had fired the first shot, and she had missed. The clang she heard was the bullet ricocheting off of a metal table behind one of the bodyguards. Ignacio's gun went off next and hit the very bodyguard she may or may not have been subconsciously aiming for, through the forehead. After that, things progressed quickly.

Streams of bullets began flying in their direction. Ignacio pulled Sam down to the ground and they both proceeded to fire back. Sam's heart pounded so loudly, she could not differentiate between the pumping of blood in her ears and the deafening bullets exploding around her.

They whizzed past her, a cloud of angry hornets with a death sting. She kept firing, peeping around the corner and firing again, until it was just her empty gun clicking.

After only a couple minutes, silence fell upon the room. She got up to her feet and slowly inched her way forward. The bodyguards lay sprawled out on the floor, both bleeding out profusely. She looked back at Ignacio. He was clutching the top of his shoulder. The blood seeped from between his fingers.

"Oh no! We need to get you to a hospital."

"What about you?"

"What do you mean?"

And then she felt it. The haze of bullets and her wildly beating heart had overshadowed everything else. Sam began to feel a pain in her side, which was rapidly increasing in intensity. She lifted up the corner of her shirt. The bullet had only grazed her, but had burned her side and taken out a small patch of flesh.

Sam glanced down at her side. "Oh this!" she said jokingly. "I'll be fine." She pressed her shirt firmly into her side to abate the bleeding, surprised by her own response. Who was this Sam that could take a bullet and just walk away?

"Sam?"

That voice.

"Sam dear, is that you?"

Her memory came back to her, as crisp as the day it happened: her father calling her from the basement of her childhood home. She was seven, bounding down the stairs with her little green notebook in hand. Her father beckoned her to look in his journal. He had written down a riddle for her to solve: I am a creature with a curious name. The mirror eyes on my back will play tricks on your brain! When a bird sees me perched, it flaps away in fright, but when you see me in the air, my dear, you will clap with delight!

Easy one. The butterfly.

And just like that, Sam remembered everything. Her other life came flooding back to her with the swiftness of a door blown open by a strong gust of wind. She could suddenly see both of her lives in totality, all the moments of childhood on, and all the emotions that came with them. The two selves had merged into one new person. She had been recreated. She was connected.

"Dad!" Sam rushed towards the glass room and swung open the door.

Her father was sitting up, in a somnolent stupor, barely aware of the world around him. She threw her arms around him with all the fervor and intensity of four lost years. The search was over. She had found him.

"Sam..." said Chip drowsily, "It's you. You've come back to me."

"Dad it's me, I mean, the other me is here too."

He held her tightly and pressed his lips to her cheek, then pulled her back and looked at her, his eyes welled up with tears.

"You mean Sarah? That means you've connected. I've missed you so much."

"I've missed you too." Sam threw her head into his chest and sobbed. A few minutes later she pulled away.

He looked at her, through the foggy haze of the drugs.

"Sam, can we be sure that you're fully connected?"

"What do you mean?"

"You remember both lives, but does Sarah in the other world?"

"You mean—"

"I mean this process of connecting is two-fold. Sometimes you connect in sync, in both worlds. Other times, your other self has to catch up... ugh..." Chip moaned, holding his head in his hands. "Sorry honey, I'm feeling a bit drowsy."

"I don't think the other me has connected yet. Listen, we need to get you to a hospital."

"No. It's too dangerous. Take me to the warehouse. I have something... that counteracts this drug."

"But Dad, they turned everything over in there."

"I know, trust me. I have secret storage spaces they would not have found... and what about you?" Chip suddenly noticed Sam's blood-soaked shirt. "You're hurt." He looked at her side, wide-eyed, wobbling back and forth on the table of the brain imaging machine. "You need a hospital yourself."

"No, it's not that serious, just a nick. We stopped them." She looked over to Ignacio who was now standing at her side.

"Not quite. Look at the screen." Chip motioned towards the computer screens outside the room.

Ignacio and Sam walked over to them, carefully stepping over the body of one of the deceased scientists who was sprawled out on the floor, his lab coat saturated with his quickly leaking blood. The other scientist was nowhere in sight.

Sam shuddered, wondering if she had killed any of them herself.

"Damn it!" Ignacio suddenly slammed his fist down on the screen, making both Sam and her father jump. "The formula extraction worked. He must have escaped through the back."

Sam looked carefully at the screen and frowned, the symbols of a chemical formula were printed all over it.

~~~

Sam squirmed in her chair as she watched the doctor that was called to the warehouse work on Ignacio's wound. Ignacio informed her that they would not be going to a hospital, as they would most likely be detained and questioned. Her wound was small and took a matter of minutes to patch up, but Ignacio's was much more extensive. He groaned in pain, his voice piercing the air with a high-pitched yelp that made Sam's hair stand up. With this short notice, his friend was only able to bring local anesthesia, the bare minimum that was necessary. Knowing she was of no use to anyone in that moment, Sam walked into the other room and put in her headphones. She laid back and closed her eyes, trying to be somewhere else, feeling the softness of the plush chair pressing against her back.

She awoke to Ignacio gently shaking her shoulder. She drowsily looked up at him through the fog of sleep and instinctively reached into her front jean pocket to pull out her tiny mobile phone, which had surprisingly stayed put through the whole ordeal.

She couldn't decide which was more alarming: the current time (5:25 a.m.) or the twenty three missed calls. It was a couple days after Elijah's assault, and he'd been on edge since it happened. He did go to the police, but nothing had come of it yet. *I must have completely lost track of time. Elijah must have sent the police after me by now, oh god.*

She pressed two to speed dial him and then immediately hung up. What would be her alibi? She racked her brain, searching for a believable story: she lost track of time, she was in a bad car accident, she got lost, she fell ill. Then it dawned on her: she would simply tell him the truth.

It was close to 6:00 a.m. when Elijah arrived at the warehouse.

"I don't know if this is a good idea," Sam's now-alert father said as Elijah came into the room.

"Dad, he needs to know. There's no way I can keep this act up. I'm sorry. Besides, we need all the help me can get now."

"Dad?" Elijah looked at Chip, puzzled and then it dawned on him, the pointed nose, the thin, curved lips.

"Sam, what the hell is going on?"

Sam sighed and motioned for her husband to sit. No longer could she look at this man, the love of her life, the one she chose, in the same way.

Sam explained the entirety of what had occurred, since the search for her birth parents began. Ignacio spent a considerable amount of time explaining himself to her father, proving his allegiance. After the ordeal was over, Elijah sat back in his chair with a blank expression. A couple minutes later, he spoke.

"I still don't understand why you wouldn't just come to me, why you all felt that I couldn't be trusted to protect her."

Sam rolled her eyes at Elijah to let him know that she didn't need his protecting.

"Now, I can put all that behind me," Elijah continued, "but Sam, listen." He took both her hands in his and looked into her eyes. "I'm here for you. I don't care how dangerous this is for me. I want to help."

"Okay," she replied.

Sam turned over this idea for a moment. Nothing in their wedding vows mentioned for danger or in the face of death. It also never occurred to her that she would be with two different men, in two different worlds. Should she permanently call it off with Joey, since Elijah was technically her husband? She doubted Joey wanted anything to do with her at this point anyway. The whole thing just felt wrong.

Sam suddenly remembered her mother dying at the hospital. This was her birth mother, who was alive and well in the waking world. She wondered how her life had been cut short, and how husband and wife were now completely and hopelessly separated, stuck on different sides of the same coin, never to meet again. She knew how much her father must be hurting.

She marveled at their relationship, how they found each other in two different worlds and fell in love. She wondered what would have happened if they didn't.

"We need to regroup," Chip began, interrupting her thoughts.

"I'm way ahead of you," Sam replied.

"What do you mean?"

"In the other world, I went to the papers. I've exposed them! Lucas helped me. I'm hoping they'll be arrested very soon."

"This is good. This is also very dangerous. Where is Lucas, by the way?"

"He's gone Dad, Dr. N's people killed him... but he took the super pill, so he's stuck on the other side."

"Oh no... I'm so sorry."

"And we didn't get Tyshawn out. Even if we expose the truth on the other side, all those poor people here will still be stuck. We need to go to the papers here too. We can't just leave Tyshawn in that hospital.

"But you don't have any inside information like you do on the other side or any connections to the newspaper here," Chip said in dismay.

"But I do," Ignacio cut in.

Everyone turned to look at him.

"I have inside information, and I am willing to say everything I know to turn that witch in. Otherwise, my sister will not be alive for long."

37. Waking Life: Intuition

Moments later, the lights went out and they were standing in total darkness.

Sarah felt her head begin to swim, pulling her mind away from reality, until she slowly found herself back, face to face, with the nightmare of the caves.

The barn owls emerged from the blackness, swooping down over her as she lay helpless and rigid on the floor. Her body was one giant, pulsating heart. She was letting go and could not tell where the owls were coming from, whether from her mind, out of the cave of Lizard's Foot, or out of the dark corners of the basement.

She felt the gentle tug of sanity leaving her body with each exhale and floating through the air before her. She was well beyond the point of caring. In fact, she felt like embracing it. Beyond the syncopated rhythm of blood pumping and wings beating, she could hear Lucas's voice calling her name softly, as if through the wall of another room.

"Sarah... Sarah! What are you doing?"

Lucas's voice grew louder and started to pull Sarah out of her hallucination-fueled daydream. She was now realizing that this was in fact a daydream. She had not experienced any visions for a while now, as she had not taken any Balixa in over a week.

"Sarah, please get up. I know you're scared, but we'll find a way out of here. I promise."

Lucas's voice was delicate and filled with promises, sweet sounding to Sarah's ears; a pleasant addition to Sarah's daydream, nothing more. She did not want to leave, though she could now feel her head resting in his lap, his hand gently stroking her hair, pulling her further and further out of the vision.

And then she felt something, much more uncomfortable: the pain in her chest, the familiar aching that had driven her here, looking for her father. Now all she wanted was to escape, to not feel the pain that had persisted all these years. She closed her eyes and began to drift off again.

"Sarah, no," Lucas pleaded, now an irritating reminder of the outside world she was growing to hate. "Sarah please, I need you. Don't check out again."

Sarah considered the option. If she was to check back in, what was there for her? A half-dead father, the black vault of the basement she was now trapped in, and Lucas... no, it was not enough.

Then another sound became perceptible. At first, Sarah thought it was her heart beating in her ears again, but no, it was much more precise, mechanical. The ticking was coming from Lucas's pocket.

The pocket watch! It's what lead him to becoming connected. Sarah thought of her father giving him this watch as a sign of hope, a promise. Sarah remembered the promises she made to her father.

No, I can't stay like this. I have to move. There has to be a way out of here.

And then, in her moment of despair, a thought emerged; she had no idea where it came from, but there it was. The words came back to her deliberately and steadily, as if someone was dictating them to her: *Look through one and you will find that you can see clearly to the other side. Look through the other and you will only see yourself staring back. The glass is a mirror... the mirror is a glass... the owls are watching... follow them to where they sleep... where they sleep... where they...*

And then she was back in the basement. Nothing around her but blackness and the softness of Lucas's lap underneath her head, his hand softly stroking her head, starting from her forehead and working his way to the back of her head, his fingers gently working through the strands of hair, lightly scratching her scalp. She opened her eyes and tried her best to sit up. Once she was in an upright position, still leaning against Lucas, she spoke.

"Look, I think I know what to do. I've been doubting myself since this whole thing started. Every time I listen to my gut, to my intuition, I get somewhere, I find something, there's a breakthrough. I had a bad feeling about Dr. Fowler as soon as we entered the house today, but I chose to ignore it. If I can just listen to my gut, like Dad said in his letter, I think I can figure out some way out of here."

"Okay, I'm following you so far. What did you have in mind?"

"Well, what my instincts are telling me right now is that Fowler was my father's closest confidant."

"Right, we established that. What else?"

Sarah rolled her eyes. "If I could just get connected, then I could probably find a way to get out of here. If I could reach myself on the other side, then I could talk to Dad about this."

"Yeah, but why do you think you haven't connected so far? What's the missing piece?"

"Not trusting myself. That's the entire reason. Here's my other thought, Balixa makes people see things from the other side, right?

So, there's something about sleep that helps you connect to your other self."

"Okay, still following."

"I remember you telling me something about the time difference between the two worlds. If it's really that late over there, there's a good chance my other self could be asleep. If she's connected, and I know you said she wasn't before you died, but if she's connected now, then maybe I can go to sleep, somehow wake her up, and she can go get help."

"Okay I get the sleep thing, because I'm pretty sure that's how memories are transferred between the two worlds. I mean, I remember stuff from the other side when I wake up in the morning each day. But, how are you going to wake yourself up? Don't you think that sounds... I don't know... a little far-fetched?" Lucas said.

"I know. I know it does. But there's no phone signal here, and we have no other ideas to try."

"You're right. I'm fresh out."

Sarah lay back down into Lucas's lap. "Stroke my hair again, it'll help me fall asleep faster."

Sarah could feel Lucas blushing in the darkness. She felt resolve, a sense of peace she had not felt before. This feeling was vastly different from the ruthless ambition that drove her all these years to find her father. It was not despair or defiance that controlled her now. Sarah knew what she must do and that no matter what happened, she was on the right path now. With her newfound confidence, she drifted off to sleep.

~~~

Thirty minutes later Sarah awoke. She yawned loudly and stretched her arms out into the blackness.

"I did it," she said after a moment.

"Did what?" Lucas said sleepily.

"I connected."

"You did? That's amazing! So, your alter knows where we are?"

"Well no, I didn't wake up Sam, but I became connected right before I went to sleep. It's strange. As I was falling asleep, all the memories came back to me. I remember everything, Lucas!"

"You did? That's wonderful! It's such a strange feeling, isn't it?"

"Yes, it's overwhelming, a lot has happened, but I can't process it all right now, I need to stay focused. I don't think she woke up when I went to sleep. I mean, I was dreaming the whole time, but it got me thinking."

Sarah sat up across from Lucas in the dark, their knees touching, as they were both sitting cross-legged.

"Yeah?"

He spoke softly, in acute awareness of how close they were to each other. "I think I can reach her in another way, or rather send her a message."

"How? You mean right now, without her even waking up? How would that be possible? How would that even be effective if she doesn't get your message until she's awake? It might be too late by then."

"I have this idea," Sarah continued, "If sleep is the bridge to the other side, and using Balixa helped retrieve memories from the other side, then there has to be some way to get messages directly to the other side, you know? In his letter, my father said that the glass is a mirror and the mirror is a glass. Well, the problem with a two-way mirror is that you can only see through it if you're standing on the correct side of it. But here's the catch: I remember playing with those two-way mirrors when I visited my father at the university. If you stood really close to one, then you could be seen from the other side, just barely, if the other person looked very closely. The illusion would be broken. My father showed me this. So maybe dreams are the bridge. Just think about it. How many times have you had a dream and remembered it the next day? And these visions I was having, they were like dreams too, just as vivid and maybe even created from the same part of the brain that produces dreams. So, using that logic, when are we closest to our other selves?"

"In our dreams," Lucas said in a voice blossoming with understanding. "Sarah, I think you may be on to something."

"Yes! Yes!" Sarah's voice grew louder with excitement. "Exactly. We sleep, we dream, we awaken in our other lives. That must be how Balixa works, it must somehow tap into that storage of memories."

"So how will you send yourself a message? And one that's memorable enough to wake you up and get you moving?"

"I will lucid dream. I will control my dream and let myself know what's going on."

"And you just happen to know how to do that at will?"

"Sure," Sarah smiled. "I've been doing it since I was a kid. You know, there's a lot of videos on the internet that can teach you how to do it. Besides, you know who my father is, right?"

"Well then, how will you ensure that your other self receives the message?"

"Here's my crazy idea: if my other self also has this ability to lucid dream, or even if she doesn't, maybe she will be there, inside my dream world. I will give her the message and then she can wake up and tell my father what's going on, then get right back to me with his instructions. Maybe she can even take something to induce sleep and get back to me faster."

"Sarah, this is really starting to sound far-fetched. That would mean the dream world is a shared reality where you two can meet, at the same time. How do you suppose such as place even exists?"

"I don't, but my gut is telling me that this is the right thing to do, and after all, it was my gut that just got me connected, wasn't it?"

"Well, when you put it that way... Okay, fine, I'm in, not that I'm doing anything. You know... I'm gonna have to up your retainer for this," he smirked. "Now, lay back down."

Sarah laughed as she settled back down into Lucas's lap, suddenly realizing that she hadn't paid him in weeks, and that he hadn't reminded her about it either.

"I am dreaming. I am dreaming. I am dreaming." Sarah repeated the words aloud while looking up to where her hands should be, stretched out before her.

"What are you doing?"

"It's one of the tricks. If I do this before going to sleep, there's a high probability that I'll repeat it in my dream, and that will be a signal to me that I'm dreaming."

"That's awesome! Well keep going then. I won't interrupt anymore."

"Okay."

Sarah began her chant again. After a few minutes, Lucas began stroking her head again, brushing her hair behind her ears. Sarah closed her eyes and began to drift off, and as she did, she thought about how easy it was with him, and at what point they had crossed that line, when she stopped being his client and became his friend, when they became more.

~~~

Sarah opened her eyes and found herself staring at her reflection in a full-length mirror. The image reflected back at her had a blurry resemblance, as if she were looking at herself without her glasses on, or through water. She looked down at her hands.

"I am dreaming."

And then she was in. She knew now that this was her dream world. *Clever,* she thought, observing her reflection. *I wonder if...* She walked closer to her reflection and put a hand to the glass.

"Ah!" Sarah let out a scream and jumped back, as the movement of her hand's reflection did not mirror her own.

It's a two-way mirror! Is that my other self? She can't see me... Sarah began looking around for a door and could find none. Then she remembered, this was her dream and she could manipulate it any way she wanted. In her mind, she imagined a door and began walking towards where it should be. Out of her black universe emerged a door, flying wide open before she could open it, filling the room with light.

"It's you!" Sarah said in shock.

Before her stood a slightly altered version of herself. This self had more roundness to her cheeks. Her hair was straight-ironed, and she wore bright red lipstick, a sleek leather jacket, skinny jeans, and black combat boots. It was a stark contrast from how she dressed herself.

"Why am I looking at myself?" Sam asked. "I must be dreaming."

"You are dreaming. Listen, I have a message for you. I got connected on the other side and found a way to reach you through lucid dreaming. Lucas and I are trapped in Dr. Fowler's basement. He locked us in there. You have to tell Dad! Ask him if there's a way out. Sam we're in danger! I promise you, this is not just a regular dream. Do you understand?"

Sam stood there, wide-eyed.

"Sam, do you understand me?!"

"Yes," she finally spoke, clearly shaken up, but nodding in affirmation.

"Good, now wake up and tell him. Wake up, Sam! Wake up! Wake up! Wake up!" Sarah took Sam by the shoulders and began shaking hard.

And then Sam was gone.

38. Dream Life: Brainstorming

S am awoke in a heated sweat. The pillow was drenched. Elijah moaned and reached up from the floor to the couch where she lay, whispering in his hoarse morning voice.

"It's okay honey, you were just having a bad dream."

Sam and Elijah were bunkered down in Ignacio's studio apartment in Brooklyn. Chip was there too. It was the safest place they knew to go for the time being.

"It's not a bad dream." Sam threw off the covers and got up from the couch, "it's a message."

She made her way into the living room, near the front door where Chip insisted on sleeping, so he could be alerted to any signs of trouble throughout the night. She laughed when she looked at her father fast asleep on the couch. She remembered all those nights he stayed up, fighting off sleep. She would eventually always find him down in the basement, head on his desk, drooling over his notebooks.

Elijah was right, her sleep wasn't peaceful, even before Sarah had reached her with the message. It was in those moments between sleep and waking, somewhere on the edge of consciousness that she would often come to her truest realizations. And sometime before she fell asleep, it dawned on her that everything was forever changed. However, now was not the time to dwell on these thoughts. Right now, she needed to help Sarah.

She shook Chip's shoulder gently. "Dad... Dad wake up."

Chip roused with a snort and blinked his eyes at Sam. "What is it sweetheart?"

"There's something you need to know."

"What is it?"

"Sarah and Lucas are in trouble on the other side. They're trapped in Dr. Fowler's basement right now and someone's coming for them. Dr. N's people, I think. We need to help them get out of there. Do you know a way?"

"Uh... let me see..." Chip propped himself up on one elbow. He frowned and rubbed his cheek pensively for almost a minute, wrinkling and warping the skin on his face like putty.

"Yes... I believe I do. Fowler has a failsafe in case he accidentally locks himself inside the basement and can't get out. He hides the key under a floor tile. I caught him putting it away once."

"So where is it exactly?"

"There's a tile in the back-left corner of the room, that lifts right up. It might take a fine tool and some prying, but it will give. The key is in a small box underneath that tile."

"Great! Now, is there something I can take to help me fall asleep so I can relay the message to her faster? I'm wide awake and it would take too long naturally."

"You're in luck, my dear!" Chip reached into his cargo pants pocket. "I carry a small pill canister with me wherever I go. Let's see…" He fumbled through the small tin. "Blood pressure, allergy, ibuprofen, ah, here it is, I have a few Balixa in here. If you take two and lay back down, they should kick in within fifteen minutes. Take them with a glass of warm milk."

"So, I'm guessing you don't have anything that can just put me out?"

"Unfortunately, not."

"Okay, thanks."

Sam took the pills and began making her way to the kitchen.

"Sam, wait." Chip looked at her quizzingly. "How did you wake so suddenly, just in the nick of time and know what to do?"

"She found me using another channel, dreams."

"Incredible! And do you know how to lucid dream as well?"

"Well, of course, you taught me!" Sam smiled at her father, knowingly.

Chip beamed up at his daughter. "Marvelous!"

~~~

The breaking of dawn had not eased the heaviness in Sam's head and limbs, an unfortunate side effect of Balixa. She had awoken with a pang in her heart.

The first nightmare she had that night after relaying the message back to Sarah, was being stuck in that horrible, hollow, tree trunk again. She could see Elijah reaching for her, but it wasn't enough to pull her out. The truth was, he wasn't enough anymore. No one was. She would never bring herself to admit this to him, but when she became connected, her emotions on the other side became real also. Everything came back to her: her relationship with Joey and even more surprising, a growing spark of affection for Lucas. How could she possibly reconcile these feelings with Elijah? She was only fully his before she became connected.

She imagined how the conversation would go. Elijah would promise to become connected, so that he could find her on the other side. The funny thing was, he would undoubtedly have someone already waiting for him there. How could he not? Elijah was a catch by anyone's standards.

But it wasn't just her relationship with Elijah that was troubling her. She couldn't look at her father in the same way she did when she was separated from her other half. The anguish of the years she had spent looking for him were now juxtaposed with the happy memories of growing up with her adoptive family.

A resentment had built up in her. Her father knew exactly where she was and didn't even attempt to reach out. She was even angrier that her idealized version of him was forever shattered. Her life was so much fuller and emptier, all at the same time.

She touched her cheek to find a warm stream of tears. She was infuriated. Something felt hopelessly lost in the process of becoming this new person. She wanted her pain back, the old pain of her former life. This new pain was too much to comprehend.

It was like two people were fused into this Frankenstein's monster of a person. But the truth was, she had not lost any memories. Her skills, abilities and talents were overflowing, bursting at the seams. No, she lost something much more important: her soul.

Sam let out a loud sob.

"Oh, honey," her father spoke, awoken from his sleep. He made his way to Sam and sat down on a chair across from the couch. He spoke quietly as to not wake Elijah. "I remember those pains. The loss you feel right now is only temporary. The transition after connecting is never easy."

"But..." Sam choked over her words, "I've lost my soul."

"Oh no, Sarah, not at all. Your soul has simply, fully awoken. You see, it was always much bigger, much fuller than you were aware of. You are still you, but a more complete you, and it will take time to sort out your lives, figure out what you truly want. Give yourself time... It's true, there will be losses, some ties will be severed, and new ones will be forged. Just remember, the people that love you, who truly love you, will understand. Just please, try to take it easy. You don't need to make any life-changing decisions right now."

Chip stood up from his chair and wrapped his arms around Sam, stroking her head.

Sam melted into her father's arms, feeling the same sense of safety she did as a kid, when she would wander into the basement at night after having a nightmare.

She pulled away after a couple minutes. "I'm okay. I'll be okay," she sniffled. She believed what he said, after all, he had been through it himself. "I think I'll go make some coffee. You want some?"

"No, that's alright. I think I'll lie down a bit longer... Are you sure you're alright?"

"Yes. Thank you," she said, smiling weakly at him.

As she brewed her coffee and smelled the piping hot steam, she remembered an earlier idea. She had momentarily forgotten about it, but it was coming back. It had come to her in her moments of waking. She would go straight to the local paper, all of them if she had to. She would find a reporter that was willing to listen. They would all have to go as a collective unit, her father too. There was power in numbers. They needed to come out of hiding, into the light. At this point, she could see no other way.

Elijah was the first to wander into the kitchen, rubbing the sleep from his eyes. He was wearing the same clothes he had on yesterday. They all were. He sat down in a chair around the small, white kitchen table. She smiled awkwardly up at him and leaned one elbow against the kitchen counter. Quickly realizing how insincere her smile was, she fought harder to conceal her feelings from him, walking across the kitchen and sitting down in his lap. She wrapped her arms around his neck, burying her face in his shoulder.

"Are you feeling better?"

"Yes, I am. And I've been doing a lot of thinking. I've got some ideas of how we can move forward with all of this."

"Really?" Ignacio's voice rang from around the corner. He walked over to the kitchen cabinet, took out a ceramic blue mug and poured himself a cup. "What are your ideas?"

He sat down opposite Elijah and smiled at Sam, taking a big gulp of coffee.

"I think we should wait for the others," Sam responded.

Chip finally made his way into the kitchen about an hour later.

"I was thinking," Sam began after he sat down with his cup, "that we could put our talents together in a more constructive way, and expand our reach, so to speak."

"Ah! You mean using our talents and resources from both worlds?" Chip asked.

"Exactly," Sam enthusiastically waved her coffee mug at Chip, splashing a little onto the floor. "We would use our connections, our abilities, all our resources, pool them, grow them."

"But will that be enough?" Elijah said. "From what you've said, Nathaniel Wood, or Thomas Remmer, has a lot of high-powered people working for him."

"That's why we need to gather the others... from the hospital."

"Yes," Ignacio said. "I know firsthand that several of those people would be very useful to corroborating our story. But we need to get them set free first."

"Exactly, which brings me to my next point: we need to move quickly on this with the papers, because if Dr. N has caught wind of this in the other world, she will start covering her tracks here. We should go to the papers today."

"You're absolutely right, they probably already started an investigation in the other world," Chip said, growing worried.

"And what about you Ignacio?" Elijah said. "Have you been holding out on us? From what you've told us, you have some information on the hospital as well."

"On the hospital, yes. On the witch, yes. I don't think I recorded any of her phone conversations though."

"Well, maybe you can help us get together a list of the people they are holding in that room," Sam suggested. "Once the story gets out, maybe they'll be released?"

"Yes, I might be able to help with that."

"Good!"

Chip sat staring into a vacant corner of the kitchen, scratching his beard. After a few minutes he spoke. "You're right, Sam. We are way past the point of not involving other people. We can't do this alone anymore. The problem is, they already have my formula and we still have no clue what they're planning do with it."

"We need to get Lucas involved somehow, from the other side," Sam said, pacing the floor of the kitchen. "He has FBI and police training."

A power unbeknownst to her seemed to have taken over and was propelling her forward. She could feel her resolve building. The three men sat there staring at her. She stopped her pacing for a moment and looked at them.

"What? What are you all looking at?"

"Nothing." Elijah began, "I just, haven't seen you this... determined in a while."

"Yes," Chip beamed, "Sam is discovering her true purpose."

39. WAKING LIFE: SWEET ESCAPE

S arah sat straight up in the darkness and immediately began crawling towards the back corner of the room.

"It worked? What are you doing?" Lucas grabbed for her in the dark.

"Yes. There's a key. It's underneath the tile in the back-left corner of the room."

Lucas carefully stood up and began walking towards the back of the room, arms stretched out before him.

Sarah felt around the edges of each tile for a crack, a loose one.

"All of them are stuck! My nails are too short. See you if you can find something in this room with an edge."

"I've got a better idea." Lucas pulled his keys out of his pocket and placed them into Sarah's hand. She carefully prodded and pulled on each tile, making her way around the room in a clockwise manner. Finally, about eleven tiles later, Sarah felt one give a little.

"I think I got it!" She wedged the key further underneath the tile until she could get a finger's grip around the edge of it. "God, it's heavy!"

Lucas came to her side and wrapped his fingers around the tile's edge, inching his way to the other side of it, for better leverage.

"You're right, these are not regular tiles, much thicker, and what in the world are they made of?"

"I don't know," Sarah responded. "Let's lift on three. Ready? One... two... three!"

"Ughh!" Sarah and Lucas moaned in unison as they lifted the tile and dropped it on the floor.

Sarah reached inside the shallow cavity and sure enough there was a small box inside. She pulled it open and took out the key.

"Come on, let's go!"

The door opened without any issues and without more ado, they were free.

"Shhh," Lucas hushed her. "He might still be around, be quiet."

Sarah and Lucas made their way down the hallway and rounded the corner to the living room. Lucas held his gun out for protection. Sarah could hear the television. Lucas instinctively pushed her back and peeked into the room.

"No one's here," he said, when he had the room in full view.

"Really, then why is the tele— Lucas! Listen, it's my story!" Sarah grabbed the remote on the end table and turned up the volume. The news anchor was an old colleague of Sarah's. Actually, one that she had envied for many years. She was always getting to cover the most interesting events. "Mr. Chesterfield must have released the story already!"

"Amazing!" Lucas exclaimed. "Look, there goes Dr. Neely in handcuffs!" Lucas slapped the side of his head in disbelief. "They must be bringing her in for questioning. Just look at the look on her face!" He laughed. "She's livid!"

Sarah was excited too but did not immediately feel like celebrating. Yes, their plan had worked, and a lot faster than she had anticipated, but what would this mean for them? The senator's people were undoubtedly going to retaliate.

"Apparently Remmer's people got away with my father's formula. Ignacio and I couldn't stop them, even though we kicked some ass," Sarah's smile dropped, "or rather... killed"

"You killed someone?"

"Yeah, I guess I did... So, what do you think they're going to do? The senator probably has the formula by now and is hatching his plans."

"I guess all we can do at this point is wait."

"No. We can't just wait," Sarah raised her voice. "We're sitting ducks. We have to act. But we need help: Jeremy and Nikki and you and my father and the rest of them."

"The rest of them?"

"Don't you see? This is our chance!" Sarah exclaimed with growing enthusiasm, the ideas bubbling to the surface more rapidly than she could grasp on to. "All those people they hid away undoubtedly knew something about this other world and were considered dangerous enough to be locked up. We need to talk to them, get them on our side. Build up an army."

"An army?"

"Yes! An army of people who are connected. Who knows? Maybe not everyone they hid away was completely crazy, I mean, look at Jeremy! Maybe Dr. N convinced their loved ones that they had lost their minds."

"Sarah, slow down," Lucas frowned.

Sarah could tell that her excitement was unsettling him, but she didn't care.

"No, I can't. There's no time for that. We have to act now. I don't know all the details yet, but I know we'll have power in numbers and the senator has numbers on his side. We need knowledge and manpower. Think about all the blindly unaware voters this November!"

"What are we supposed to do? I mean, there have and always will be blind voters. His campaign has been going strong so far. At least half the people I know are voting for him. So, if he uses the formula for... what do you call it? The super pill? That sounds too Sci-Fi... how about Balixa 2.0?"

"That's stupid. It's not even a sleeping drug."

"Oh, isn't it, Brainiac?"

"Shut up." Sarah rolled her eyes. "Just call it the super pill for now. I'm sure my father will come up with a name for it when he's ready."

"He's going to use the super pill somehow, but how? He wouldn't tell the public about it."

"No. They would think he's crazy. How could he possib—"

"You're right," Lucas cut her off mid-sentence, the way he did when understanding dawned on him.

Sarah laughed to herself and shook her head. *No wonder business wasn't going well for him when I met him. He seriously needs to work on his social skills!*

"He probably has a lot of resources and money at his disposal. What if he takes total control over this formula, over who gets it and who doesn't? Do you know how much power he would have? He could tell people anything he wanted."

"Okay, but what about others like us, that are naturally connected?"

"Who knows? Now that he has the formula, he can hire a team of scientists to alter it anyway he wants. I mean, look what you just figured out with your lucid dreaming thing. I bet he has a team of scientists right now, testing this formula every which way. He can tell the public that this is the only way to get connected. You know what kind of brainwashing these guys are capable of."

"That's scary...Well at least we have the media on our side now, so don't discount that. Now if there was some way we could tie Remmer to the hospital cover up..."

"Yeah, how?"

"Well I guess we'll have to go find him," Sarah snapped back, her words cutting the air.

Lucas sucked in his lips and fidgeted with his hands for a moment. Suddenly he rushed towards Sarah, taking both her hands in his, and looking deeply into her eyes in a way that made her feel like she should turn away. But she stared right back at him.

"I know you think that I think you're crazy, but I don't... I want to make this happen too. Don't be upset. It's going to be difficult and dangerous to say the least, but believe me, I understand how important it is for this man to be stopped. I'm with you."

Sarah gave him a thin smile, surprised and touched by his awkward display.

After a moment, Lucas continued. "He's a money mongering, megalomaniac. Do you remember that urban development project from six years ago?"

"Yes." Sarah felt her body begin to loosen and relax in Lucas's grasp. She also felt his grip loosening. Lucas let go of her hands. "I remember he was competing with the CEO of that mall. Wasn't that guy planning on building it right in the middle of that mobile home community?"

"Yes, even after Remmer stopped the project from going through, he turned it into a park, and displaced all those people."

"I remember, he said it was for the beautification of the community, a place for people to enjoy and have access to clean air and nature, or some bullshit like that. He just went and bulldozed all those trailers after he promised those people he would save their homes."

"Exactly!" Lucas had let go of her hands but was still standing very close. "It was just a show of power, once he squashed the other guy, he just did whatever he wanted, regardless of the voices of that community. He's a threat to our country."

~~~

A couple days later, the gang was reunited at Nikki's house once again. Jeremy had suggested that they research each and every member recently released from the hospital and get in touch with them via social media, in person, or by phone. So, they split up the list amongst themselves, a staggering thirty-two people. Sarah did not remember seeing so many people in that room.

Each person was put in charge of contacting ten to eleven people and assembling them together at Nikki's house. Additionally, Sarah was in charge of keeping track of any public appearances the senator would be making that might afford an opportunity for surveillance.

They all realized they had to move fast. The hospital exposure would grant them a small window of time to move stealthily and quickly, and to pick up on the momentum of the media.

Mr. Chesterfield had given Sarah her job back, and although her redefined purpose in life would require her utmost attention, she realized that if she wanted to keep her job and pay the bills, she would have to blend in, not make a stir, and keep the stories coming. She would be building up for the ultimate story, this of course meant she would have to work twice as hard, between planning with her newly assembled crime fighting team and keeping up with her daily work tasks.

Additionally, Sarah had talked to her mother, Addelyn, who, as she figured, thought she was going crazy after the connection processes took hold. After she explained everything to her, she was more or less convinced, though this new information would take a lot of getting used to. Her worldview was shattered much like Sarah's, but she was not alone, there was a community forming of those who were connected.

In about a week, they had contacted everyone released from the hospital and congregated them at Nikki's house, which she begrudgingly agreed to. The assembled masses were less than promising. Although most of the people were still in their right mind, a handful of them had serious mental health issues, either from Dr. N's brain scrambling or from a biological predisposition. The majority of them were scared, if not completely unwilling to fight back.

What they had gone through at the hospital and not to mention with the media, had completely spent them. Most just wanted to go home and never open their doors again. There were, however, a promising handful of people who seemed passionate and angry enough to incite this crowd.

Nikki's den was small, but people were willing to improvise, some sat on the couch, some on chairs, on the floor, or simply stood in the doorways, but they were all there.

"We need to take them down. All of them!" A tall, burly man with dark curly hair in his mid-thirty's exclaimed, slamming his glass of Coke on the table, after Sarah, Jeremy and Lucas took turns bringing them up to speed.

"We're really need to pool our minds and resources together to have any chance of defeating them," Sarah responded to the inflamed redhead.

"Exactly! Come on people, put your money where your mouth is!" The riled-up mountain man growled, standing up and looking around the room.

"And how do you propose we do that?" A small woman with a platinum blonde pixie-cut retorted.

"Well I know of someone, an uncle who works for the secret service," squeaked a squirrely man in his mid-forties.

"Really?" Lucas quickly picked up the conversation. "And in what capacity do you think he could assist us?"

"Oh, in many ways, many ways. He's black ops, you know, doing undercover work for the president. He can set up surveillance. He's got eyes everywhere, you know," he rambled on, his voice and eyes darting around the room. "Even in here! They're watching us you know, through the television. They use satellite signals to spy on us. In fact, we need to unplug it. The microwave too." The man stood up and moved towards the television set, obstructing his face with his hand from the supposed viewers inside.

"Okay!" Nikki stood up and got between the man and the television. "Please sit down, sir, I'll take care of the television."

"And the microwave."

Nikki gave Jeremy one of her *I will murder you* stares and walked to the kitchen to appease the paranoid man.

Lucas gave Sarah a sideways smile. "Thank you for that contribution Mr. uh....?"

"White. Ben White."

"Mr. White, thank you so much for that information. We'll talk more about specifics later, you know, in private."

"Ah, yes! Naturally."

His delusion acknowledged to his satisfaction, Ben went back to intently reading the book he had brought with him.

"I may know of someone who can help," spoke a middle-aged woman with a long black braid, pulled back with a Native American style beaded hair piece. "You see, my father worked for the senator one year, he was treasurer for the state, until he got fired over false charges... Anyway, he spent a great deal of time with the senator and was privy to some of his more personal information. I'm sure that if I reached out to him, he would help us."

"That's exactly the kind of resources we need!" Jeremy waved his hands before him in confirmation. "Now the rest of you, what are your talents? Please, tell us everything, anything."

"I'll put on a pot of coffee," Nikki said, getting up.

One by one, the group of former captives brought their stories forward. Several of these folks had no families, or did not keep in touch with them, so it was no surprise that no one came sniffing around the hospital looking for them. Still, others seemed to be well-loved members of society; mothers, husbands, businessmen and women, all of whom would be missed.

Maybe they all had that streak, Sarah thought, the knack for sudden bursts of brilliance or ideas that could easily be confused with psychosis and make it conceivable for them to end up in a hospital.

Most, though not all of them ended up at the hospital because they were falsely diagnosed with symptoms of psychosis, more specifically with delusions of living another life. These well-meaning people unintentionally lead their families to believe that they had reached their tipping points and fallen off into the abyss, much like in Sarah's situation.

There were however a handful of people who were originally hospitalized for different reasons: suicide attempts, self-harm and even case of severe anorexia.

All of these people had somehow ended up in the "sleep lab" living out their days as vegetables. Sarah wondered why she didn't end up like them. Dr. N must have known who she was, who her father was. Why then, didn't she try to stop her? She considered that maybe it wasn't a risk she was willing to take, or maybe she was using her as bait.

By the end of the evening, after everyone was thoroughly spent, a skeleton plan began to emerge. These pieces of information, insights, and connections would turn into e-mails and phone calls. They would become an army of more than thirty, and unlike the senator's people, Sarah's enlightened men and women would create a network of truth and light, working in both worlds, tethering others to their cause.

40. Dream Life: A Changing Country

A few days after Sam had submitted the story to the local news station, the investigation began. An eager new reporter who was dying for a good story agreed to do her best to run it by her chief. They had all gone together: Sam, Ignacio, Elijah, even Chip, as promised. They all knew that this was their best chance now. Elijah called the police back and added to his report, and they all corroborated the information. Even Lucas, who now only existed on the other side, provided the team with specific instructions on how to get the FBI on the case, via the newly connected Sarah. They worked quickly and efficiently, and in a matter of a few weeks, Dr. N was arrested, and the patients being held at Northern Weaver Psychiatric Hospital were released. While Tyshawn was a lot skinnier in this world from his time in captivity, at least he was free. He was at his cousin Taliyah's (known as Nikki in the other realm) house, recouping.

~~~

The light angled at Nathaniel Wood for effect, washed out his face in a brightness that seemed to make him look angelic, his sharp features softened.

Sam shuddered as she thought of the Lucifer of the bible, and how his name meant, "bringer of dawn." *Clever trick.*

He looked down at the podium and cleared his throat, adjusting the microphone to the height of his lips.

Sam pulled her black hoodie closer around her face to keep the biting wind off her cheeks. She rocked back and forth on her heels and waited for the inaugural speech to begin.

It had been a long campaign, but as it turned out, Nathaniel Wood had won the popular and Electoral vote in a landslide election. Interestingly, Wood had not mentioned anything suspicious or out of the ordinary during his campaign. It had been a busy, but largely inactive few months. The reinforcements were gathered. She, along with Ignacio, Chip, Elijah, Taliyah, Tyshawn, and Lucas, in the other realm, had long since assembled a network of more than forty people.

They had the intelligence, weapons, equipment, and know-how, all they were waiting on was the now soon-to-be president to announce his plans for the future of America. They had learned nothing of great significance since the formula was stolen and Dr. N's arrest. Dr. Fowler had fled.

Now in Washington, D.C., she stood wondering if she had been on one giant, wild goose chase. *So, he has the formula. Why has he not done anything with it already? Will he even tell the public or just use it to his own advantage?* These were the types of questions Sam pondered, along with the many existential ones that had been springing up since her connection, like was she really to spend her days following this man around, waiting for him to reveal his diabolical plans, as if she had no life of her own to live?

"Ladies and gentlemen of the press, fellow Americans," the president elect began.

Sam directed her attention towards the angelically lighted man in the sharp grey suit at the podium.

"I want to say that I am deeply humbled that you chose me to lead and to guide you as your new president. I promise, I will not let you down."

"Promises, promises," Sam mouthed amidst the cheering crowd. She was tired of the same old presidential banter.

"My plan for this country is far reaching. I want to live in an America where every man can get his fill to eat," Wood paused for the moment as the crowd cheered, then continued, "where every child can get an excellent education, where jobs are plentiful, industry is booming." The cheers continued.

"I have promised you many things, among them, better jobs, higher wages, affordable and comprehensive healthcare, and reduced crime. We are in need of comprehensive reforms that I will make happen, life changing reforms." He stopped for a moment and observed the crowd who were standing in full attention. "I plan to bring this country back from the brink of death! We have had enough, and we are ready for a change, a substantial change!"

The people began cheering louder.

Sarah began to squirm. The words *substantial change* coming from this man could not mean anything good.

"And I'm starting with a healthcare reform plan that is earth-shattering in its proportions, a comprehensive plan that everyone can afford, that will address the various issues that plague the people in this country."

She texted the group: *healthcare plan?*

Sam's phone was vibrating non-stop in her hand. She looked down to find a string of messages from her team: *It's his plan. He's going to put everyone on this plan, maybe this formula is going to be incorporated somehow? What is he doing? What are we going to do?*

~~~

A few weeks later Sam woke up to the sweet smell of coffee and blueberry pancakes.

She decided to tune out the world for a while and told her team that she was going away for a much-needed vacation. Where she really went was her parents' house, because surprisingly, it was the only place where could she find the kind of peace of mind she was after.

The smell of bacon wafted up the stairs along with her father's rolling laughter. His voice reminded Sam of a herd of clumsy cattle running through a field. Then came the infamous slap of her father's hand across her mother's bottom. A small eruption of laughter ensued. Sam giggled and rolled face down onto her pillow, breathing in the foresty detergent she had woke up smelling her entire childhood.

For a moment she forgot everything that happened in the past few months. All she knew of life was her childhood bed, tie-dye pillowcase, mom's blueberry pancakes, and her father's megaphone laughter. Heaven was palpable, so palpable that after a minute she found silent tears running down her cheeks, followed by the familiar ache in her chest. Again, the physical sensations preceded her awareness of her emotions, and the painful thoughts that followed. She seemed to live in a world of perpetual catching up, like her mind was fighting to keep the moment from passing. She wanted so badly to hold onto the simplicity of it all, the pleasure and comfort.

She squeezed her pillow tightly, like she did the night when Freddie Blanchett broke up with her in eighth grade. She battled against the disturbing thoughts creeping up on her from every corner of her mind, whispering to her that all of her life's normalcy was over.

Not today, Satan.

Sam sat up in bed and rubbed the sleep from her eyes. Fumbling for the remote at the end of her nightstand, she flipped the television on. It was set to the local news station. They were covering the hospital scandal and would be for weeks. Sam instantly recognized the woman being interviewed. In the other world, she had convened at Nikki's house with the rest of the released patients, but she didn't talk much then. In this world, her name was Rosie. She was a young woman with bright green eyes, somewhat gaunt cheeks, and a complexion to match her namesake. Her mascara was smudged and running down her cheeks as she wiped at her face and choked over the words. Sam teared up. She could not believe what this woman had endured, what they all endured in that hospital. She shuddered as the woman said, "They kept us sedated at all times, so that we didn't know if we were asleep or awake. Moments of lucidity were so rare that we were losing touch with reality. We are not seeking vengeance, we just want our stories to be heard, we were silenced for so long." Sam watched for another fifteen minutes until her mother called to her that breakfast was ready.

Sam put on her best camera-ready smile and made her way downstairs.

"Morning kiddo!" Her father greeted her as she made her fast-paced shuffle down the stairwell. "Sleep well?"

"Yes, like a rock."

"That's the best kind of sleep: the sleep of inanimate objects!"

Connie left the pan of sizzling pancakes and came over, wrapping her arms around Sam, pulling her close. "It's good to have you home, sweetie. We've been worried about you."

Sam didn't even pull away or give her usual retort. She just stood there, eyes closed, head pressed against her mother's neck.

Ben came over and laid a hand to Sam's forehead. "Wow, maybe we really should be worried about you."

"Benjamin!" his wife snarled back, "Can't a daughter just be happy to see her mother?"

Ben gave Sam a sidelong glance before sitting down at the table.

She gently broke free from her mother's embrace. "I'm fine, really, I am. I'm just tired and glad to be home."

"Mhmm..." Ben began again.

"Dad! Please just stop," Sam said in exasperation.

"There she is! Okay, okay. I'll take your word for it."

"Honestly, Benjamin, let the child have some peace and enjoy her breakfast."

Connie set down a plate of bacon, eggs and pancakes in front of Sam, while simultaneously placing a heaping platter of pancakes in the center of the table with the other hand.

"Thank you, but this is a lot of food, Mom."

"Well honey, I don't know how you're feeding yourself these days. Are you cooking at all or still going out to eat all the time?"

"I'm eating just fine."

"And what about work, is that going okay?"

"Mom, can we please just not talk about me for a while? Nothing bad is going on, I promise. I just don't want to think about work right now. It's exhausting. I'm exhausted and I would rather talk about you guys."

"And what makes you think that talking about our work is any less exhausting?" Ben asked.

"Ben, the girl needs a break, she's tired."

"Well, then, why don't we talk about something else altogether, like…. oh! I got it. Your mother signed us up for the new healthcare plan that came out today."

"What? The new plan came out today?"

"It's okay, Sam," her mother stared at her. "You still have time to sign up."

"Yes, I signed us up for it right away," Benjamin continued, "You know, the fee for not signing up in time is astronomical! But honestly, it's an amazing plan, very comprehensive. You really should look it over soon."

Sam put her fork down and swallowed her food. "So, you're saying there is no option to opt out of this plan?"

"That's right. To opt out would be ridiculously expensive, but this plan costs us practically nothing! I've read through the fine print. The man is a genius."

"And his end of life plan for everyone is amazing," Connie continued, taking a bite of bacon. "Affordable housing and medication for everyone over sixty-five. Just incredible! Not that we would ever give up our house. Everything from surgeries to women's health, it's all included and covered in this plan. I would have elected him four years ago if he was doing this."

"Are you alright Sam, you're white as a sheet," Ben interrupted Connie's diatribe.

"I don't feel well. My stomach really hurts. I think I'll go back upstairs and lie down."

"Oh no! You *are* ill. Let me get you some medicine."

"No mom, I don't need medicine. I just want to lie down and be left alone for a while."

"Ok honey, I'll come check on you in a little while," Connie placed her hand on Sam's forehead. Well at least you don't have a fever."

Sam got up from the table slowly and made her way up the stairs, deliberately, one painful step at a time, counting them under her breath, a grounding technique she did as a child, when she needed to focus on not killing her brother after one of his pranks.

She tucked back the curtains of her bedroom window and looked outside. The cars whizzed back and forth on the busy street below. A yellow cab honked and flew around a blue Lincoln Town Car that had come to a sudden stop, only to be abruptly cut off in the next lane by a black Honda. It was a typical weekday morning traffic jam.

Sam laughed to herself as she thought of how futile getting away would be, how ridiculous for the cab driver to even consider getting their client where they needed to be on time. She looked in both directions, the jam seemed to stretch out as far as the eye could see. The cars were a swarm of angry hornets hovering on the street in a confused mass, completely unaware of what they got themselves into.

And then she felt it, more awake and aware than ever before. Chip was right, she wasn't broken, and her soul wasn't lost. It was simply filled with more insight and awareness than she knew what to do with. It was fear that held her back.

She thought of her parents, misguided, with their growing enthusiasm for this new president and his seemingly unifying policies. She could see the stealthy chaos setting in around her, but she was not helpless. She was not alone. She had an army of newly forged friends and family beside her whose eyes and souls were wide-open, connected. They could see from both sides of the glass. A wave of relief set in, as her cell phone buzzed in her pocket. It was Jeremy. The text read: *When are you coming back? We need you here.*

BEFORE YOU GO

Thank you for reading Mirrors by Sonya Deulina Williams. If you enjoyed the book, please do us a favor and leave a review. It doesn't have to be a dissertation, just a few lines about what you liked. It goes a long way and we'd really appreciate it. You will feel an amazing sense of satisfaction because you're helping new authors to the genre and a publisher that is pretty cool. You can learn more about us, our books, and authors on our website: www.chandrapress.com

If you like free stuff, early access to new releases, sweet deals, discounts, giveaways, and exclusive offers, please join our awesome newsletter. Just type this link into your browser: www.chandrapress.com/newsletter

Made in the USA
Columbia, SC
18 December 2019